STONE CREEK

Canoes in Winter – Book 3

Bob Guelker

Printed in the United States of America
ISBN print: 978-0-9977457-4-0
ISBN ebook: 978-0-9977457-5-7
5 Pines Publishing
16910 County 13
Nevis, MN 56467

Cover Art by: Amelia Woltjer
Cover Design by: Eled Cernik
Song Credits:
How Could Anyone: Words and lyrics by Libby Roderick, copyright 1990 by Turtle Island Records

Then You Can Tell Me Goodbye: Songwriters: John Loudermilk / John D Loudermilk, Lyrics © Sony/ATV Music Publishing LLC

Publisher's Cataloging-In-Publication Data
(Prepared by The Donohue Group, Inc.)

Names: Guelker, Bob.
Title: Stone Creek / Bob Guelker.
Description: Nevis, MN : 5 Pines Publishing, [2017] | Series: Canoes in winter ; book 3
Identifiers: ISBN 978-0-9977457-4-0 (print) |
            ISBN 978-0-9977457-5-7 (ebook)
Subjects: LCSH: Wineries—Minnesota—Fiction. | Families—Minnesota—Fiction. | Bullying—Fiction. | Country life—Minnesota—Fiction. | Child welfare workers—Fiction. | Horses—Fiction. | LCGFT: Domestic fiction. | Romance fiction.
Classification: LCC PS3607.U45 S76 2017 (print) | LCC PS3607.U45 (ebook) | DDC 813/.6—dc23

DEDICATION

To Barb, Linda and Deidre, who were so generous with their time to read the first very rough draft of Stone Creek. And then kind enough to offer encouragement to get it polished and published. You are the best people any writer could ever be lucky enough to call his friends. Thank you from the bottom of my heart...

CONTENTS

CHAPTER 1

CONSEQUENCES ~ APRIL 15, 2016

"Dammit Sally, I will never forgive him, even now that he's frickin' dead, and even though we never have to worry again about another parole hearing or appeal that could cut that son of a bitch loose."

Sam squeezed his eyes shut and sucked in a deep breath through his nose. He clenched his teeth and crumpled the newspaper clipping into a ball, squeezed it tighter and smaller, like he was trying to turn a lump of coal into a diamond. He tossed it into the wastebasket but then snatched it out. He grabbed a couple of sheets of newspaper off the top of the antique wood-burning kitchen stove, wadded them up, and tossed them in with the clipping.

Sally watched, her eyes moistening as Sam opened the firebox and stuffed the ball of papers in among the ashes then struck a kitchen match to light it. "He was so goddamn evil. Not an ounce of remorse. It was like we all asked for it, like somehow it was our fault!" A wisp of smoke leaked out around the burner plates. Sam reached to the stovepipe and opened the damper.

He turned, and Sally invited him into her arms. "It's okay, honey. It's okay," she said through her tears, patting him on the back. "It will be better."

Sam's oldest sister, Jill, had sent him the newspaper clipping.

Child Molester Duane Whiting Dead of Apparent Suicide

Duane Whiting, convicted serial child sex abuser, was found dead in his cell at Oak Park Heights Prison on April 10, 2016, of an alleged self-inflicted stab wound to the chest. Authorities say Whiting had smuggled a kitchen knife into his room. He had been denied parole the day before.

Whiting was convicted in 2004 of 21 counts of Criminal Sexual Conduct for having sexual contact and penetration with boys over and under the age of 13. The investigation began when a man, who was 54 in 2003, informed Anoka County authorities he had been raped by Whiting when he was 8 years old. The man, who chose not to have his name released to the public, told authorities he came forward after all those years because he suspected that a young boy on the youth baseball team Whiting had coached during the summer of 2003 had been sexually abused by Whiting. Based upon that boy's accounts, Whiting was arrested and charged with the first six counts. Whiting was determined to be a high flight risk, and bail was denied.

A six-month investigation followed, and 12 more victims came forward, ranging in age from 14 to 47. The earliest victims' claims could not be charged because the statute of limitations had passed. In all, Whiting was convicted of having sex with 6 different boys who had been under 18.

During sentencing, the judge noted that Whiting sat stone-faced throughout the week-long trial, and when given the opportunity, he made no apology for his actions. Whiting was sentenced to 21 concurrent terms, the maximum being 30 years, and the maximum fines, which totaled $450,000. The judge ordered that if Whiting, a successful car dealership owner, did not have the $450,000 immediately available and did not pay the fine within one year, the court would seize his assets.

Whiting's appeals in 2004 and 2007 were unsuccessful. Whiting's wife subsequently sold their car dealership in Coon Rapids, and their lake home in Cross Lake, where many of the alleged offenses had taken place. The lake home was purchased by one of Whiting's alleged victims from the 1960s, who remains anonymous. He had the home razed and turned the property over to the city of Cross Lake to be annexed to an existing city park and beach.

———————

May 9, 2017

"Mr. and Mrs. Ryan," Esther Kellogg, the Stone Creek School principal, warned in a steady, stern monotone, "there will be consequences." She pointed out the window toward the 120-year-old Norway pine in the center of the courtyard. "You've got to put a stop to this nonsense."

Seven junior high girls were sitting around the giant tree, holding hands, eyes closed, their faces raised to the upper reaches of the pine. The Ryans' daughter, Angel, was among the group. Other students of all grade levels dotted the courtyard, sitting on benches or lounging in the grass, standing, visiting, reading, awaiting the bell to signal them to the classrooms. Only a group of four boys about the same ages of the girls in the circle paid any attention to them. The boys huddled, heads close together, the way young boys do when they're plotting.

Sam's lips were pursed as he fidgeted with the brim of his hat and stared out into the courtyard. Sally inhaled deeply and audibly through her nose. She turned back to Kellogg. The 60-something-year-old principal was all business, from her beige skirt and brown blazer with a white blouse buttoned all the way to the top, to her arms folded across her chest, her wire-framed glasses on a lanyard, her gray hair knotted into a neat bun. She turned to meet Sally's gaze.

"Angel," said the principal, "is the ringleader. You know it and I know it."

"Mrs. Kellogg…" Sally began.

Kellogg immediately interrupted her, lips pressed thinly together. "That's MS., thank you."

"Sorry, MS. Kellogg. I was going to say, my sister's wife, Joan Adair, is a lawyer, and a darn good one." Sally continued in a calmer voice. "She said that although public schools can't be any part of sponsoring school prayer, it is legal for the students to organize it themselves."

"Ah, while that might be true," said Kellogg as she lowered her glasses to rest on her chest and pointed forcefully out the window, "what we see out there isn't prayer. Angel herself admitted she doesn't believe in God. I asked her what she was doing. She said it's a *healing* ceremony, that Cindy's great-grandmother is sick…cancer. Angel said they imagine themselves surrounding this woman in her bed and holding their hands above her. And light from what she called the Universe flows through their hands and into the grandmother. Angel said that you, Mr. Ryan, taught her that."

"I'm not gonna argue with you about what it's called," Sam told the principal as he stared at the floor and massaged his brow. He reached into his back pocket and tossed three folded papers onto Kellogg's desk. "After you hauled Angel in here the other day to grill her about what she and the others are doin' around the tree, that's when we talked to our sister-in-law. She gave us these—court cases."

A sudden commotion erupted in the courtyard. One of the four boys was riding a broom like a hobby horse, circling the seven girls. He didn't get far before another student tackled the broom jockey. The tackler straddled him and rolled him over face up. In an instant, he had his fist cocked. The girls had jumped to their feet. Six of them fled, but one stood and hollered. Too late.

"Danny!" Sally shrieked as their son flattened the other boy's nose. The injured boy rolled onto his belly, and blood streamed from his face. Danny stood over him, his fist still cocked and his feet dancing like Muhammed Ali in the boxing ring. Angel was screaming at him, while Cindy stood a pace behind, her hands covering her face. He ignored both girls and jerked his head back and forth, searching for the other three boys, but they were long gone.

Suddenly, two senior high boys grabbed Danny from behind. A young male teacher ran to the bloodied boy and knelt beside him. The bell rang. The senior high boys handed Danny off to another teacher—a larger, older man dressed in a sweat suit.

"Oh no," Sally sobbed into her hands.

Sam shook his head and closed his eyes. Kellogg picked up the papers he had tossed onto her desk.

"Had you read a little further, Mr. Ryan," Kellogg said smugly, "the law also says schools can forbid religious activity if, in fact, it is deemed in any way disruptive." Opening her fingers, with a flair, she dropped the paperwork into the wastebasket next to her desk. "I'd call Danny standing up for his sister in that way pretty disruptive."

———

Danny was only 10 months younger than his sister. Angel's hair was dark and wavy like their dad's; Danny took more after his mother's side, with sandy hair that was unruly-curly but handsome. He liked to wear it down to his collar, like his dad did. It looked like you could never get a comb through it, or would ever want to in the first place. He had become a tall kid for being only 12, having shot up past his sister.

Sally and Sam, from the kids' earliest days, joked that their children had come from the same planet but landed here one after the other, as if the kids had planned it that way. Or maybe they had traveled here from the same century, Sam suggested.

When Danny was barely walking, they had found the kids in the living room whirling as fast as they could and howling. A couple of Rumi's whirling dervishes from thirteenth century Turkey, Sam suggested. Sam's mother had called him the same thing when he was a toddler and would go by himself to wherever compelled him, to sing gibberish and whirl in oblivious ecstasy.

The Ryan kids played together and worked together like one, finishing each other's sentences, and rarely arguing or getting angry with each other like normal siblings did. "Yup, those are our little soul twins," Sam and Sally often joked.

After Danny had sailed through first grade, and spent much of that school year being a pint-sized teaching assistant, his teacher recommended he skip second grade and proceed right to third. When Danny's teacher called and they went to the school to discuss it, the news was déjà vu all over again for Sam. Sally had her reservations—not about the siblings being in the same grade, but whether it might be too big of a jump.

The teacher smiled and said, "No, Danny needs to be challenged. Second grade would bore him to tears!"

Sam recalled when he had been in therapy with Laura back in 2003 that they'd unearthed what a devastating blow it had been to his self-esteem and sense of fairness when his folks arbitrarily had not allowed him the same honor and privilege.

"Trust me, this may be the best thing that ever happens to Danny," Sam said.

The siblings were ecstatic to learn they would be in the same grade. From then on, more than ever, strangers assumed they were twins. And the kids loved it.

Danny had decided not to play junior high baseball that spring of his seventh-grade year, although he had been one of the best pitchers in the peewee rec league the summer before. They had to work the new team of Percheron horses—Stevie Ray, the three-year-old, and Prince, the two-year-old—which they had from the time they had been broke and had started training at a horse ranch down near Alexandria.

Like his dad, Danny would rather ride behind in a wagon than sit in a saddle. By the time Danny was nine, he could hitch the team, except his dad had to slide the heavy breast collars over Elvis's and Roy's heads. Danny insisted on putting the bridles on, even though he had to use a step ladder. He darted under and around the team like a ghost, running the lines and hooking them up. Sally would cringe as she trusted her baby to those giants. By the time Stevie Ray and Prince had arrived that spring, Danny had been more than man enough to hitch them himself, even without a step stool. He planned to be the first person to drive them as a new team.

There was also Danny's new puppy. In March, the little yellow fur ball, the daughter of one of Deja's pups, arrived at the farm just seven weeks old. It had broken Danny's heart when they'd had to finally put down the family's old Lab, Deja, the September before. Shortly after

Deja had passed on, he'd called the owner of one of Deja's female progeny. The owner said he was going to have his Lab bred. Finally, in January, it was time for the pups to be born. Danny marked a calendar from 1 to 63, and crossed out the days, as they ticked off as slowly as molasses runs in winter. He'd never experienced such an interminably long wait; it felt more like 63 years.

Two weeks after the litter was born, he and Sam went to see the new arrivals. One pup, her eyes squinting open only to slits, abandoned the lunch it was jostling over with its littermates. It crawled right over to Danny, then grunted and nuzzled his knee. He picked her up gently, noticed the pup was a female, held her close to his face, and smelled her sweet puppy breath. Danny looked at his dad with a huge grin.

"Misty," he whispered as he held the puppy up toward Sam, "meet my dad."

Sam hadn't realized that Danny had brought along a marker, which he fished out of his pocket, marking a little red X on her rump.

"We'll be over often enough to keep her marked. At least twice a week—right, Dad?"

Danny had sat with Deja every second he could manage—doing homework, eating supper—as the cancer grew inside her. Sometimes he even slept with her on the couch all night. When the time came for the vet to come out and administer the final shot, Danny held her tight, his arms around her neck, her head in his lap. The last thing Deja felt on this Earth was a tear from Danny falling onto her closed eye.

Sam asked quietly, "You want to help me dig the...?"

Cutting his father's offer short, he replied, "Nope. I'll do it myself." And he did. It took him into the evening, as he prepared a spot on the hillside below the fire ring, next to the marked grave Sam had dug for Sally's Sheba several years ago.

At suppertime, Sally walked up to check on her son.

"Almost done," Danny said over his shoulder, as he shaved one side of the grave with a square-nose shovel. He hadn't dug just a hole in the ground. It was a real grave, about four feet deep, three sides already sculpted perfectly vertical, and all the soil in one neat pile.

He surprised his mom the way he talked—all business when there was an important job he had to do, like an engineer building a dam.

"Can you guys hitch the team and bring 'er up in the wagon?" Danny asked with an even, businesslike tone. "I'll finish up. Let's have supper up here. That's what you do after a funeral, right? You eat and tell stories about the person who's gone."

"Umm...sure, honey." Sally wanted to run up and squeeze him hard, but he kept to his task, not looking up again. If he had, he would have seen tears trickling down her cheeks—her boy becoming a man so young.

———————

"Waddya think?" Angel asked her brother, as she held out the two-foot-by-three-foot cross made of one-inch-thick cedar boards. "Daddy and I made it." The words and letters had been routed out in shallow trenches. Danny nodded as he ran his fingers across them.

OUR BELOVED DEJA. R.I.P. 2003–2017

"Perfect," he said, like he was approving a piece of art he had commissioned. "Let's get this done." He lowered himself into the grave. His mom, dad, and sister, down on their hands and knees, slid their hands and arms under the blanket Deja was wrapped in, and lifted her into Danny's waiting arms.

"Sleep tight, girl," whispered the boy as he settled his dog into the bottom of the grave.

Together, in silence, the family filled the grave with the square-nose shovel and the spade, handing off to each other after several scoops. Finally, Danny gently tapped and rounded the mound smooth. Before climbing the hill to the fire ring, he paused at Sheba's marker and cocked his head. He'd seen it a couple hundred times, but paused and looked at it now as if it were the first time.

The parents had never explained to the kids how Sheba died, nor had Danny or Angel inquired. In fact, the only thing the kids knew about Sally's old life was that she had been married once before, her husband had gotten into an argument, and the other guy had shot him. Sam and Sally had decided that the kids would hear something from someone out there soon enough, and then ask questions. They had agreed to be honest and forthright when the time came.

Still, as Danny held his long, metal roasting fork with a venison sausage out over the fire, it was a bit of a surprise when he said, "Tell me about Sheba."

And the floodgates holding back the story about how Sam and Sally came to be were open—history revealed in front of a roaring campfire until well after dark, the new moon only a day away. Like they had promised each other they would be, they were frank with the kids.

The kids reacted with a wide range of emotion and comment, or sometimes silence. From their parents' fateful meeting in the gravel pit. ("Oh, good grief, Mom!" said Angel.)

About falling in love when they really shouldn't have. ("It was meant to be," said Danny.)

The night Sam had saved Dakota—including sleeping together, and Sally saying goodbye forever. (No comment from either kid, but Angel and Danny stole sideways grins at each other.)

All about Sally's father-in-law, Pop. ("Gosh. I wish I could have known him," said Danny.)

Then about Bill killing Sheba and the terrible things he did to Sally. ("That fucker!" Angel said under her breath.)

And Sally escaping into hiding, letting everyone believe she was getting an abortion, when she knew she could never do that. (Silence from the kids.)

About how Sally and Sam had reconnected long-distance because of the Percheron team ("Oh, now it's getting too sappy," teased Danny.)

And about the day Angel was born. How they'd found out from Judge Friday just in the nick of time that she was Sam's daughter after all, and when they did the test on the faucet with the remaining condom from the out-of-date three-pack. ("Point well taken. Don't want to get myself accidentally knocked up," Angel said, as she pointed a thumb in her mother's direction, "like somebody I know.")

"Now wait a minute, young lady!" Sally scolded.

"Sounds like they might be ready for the tape when I was learning to run the camcorder that day over in Detroit Lakes," Sam teased Sally.

The kids giggled into their hands.

Angel imitated a TV news reporter, "Those might be the two nicest butts in Becker County!"

"WHAT?" Sally shrieked. "You little... whatchamacallits!"

"Hey," said Danny, "the evenings get pretty long out here when you two are in town, the mosquitoes are nasty, and there's nothing good on cable."

Angel cut in. "That's the only tape we found with Pop in it. We've watched it at least 20 times. Oh gosh, Daddy, when you accidentally recorded Pop watching Mom... whew. I could see his soul wrapping its arms around you, wanting to protect you. Boy, did he love you, Mom."

"But, Daddy, you sure were a bit of a perv back then!" she added.

Sam chuckled a little and then composed himself. "Seriously, about your mom and me back then... Okay if I tell 'em?"

Sally nodded, smiling.

"At first, every time I saw her I couldn't believe my eyes—and I still can't—that she would even talk to an old fart like me. And sure, I dreamed about where we might end up, even though she was married at the time. And as I learned more and more about Bill, I just tried to concentrate on being her friend—no strings attached—and not make it any worse for her. But the things Bill said, the things he did to your mom..." His jaw clenched and he shook his head.

"Mom," Angel asked, "is that what the nightmares are about? Are you going to have one tonight because of talking about how things were back then? I'm sorry...we can stop."

Sometimes Sally would scream so loud in her sleep that the kids would awaken and come running. She would sweat and thrash about, her face twisted into abject fear. Sometimes it took a couple of minutes for her to realize where she was. The kids and Sam would hold her tight and gently talk her back to reality. But even when Danny and Angel had been barely big enough to climb out of bed by themselves and run to their mother, it had never scared them. When one of yours was hurting, you gathered them in. It was what a family that close did.

Sally nodded. "Don't worry. You kids needed to know about that. I don't know if I'll have one tonight. Sometimes they just happen when things are going great. But I'm so thankful to have you guys all put your arms around me when it happens." She rubbed under her eyes with her thumb and pointer finger and held back tears.

"Would it be okay if me and my friends sent you some healing?"

"Sure, honey, that would be fine. Thank you." Sally wiped her eyes with the butt of her palm.

Danny turned to his father. "What were you feeling, Daddy, when Mom left—when she disappeared and didn't call or anything?"

"Sometimes you just have to let go and trust that things will work out, even if feels like you're being punished."

"Group hug," Sam suggested. "Over here, by the north rock, where your mom and I got married."

As they squeezed each other, patting backs and swaying, Angel said, "Thanks for hanging in there, both of you."

"It's been a long day," Sam said. "How 'bout we pack this picnic up?"

"I'll drive," said Danny, as he stood up and poked at the fire with his roasting fork.

"Shotgun!" shouted Angel.

It was darker than the inside of a cow, except for the stars and the firelight. Angel rode copilot on the wagon seat with her brother. Softly, she sang Roy Orbison's "Only the Lonely" in time with Roy and Elvis's steady gait. The kids swayed together.

Sam and Sally sat on the back of the wagon, their legs dangling as it rumbled and bumped over the uneven ground of the trail. She laid her head on his shoulder, he put an arm around her waist. Sam thought he heard Sally sniffle, and kissed the side of her forehead.

"How did we get two great kids like this?" she whispered into his ear.

He whispered back, "Well, I put my penis inside your vagina, and then…"

"Correction," Sally teased. "As I recall, you were in pretty tough shape that first time. I did the putting…" They flopped onto their backs and rolled onto their sides, laughing and then kissing.

Angel didn't turn around. She wouldn't have been able to see in the pitch-black darkness anyway. "Oh Danny, we can't take these two anywhere, can we? Now they're making out."

Danny just shook his head and smiled into the darkness. He held the reins loosely. No need to direct Elvis and Roy, even in the dark; the steady, loyal team had made the journey between the fire pit the barn hundreds of times. He could have put blinders on them, and they'd still plod down the last hill into the yard and turn into the barn alleyway perfectly, stopping right in front of the tack room.

———————

But the damn nightmare struck that very night. It took all three of them to gently nudge Sally out of it, hold her, and comfort her. After Danny and Angel shut their parents' bedroom door and moved down the hallway, they vowed in a whisper to never again speak of Bill, or say or do anything that might remind their mom of him. The hooked their little fingers of both hands, and touched their foreheads together, whispering, "This we promise to the Universe…to keep our mom safe from those nightmares the best we can."

———————

As Sam sat in the school conference room awaiting the deputy sheriff, his mind wandered back to when the kids had been five and six.

They had insisted upon sleeping in the same bed.

"Why?" Sally asked.

"So we can go there together!" Danny answered, giggling.

"Go where?" Sam asked.

"To the place," Angel said, elbowing her brother in the ribs.

"What place?" their mother asked.

At that moment, Sam grew faint, his spine fluttering. He knew what they were going to say. His stepdaughter had told him about it when she was little—her nighttime journeys to a very special place. She'd fall asleep and her "friend," a young boy her age who she called Joe, would come get her. And just like Peter Pan, they'd fly up to what she called the Village of Children.

There were no adults. Just kids. Some like themselves. Others of all colors. Some crippled, but still filled with joy, who the healthy kids would willingly take care of. And every beautiful bird and butterfly and kitty and puppy or other cuddly animal you could think of—all wanting to land on your hand or be petted or hugged or kissed. And the flowers were every color of the rainbow, and the trees shined and shimmered with gold and silver.

When Sam had driven a school bus in Minneapolis one winter 20-some years before, he noticed one little third-grade kid who never joined in with the others' mischief. When they'd pass a certain tenement every day, Julio would strain to see it as they approached, then stare at the run-down building as long as he could. The kid's eyes would moisten every time.

Sam was struck by the boy's gentle countenance and mysterious presence. Julio was the last stop on his route. One day when Sam didn't open the door right away, Julio turned to Sam, with a curious look.

Sam asked, "What is it about that apartment house back there?"

Julio lowered his eyes to the floor. "That's where my mom killed herself."

"I'm so sorry, Julio. Do you have anybody to talk to about that?"

"Yup." Julio bobbed his head up and down. "John. But he don't come see me as much lately."

"Why not?"

"John said when I get older I won't be able to see him. I miss going there with John."

"Going where?" Sam asked.

"There's this place he used to take me almost every night after I went to sleep. Just kids…and God."

Julio went on to describe a place exactly like the one Sam's stepdaughter had told him about.

Now, more than ever, Sam missed the times when Danny and Angel had been so innocent, recounting their fanciful nighttime travels.

Danny rubbed his bruised knuckles. "Those four boys," he said to his parents, "they've been calling Angel a witch. And doing other stuff."

The boy and his parents were alone in the school administration conference room, awaiting the visit from a deputy sheriff.

"I warned them plenty, but they just kept it up, sometimes walking behind Angel and her girlfriends, hissing and cackling like witches. I warned them…" Danny stared out the window, his lips tight and eyes narrowed. "And I'd do it again."

"Now stop that talk!" Sally pleaded. "Sam, you tell him!"

"Son…"

Before Sam could speak whatever it was that he didn't know how to say, there was a knock on the door. The knob turned, with Kellogg entering first, followed by a deputy sheriff. They walked to the opposite end of the long table and sat down. The deputy was young, in his late twenties or early thirties, and decked out in all the law enforcement garb: belt with holstered weapon, mace, cuffs, taser, and other tools of the trade. A microphone was pinned to his epaulet, and he wore a bulky bulletproof vest under his tan service shirt. His head wasn't shaved shiny, like so many deputies did. He was the opposite of imposing. He had medium-length, wavy, dark hair, and a kind, handsome face.

Kellogg made the introduction. "Deputy Elliot, this is Mr. and Mrs. Ryan."

"Hi, Jammer. Hey, Sally," the deputy said cheerfully.

Kellogg's head snapped up from her paperwork.

"Hey, Shawn," Sam said. "We got us a little situation here."

"How do you know each other?" Kellogg demanded.

"Sam here was my school bus driver back in the old days."

Kellogg furrowed her brow. Having been at Stone Creek School less than a year, and not having paid much attention otherwise, it hadn't sunk in how close-knit the community was.

———————

Shawn Elliot was a local product. Fatherless and with a mother who spent more time in the bars than at home, Shawn had been a rudderless, certifiable hellion in his early high school days. Obviously intelligent, but a terrible student. He had rebelled against any kind of authority, like when he'd been told the school dress code required him to button his shirt if he wasn't wearing a tee underneath. James Dean, in the movie *Rebel Without a Cause*, was Shawn's hero. He had gotten caught smoking around the corner from the janitors' entrance when he was a sophomore, then again while drinking whisky in his car in the school parking lot his junior year.

But a deputy sheriff, who had been called out for the drinking incident, had seen something behind those angry eyes and a jaw set like steel. He had told Shawn that if he'd come to his after-school youth group for students considering a law enforcement career, he'd see to it that the judge went easy on him. That man, now county sheriff, was Frank Davis.

Apparently, Shawn had needed just that one break. His senior year, he made Honor Roll both semesters. The fall after graduation, he enrolled in a community college associate degree program for law enforcement. He graduated with honors in just two years. Before he had even turned 21, he was hired as a part-time jailer. The next year, he hooked on full-time, his duties split between positions as court bailiff and jailer. Davis was elected sheriff, and Shawn volunteered to take over his youth group.

The following year, he earned a spot on patrol. In five years, he tested for sergeant and won that position. Three years ago, when the city of Stone Creek had disbanded their one-man police department and contracted with the county sheriff's department for a full-time patrol position, Shawn posted for it, even though he knew taking it would cost him his sergeant stripes and a considerable amount of pay. He wanted to serve the place he called home and the people who had helped him grow into a man.

On the Stone Creek patrol, in only two months' time, he had introduced himself to every business owner and compiled a list of key holders. His monthly reports to the city council detailed his contacts with the public and business security checks, even how many miles he put on his squad car—facts the council had never received before Shawn Elliot came back into town.

Before Shawn had been called to Stone Creek School about Danny, the buzz around town was that the young man had already applied for the sheriff's investigator position. The concern about that was the next guy might not be like Shawn.

———————————

"Hi, Danny," Shawn said softly. "I'll be taking your statement. I hate to say this, but Danny, what you did to Billy could potentially be prosecuted as a criminal assault. At least, that's my understanding, after talking to the ambulance crew about the damage to Billy's nose."

Shawn remembered his big break from Frank Davis. He had always wanted the chance to pay it forward, but the right kid and the proper circumstances hadn't shown up.

"Shawn, really, this was just a schoolyard fight," Sam pleaded, "not a criminal assault."

Danny said, "Dad, these guys—Billy and the other three—they've been after Angel and calling her names. They even slip drawings of witches into her locker and tape stuff to the outside, like black cats and Halloween pumpkins. And when no one is around who will tell, they're after me all the time. I've been elbowed in the ribs so many times, I can hardly breathe."

"Goodness! Well, honey, why didn't you report these things to Ms. Kellogg?" Sally asked, giving the principal a questioning glance.

"I did! Five or six times."

Shawn, Sally, and Sam all trained their eyes on Kellogg.

"Now, Ms. Kellogg," Shawn said, "I assume you have a record of these complaints?"

"Actually, I do have several complaint forms—regarding Daniel. The other boys filed them." She held up six forms. "They came to me first, telling me in every instance that Daniel was after them, and warning me that he would probably come in and say the opposite."

Shawn asked, "So, did you call Danny in with regards to these other boys' complaints?"

"I didn't have to," Kellogg said, her hands folded in front of her on the table. "It wasn't long until Daniel came to my office and tried to tell me exactly what the other boys said he would."

"Either way, why didn't you notify us?" Sam asked, staring Kellogg straight in the eyes.

"Frankly, I wasn't sure who to believe then, although I certainly do know who to now," Kellogg said, clearing her throat nervously. "I didn't want to open a can of worms and get parents involved unless there really was something to it. I can't make those kinds of judgments, you know—just accuse students based on hearsay."

"Danny," his mother covered his clasped fists with her soft hand, "why didn't you come to us?"

He threw his hands in the air. "Yeah right! Just so you'd tell me to ignore them harassing the crap out of my sister?"

Elliot asked, "Why do you think they're harassing your sister, and doing those things you said?"

"My sister is a *healer*. She's got this gift, like our dad has, but times a hundred. And other things. Dreams. Déjà vu. Kids come and ask her to help out their family, or their pets. She says we can all do these things, but we just don't know it. For me, it doesn't seem to work, but she's teaching other kids how to remember. They have a healing circle every morning before school if it's not raining, around the big pine tree in the courtyard. A couple of weeks ago is when those boys started after Angel and her friends over it."

Kellogg rolled her eyes and sighed loudly. "Well, yes, I did try to get the girls to stop whatever it is they are doing before school out there, because it was upsetting some of the other students. And Angel is definitely the ringleader. I talked with her about it, but she wouldn't budge. In fact, she became quite belligerent, claiming it was her *right*." She took a deep breath and adjusted her glasses. "Regardless, we're here because Daniel busted Billy's nose all over his face. That part is crystal clear."

Sam said through his hand over his mouth, "This really stinks."

"Now, Sam," Elliot said, "we'll get this sorted out…"

"In the meantime," Kellogg said, taking command of the conversation, "for starters, Danny will be suspended from school for three days. I'll be calling the disciplinary committee to meet ASAP to decide if the suspension should be longer, or if Danny should be expelled permanently. What may not play so well with the committee is the fact that these boys came forward saying Danny threatened them and vowed to get even—six times." She thrust the complaint forms in the air.

Just then, Angel entered the conference room. Her eyes were wide and her mouth slightly agape as she scanned the faces, all serious. Her concerned gaze settled on her brother. "Danny, I told you not to do anything. I don't care what those boys say." She took a seat next to her mother.

Kellogg said, "I asked Angel to sit in. I want everyone in the family to realize that this nonsense—whatever it is they're doing around the tree—has to stop."

"What's gotta stop," Sam interjected, leaning forward and pointing at the principal, "is you allowin' bullies to harass our kids! What's goin' on here is you don't understand or accept anything beyond the tip of your nose, so you're lettin' dog eat dog!"

"Wait a minute," Angel held her hand up in her dad's direction. "Why are *you* here, Shawn?"

Elliot set his pen alongside his notepad. "Well, I have to file a report with the county attorney. Danny could possibly be charged with assault and might have to go before a juvenile court judge."

Angel turned to her brother, shaking her head. "Juvenile court? You mean, like Danny could have a record? They could send him away?"

"Assuming the other boy files charges, it's up to the judge. Sorry to say, I've seen kids sent away. To juvenile hall or foster care. Sometimes the judge orders a psychiatric evaluation. Restitution. Community service." Turning toward Danny, he continued. "Now I can't give legal advice, but I have seen it go a long way toward leniency if the perpetrator admits his guilt and shows remorse ahead of time—apologizes, tries to make good, and has some sorta plan going forward to stay out of trouble..."

Danny said, "So what if I do all that and they keep talking trash about Angel? What if they keep after me? Then what am I supposed to do?"

Elliot resumed writing his notes. "I sure wish there was a record to support your story. All I can say is, you gotta keep your nose clean, Danny."

Kellogg said, "In the meantime, I am proceeding with the suspension; I simply don't have any choice. It's in the handbook. I'll have the secretary let your teachers know that you won't be with us for at least three days, and they'll email you the assignments. I suggest you get the books from your locker on the way out. And, Danny, spend your three days thinking about what Deputy Elliot said about keeping your nose clean."

She turned to Sam and Sally. "Mr. and Mrs. Ryan, I'll call you after I set up the disciplinary committee meeting. It will be within two or three days. You are strongly advised to attend, but Danny won't be allowed."

"You're darn right, Sally and I will be there," Sam promised through clenched teeth. "And we will be bringing our attorney."

"Have it your way," Kellogg said, setting her glasses back on the bridge of her nose and shuffling the paperwork in front of her. "You can work with us, or not. The disciplinary meeting is a chance to move forward, with steps we will decide upon together to ensure this never happens again and to minimize the consequences. But no attorney can make a broken nose disappear into thin air."

Elliot insisted, "Trust me, Sally, Sam—a judge loves to see plans developed by the parties from both sides, instead of having to listen to arguments like it's a trial and having to come up with a course of action himself. They are big on using their rubber stamps on compromises and joint plans, like Mrs. Kellogg is suggesting."

"Excuse me, Deputy Elliot, it's *Ms.* Kellogg. Continue, please."

"Beg pardon, ma'am. And one more thing—there's not a lot of time. My best guess is that Danny will be summoned before a judge next week. The wheels of justice turn pretty fast when it comes to juvenile cases."

Angel fixed her narrowed eyes on Kellogg's. "So have I broken any school rules? Yes or no, please."

"Well, no," Kellogg answered. "Not yet, anyway. But your actions did cause your brother to get into this trouble. And the law says that based upon his actions, I can forbid you to conduct whatever that ceremony is you lead."

Steely-eyed, arms crossed, Angel asked, "Are you forbidding me and my friends?"

Sally curled her arm around her daughter and gave her a gentle squeeze as she held a finger in front of her lips.

"Well, if it has come to that, yes. Yes, I am forbidding you from conducting or participating in any more such… gatherings," stammered Kellogg. "I'll be contacting the other girls' parents as well."

"You better call the National Guard, too," Angel advised. "This is baloney! I know the law. With my brother as the scapegoat and forced out of the picture for now, you don't have a case. You don't have any more disruptive forces left to blame."

Kellogg smiled at Angel, and feigned a swoon by patting her chest lightly and raising her eyes to the ceiling. "Meeting adjourned," she announced as she slid her chair back and turned for the door.

"Ms. Kellogg, I'll see you at the big pine tomorrow morning."

———

Growing up, Angel was never really trouble for her parents exactly. But she always had a way of making her point. She wasn't much of a negotiator. Her manner of resolving disagreements or getting her way was more, "Show me. You'd better have your ducks in a row." That propensity was obvious even before she could speak. She said it with her deep, green eyes—fixed and questioning. By age three or four, she had already become a three-foot-tall Judge Judy.

Sally often recalled fondly Angel's first horse, Lady. Angel had been barely 4 years old; Lady had been going on 20. A guardian angel of a horse. Angel would pester her mom nearly every day during riding season to put Lady's bridle on. Then Lady would obediently trail Angel to the closest vehicle or barrel or stump, anything she could scramble up on high enough to get a leg over the horse's swayback.

Or sometimes Angel would belly flop onto her horse, and grab the mane to right herself. The horse never moved a muscle while Angel scooched forward and stretched over her neck to fetch the reins. And away they'd go, walking around the yard, Angel off in her own little world, talking to no one in particular or singing, sometimes leaning forward and wrapping her little arms around Lady's neck. Sometimes she even fell asleep atop her special horse. On and off her equine buddy several times a day. In between, Lady nibbled grass, with the reins dragging below her, never tempted to get into any kind of trouble. The next time Angel emerged from the house and whistled up her horse, Lady would automatically stroll to the nearest stump or vehicle.

But there came a day when Angel was six and knew she needed to trade up to a horse that could move out and run the rodeo games her mother was teaching her. Still,

Angel did not want to part with her beloved Lady. Sally had attempted to reason with her daughter, explaining that they couldn't manage two horses for her—short on stall space, not to mention the expense. And besides, there were other girls, littler than her, who needed a good horse.

"Wouldn't it be nice to share Lady with another kid, like someone shared Lady with you?"

But they went ahead and bought Angel a bigger, younger horse, keeping Lady in the pasture. As she and Angel were driving to Detroit Lakes and passed a small farm, Sally finally broke the news, "I'm sorry, honey, but I sold Lady to these folks. They're picking her up Saturday."

Angel was never much for putting on tantrums. Nor was she much for giving the silent treatment. Instead, she usually had an instant comeback that often seemed too profound for a tyke her age. But this time, she had sat perfectly quietly, her arms folded tightly across her chest, her jaw set, gazing straight ahead. Finally, after about 10 minutes, she asked her mother in a steady, measured voice, "How would you like it if I sold YOUR horse?"

Since then, Angel had gotten three more horses, including the one she had now, which any competitive rider would die for. Every two or three years, with her skill level advancing a few more notches and her competitive spirit growing, she'd announce, "I need a faster horse. I'm sure some little cowgirl or cowboy will really appreciate having mine..."

Sam and Sally were humbled, holding each other tight and counting their lucky stars. They'd never known anyone of any age or upbringing or social status who put others so selflessly before herself. Angel gave of her gifts to anyone who asked.

Not that she automatically emptied her closet to the poor or threw the barn doors open for whoever wanted a new horse. But Angel lived the gift of inclusiveness and sharing, and showed a soldier's fearlessness when standing up for others. Yes, her mouth had gotten her into a few tight spots, but thank God, they often prayed, her heart is way bigger than her mouth, and folks know it.

Direct, yes. Selfish, not a bit. Demanding of complete honesty from everyone, especially adults who are in a position of authority, like Kellogg. Angel practiced it to what some folks thought was a fault. But if you were going to baffle her with bullshit, you might as well learn right up front to bring your own scoop shovel and clean up after yourself. Or Angel would kindly advise you to do so.

———————

On their way out of the conference room, Danny whispered playfully into his dad's ear, "The good news is—three days off, the morels are still popping and the suckers are runnin'!"

Sam tried to hide a grin, but Sally caught him and rolled her eyes. "Oh, you two. I don't want to know..."

CHAPTER 2

THE HONORABLE THING TO DO

It was a deathly silent 10-minute ride back home. All three seemed lost in thought over the sudden direction they found the Ryan family heading, on an otherwise beautiful spring day. Sam thought back to his own teenage foibles, and the mischief he'd gotten into when he had been even younger.

His father had ruled with an iron fist. He had never used a fly swatter when a sledgehammer would work just as well—a learned behavior that Sam had to consciously prevent himself from repeating with his own children. Still, with his kids Matt and Ellen, he had often failed as an understanding and forgiving parent. He often overreacted angrily on the spot.

Like with his folks, a lot had been going on in his life when he'd begun raising his first set of kids. He realized that his folks had just been trying their damndest to make ends meet and keep some semblance of order in a small house with seven kids. Sam's excuses had been that he was in a dead marriage he was trying to make the best of. It didn't help that his new business had gone bankrupt, which made the marriage even more stressful. Somehow, he had never connected that being molested by a neighbor kid at the age of eight had anything to do with the anger that too often spilled out.

After the divorce, when Matt was 14, Sam would drive halfway to the city, where he and his ex-wife exchanged their son for a weekend visitation at Sam's. Matt was at that age when he didn't want much to do with his dad, and one weekend he begged to stay with his friends instead. Sam had hoped he would want to go duck hunting with him and his own boyhood pal, Rick.

That Saturday evening, the phone rang. It was the city police. Matt and his buddy had been picked up for shoplifting. Thankfully, only Matt's buddy had any stolen goods on him, so they weren't going to charge his son.

Sam was boiling, loaded and cocked, with all manner of unforgettable, unforgiving punishments rolling around in his head that would guarantee Matt never did anything so damn stupid again, at least not under his father's supervision. Sam had stuffed away the fact that his father's sledgehammer had only made him angrier and distrustful of authority. In fact, it had turned him to self-destructive behavior like smoking cigarettes, driving his car recklessly, and drinking, even in junior high.

Sam looked at the phone in his hand and turned crimson, telling Rick, "He shouldn't have been there in the first place!" He slammed the phone into the holder. "He should have just left his friend and called me when he saw what was going on! How in the hell can you NOT KNOW your friend is stuffing his pants and shirt full of some store's junk when you're right there with him?"

Rick, who knew Sam's history with his father well, ignored the tirade and advised calmly, "Whatever you do, don't be your father. Stand by your boy."

And Sam did just that, even though the demons were clamoring to burst out and engulf his son. On the way home from the police station, Matt asked if they were still going duck hunting in the morning, saying he'd like to go.

The three of them got up at 4:30 the next morning. It occurred to Sam, waiting for the daylight and the ducks, that standing by his boy also meant sitting next to him in a duck boat.

Matt heard his dad sniffle. "What is it?"

"Nothin'. Coffee too hot, burned my throat…"

Sally was deep in thought as she stared out the windshield on the way back from the school meeting. How wonderfully different her present life was. She rarely thought back to her first husband, Bill. *What's the point?* she reminded herself. He's dead and she'd separated herself from anything about him. She knew that if Sam hadn't literally fallen into her naked lap that day in the gravel pit 14 years ago, things would have been so different…and not for the better.

She had been correct when she'd told Sam on their wedding night that she thought she was pregnant again. Sam had just turned 55, and she had been closing in on 40. But they were as happy as kids on Christmas when the test confirmed she was pregnant.

Danny had arrived 10 months after Angel. No dramatic home birth that time, like the family reunion three-ring circus at the Ryans' house, when Angel had made her arrival in the kitchen, and Sam's grandson Sam Anthony did so in the living room two minutes later. They had taken the standard route with Danny. However, they did have Sally's nurse practitioner sister, Maureen, assist.

Sally chuckled under her breath and turned to look out the window.

"What's so funny?" Sam asked.

She laughed again. "I was just thinking back to a couple months after Angel and Sam Anthony were born. I opened the freezer to find something for supper. Remember? I held up this plastic bag and asked you, 'What part of the deer is this from?' Your mouth dropped open and your eyes got big as pie plates. You said, 'Um...that's Angel's placenta. Didn't know what to do with it. Shit! Forgot I put it in there.' "

"What's a placenta?" Danny asked from the back seat as the car rolled into the driveway.

Sally and Sam, stifling their laughter, exited the car and met in front of it. They laughed until they cried and fell on the ground. She rolled on top of him, sat up, and held his face in her hands, kissing him hard on the lips.

"You have no idea how much I love you."

"Ah, geez!" said Danny, shaking his head as he hurried to the porch. "Cowgirl-style, and right in the yard. Gross."

"Hey!" shouted Sally. "How do you know about that?"

"How do you think? The internet, a 12-year-old boy's best friend," Danny teased.

"Wait a minute," Sally hollered at her son as he reached for the front door. "Who in the heck says that?"

He grinned and pointed at his father, who was still straddled by his mother.

"WHAT?" Sally grabbed Sam's throat with her hands.

"Sorry," Sam said. "I meant just for schoolwork...."

Danny shouted as the door was shutting, "When you're done, I'll be back with a pail of cold water and a couple of cigs for you guys."

Sally collapsed onto Sam's chest and whispered, "Oh my, what have we created? These two kids of ours..."

"Well," Sam whispered into her ear, "if you don't get off me pretty soon, we really are going to need that pail of water..."

"Samuel Ryan, why did I ever marry you?"

"Remember? You had to, it turns out. It was the honorable thing for you to do."

She held his face and pressed her lips to his again. Sam loved it when she kissed him like that—just like their first real kiss, that night after Sam had saved her horse's life.

Suddenly, Danny barreled out of the house, running toward his parents, a four-month-old yellow Lab puppy at his heels and a mop bucket full of water splashing over its sides. He stopped and took aim, one hand gripping the handle and the other underneath.

"Danny! You little butthead, don't you dare!" screeched Sally.

Too late.

CHAPTER 3

THE DISCIPLINARY COMMITTEE

The next morning, Angel waited for her six friends at the big pine before school. Only Cindy came to sit with her; the others were nowhere in sight.

Cindy Palmer and Angel had been inseparable since they met in kindergarten. She was a feisty, freckle-faced redhead. Her hair was so curly it was almost kinky. She almost always wore it in a tight ponytail. Untethered, her hair was an orange afro. She and Angel rode together as often as they could. They had a friendly rivalry at the horse games, but never cared who won, nor did they keep track. Their bedroom walls were both decorated with ribbons they had won, and their dressers covered with trophies. At the end-of-year points tally, one of them would be at the top of their age division, the other second.

They lived just three miles apart and would meet somewhere in between, then set off on their ride from there. They each had a drawer of spare clothes at the other's house, in case they decided to stay overnight.

Angel glanced over at Kellogg's office window. The principal stood close to the glass, watching her, a smug smile pasted cross her wrinkled old face. The two girls sat against the trunk of the big pine. Angel was tempted to give Kellogg the finger, and started to form that gesture, but Cindy noticed and grabbed her hand tightly.

Angel knew that Kellogg had gotten to her other friends. She didn't feel slighted, for this was her fight not theirs. The principal had also gotten to Danny's friends, except his best friend, Nate Skogquist. Angel decided she would greet her friends warmly, as usual, and not speak a word of the healing circle having been busted up.

The disciplinary committee—made up of a school board member, a teacher, and a private citizen—met the next morning with Sam, Sally, and Joan. Of course, Kellogg led the proceedings. She laid out her case, including graphic pictures of Billy's battered face, much of it covered with bandages, his eyes swollen black and blue.

"Billy and his parents will be filing charges against Danny," Kellogg informed Joan. "So the results of our meeting today will be sent to the court as a matter of record. Also, Billy's parents were considering suing the Ryans, but they've changed their minds."

Joan—the wife of Sally's sister, Maureen—had been practicing law for almost 30 years. She excelled in the tougher courts: divorce, family, civil, juvenile, and defense. She'd heard it all thousands of times and didn't pull any punches.

"You're the one they should be suing," said Joan. "And I'd be happy to tell Billy's parents that. Had you performed your duties and brought Danny in at the first contrived complaint against him, instead of keeping them a secret—and if you had instead called a meeting with HIS parents—this entire episode would never have occurred. You were derelict in your duties and failed all the students involved miserably. I'm sorry, I can't state it any other way."

The two male committee members seemed unimpressed by Joan's indictment. One gazed out the window and the other looked over his cheaters at the paperwork in front of him.

She continued, addressing them directly. "Excuse me. To me, the only question we need to answer here is—Why didn't Ms. Kellogg take the appropriate steps at the first evidence of trouble?"

The school board member, a middle-aged man in a business suit, shifted his gaze uncomfortably from the window to the papers in front of him. "Ms. Kellogg is not the subject of this hearing, so please confine your remarks to the facts at hand."

The citizen, an older gentleman dressed like he was headed for the golf course, adjusted his reading glasses and picked up the stack of papers and photos. "It's clear-cut what happened. The only question is, where do we go from here?"

As for the teacher, Amy Wilson, this was her first disciplinary committee meeting. The Ryans knew her as the kids' English teacher, her first job out of college. The students loved her because she didn't talk down to them. Instead, she elevated them at every opportunity and appreciated everything they had to contribute.

Youthful and lively, she could have been mistaken for a high school cheerleader—pretty and petite, with long, wavy, dark brown hair swept up in a ponytail, eyes as blue as the sky, and high cheekbones that hinted at her tiny bit of Native American heritage. Both earlobes held plain silver hoops, her left ear also adorned with another six piercings of various colored and shaped studs. She had a tattoo on the inside of her left forearm—a half dozen oriental characters.

She spoke barely above a whisper. "I have the Ryan children for seventh-grade English, and they are both excellent students. Angel can be…shall we say, outspoken, but she's certainly smart enough never to cross the line far enough to get in trouble. Actually, I'd say she's quite charming; everyone likes her, students and teachers alike."

What Amy didn't share with the committee and Kellogg was that she'd had dozens of fun conversations with the Ryan kids about hunting and nature, at first prompted by a photograph on her desk of herself with an eight-point buck she'd taken with her bow. Angel admitted she wasn't a bow hunter herself, but loved to go with her dad and Danny, sit in a tree stand above them, and record short movies of the action on her phone. She had captured Danny's first bow kill ever that fall—a spike buck that Danny had double-lunged from 13 yards.

Sam noticed Kellogg's brow was furrowed and her lips pursed over Ms. Wilson's observation about Angel.

"Danny is quieter," the English teacher continued, "but he's not a troublemaker. This is so out of character for him. I think there has to be more—"

Kellogg interrupted. "Ms. Wilson, excuse me. I know you are new to the committee. Even if Danny had been granted sainthood status by the Pope himself last week, the question is, who is Danny THIS week."

Amy opened her mouth to respond, her hands outspread. Raising her voice and straightening in her chair, she explained, "I have to wonder if he isn't the same kid he always was—a really good guy who got pushed to his breaking point. I think if Danny had felt he had an ear out there to listen to him, none of this would have happened. And I don't think it will happen again. That is, if someone can keep those boys off his back..." Amy set her steely gaze on Kellogg.

Kellogg simply shook her head and rolled her eyes.

The school board member sighed and drummed his fingers, making it obvious he was unimpressed with Wilson's speech. He looked back and forth between Sam and Sally. "This infraction is serious enough that he could be expelled. Mr. and Mrs. Ryan, do you truly believe that if we let Danny return to Stone Creek School, he won't reoffend? And if we do let him come back and he does something like this again, haven't we failed the rest of the school? Should we really take that chance?"

Joan shook her head and exhaled loudly. "You are still missing the point, overlooking many of the facts." She pointed to Kellogg. "Should Danny pay for—"

"I believe we've heard enough," Ms. Kellogg said, as she unfolded her hands and picked up some notes. "Here is my recommendation, and I think it's a decent compromise, although I do have reservations."

She distributed a single sheet to each person. "Part 1: If the Ryans will convince Angel not to conduct any more 'healing ceremonies' or any other prayer-like gatherings, that resolves the possibility of some students becoming offended, and should also eliminate the disruptive actions."

"Wait, what?" Joan interjected. "Now it's clear as spring water that this is really about Angel and your bias toward her!"

"Well, there are many who do not approve of those ceremonies, and yes, are even offended by them," Kellogg admitted. "A number of parents have contacted me about this so-called healing circle. Stone Creek is, by a large majority, a conservative Christian community. How do you expect me to justify allowing pagan ceremonies such as this on school property?"

Joan jumped to her feet, smacking her forehead in exasperation. "You show them the law! It's that simple! And tell them that as a public institution, this school has to follow the law! And about these conversations with these 'concerned' parents, I assume you have a record of them? Notes detailing the conversations, who you spoke with, and the like? We're going to need them."

Kellogg continued, ignoring Joan's concerns. "Part 2: Instead of three days' suspension, Danny Ryan will not be allowed back in Stone Creek School until after the court has adjudicated his case—assuming the court determines that he is not a danger to other students. Part 3: If the court determines Daniel is fit and safe to attend this school, and he subsequently does reoffend at any time between now and graduation, I will recommend that he is expelled without recourse."

"You gotta be shittin' me!" Sam exclaimed. He gestured to the committee members. "Have you ever seen anything like this? Are you going to rubber-stamp this debacle?"

"Oh, and one more thing," Kellogg offered, with a thin smile. "Billy's parents said that if Danny will make an admission of guilt to the court ahead of time, and allow the judge to rule on whatever we decide at this meeting, they will not demand a hearing that will require the children to testify, which I'm sure you all agree, could be traumatizing to all parties involved."

"Traumatizing, you betcha it might be!" Sam said. "For those boys to lie under oath!"

Kellogg ignored Sam and continued, "It's time for a vote on my proposal. Two votes and it passes, then I send it to the court. Fewer than two votes, and we sit here and work out a compromise. If it comes to that and we can't work out a compromise, I will enter that fact into the recommendation. A show of hands will suffice.

"All on the committee in favor of this recommendation?"

The businessman and the golfer both seemed bored and eager to leave. Their hands shot up without hesitation.

"For the record," Kellogg stated, looking directly at Ms. Wilson, "those opposed?"

Amy set her jaw and boldly returned Kellogg's threatening gaze.

"Opposed."

"Very well, meeting adjourned."

That Thursday was the last day of Danny's original suspension. When Sam, Sally, and Joan returned home from the hearing, he was nowhere in sight. But there was an envelope from the court on the kitchen table, with the summons alongside it. Danny was to appear in court the next Tuesday at 10:00 a.m.

Sam went out into the farmyard and hollered for his son. There was no answer. He checked the barn and saw that one golf cart wasn't in its parking spot. He figured Danny was most likely out picking morels somewhere between there and Joan and Maureen's place at the other end of the woods trail.

He went back inside to inform Sally and Joan he was going to go search for him. Sam wouldn't have to check too many places; he would simply follow the tracks where the cart had flattened the new grass underneath its wheels.

He didn't have to go far, less than a quarter of a mile to the fire ring. Danny had a fire of twigs and small branches going in the pit and was sitting on the north rock, his head in his hands, sucking in breaths between sobs. His Lab puppy, Misty, was licking his hands.

From just below the rim of the plateau a hundred feet away, Sam hollered, "Danny?"

Danny stayed on the rock, his face still cupped in his hands, and shook his head back and forth. Sam hurried over to console him, and Misty ran up, her oversize feet pounding the ground. When he knelt in front of Danny, he could see his son's hands were soaked with tears and phlegm. Sam began dying inside and had to bite his lip to keep from sobbing himself. He leaned forward and held his son tight. Misty stood on her hind legs and nuzzled Danny's elbow.

Danny lost all control of his grief, laid his head on his father's shoulder, and squeezed Sam as hard as he could. "Dad, I am so sorry… When I saw the summons, it really hit me."

"You don't have to apologize, son." Tears began leaking from Sam's eyes. "We'll take care of this, we'll get through it together. Come on, son." He helped Danny to his feet. "Mom and Aunt Joan are waiting for us."

"Danny, they aren't going to let you back in school until after court," Joan said. "We can live with that until Tuesday. In the meantime, there are a couple of things for you all to keep in mind. We really have to watch our steps in order to get Danny back in school and keep him there. Pushing back isn't going to work. They hold all the trump cards."

"But this is so…so unjust," Sam pled.

"That's the other thing. It's got me stumped," Joan said. "The way people behave—and I'm talking about Kellogg—there's a reason for everything. What she's done makes no sense to us, but it makes perfect sense to her, whatever her motivation is. It will help if we can figure her out. I don't mean we need to hire a private detective, but I will have my legal assistant do some checking about her. How long has she been at Stone Creek?"

Sally answered, "This is her first and only year. When the school lost its last principal to a better offer without warning just before the beginning of this school year and was in a bind, she came out of retirement. I don't remember from where. They gave her a pretty sweet deal, if I remember right. But she told them it was only for one year."

"So why would she throw down the gauntlet over this?" Joan asked. "She has no stake in anything regarding the school. And she has only three weeks left there."

"A good question," Sam agreed.

"Another good question," Joan added, "is why aren't Billy's parents suing? And why are they avoiding a trial?" She sighed. "At any rate, in the meantime, kiddo, we need to work on your plan, your promise to the court about how you won't let anything like this happen again. I don't think this is the time to argue how Kellogg effed this up so bad. Let's just get you back to school. I also think it would be a bad idea for me to attend the hearing. We don't want to appear intimidating in any way."

"As far as Angel is concerned," Joan turned her attention to Sally and Sam. "Do you think she'll be okay not making any waves for now?"

"Well, she's certainly got a mind of her own," Sally said. "But she loves her brother more than anyone."

"I'll talk to her," Danny offered. "You know, I think she's really going to like the part about figuring out Kellogg. You know what a whiz she is on the computer."

Danny turned to his father. "So I've already wasted my first two days off doing schoolwork and feeling sorry for myself. What will it be today—working the team, spearing suckers, or picking morels?"

"Got plenty of morels, and the yellows still haven't started. So suckers, I suppose. Working the team can wait."

"Mom, you take a kayak and herd them toward me and Dad in the jon boat."

"I'll pack the lunch," Sally said.

"To the river!" Danny shouted. Misty, who had been curled up on the couch in the living room, already knew that signal. Giant puppy feet thumped onto the floor, rumbling to the kitchen and sliding to a stop against the table leg. The gangly pup scrambled to regain her footing and jumped to put her paws on Danny's thigh, her eyes bright and her tongue hanging out the side of her mouth.

Danny shook a finger at his puppy's nose. "You're doing great when I tell you to get in the boat. But not so great with 'Stay in the boat'. Mom, we'll see, but she might have to ride with you. You should probably bring along a towel and some dry clothes in a plastic bag. She's really growing, isn't she?" He nuzzled his dog and squeezed her hard around the neck. "You're just like your Grandma Deja."

He looked to his parents and added, "Isn't it funny how genes get handed down from one generation to the next, and in many ways, we end up almost carbon copies? So who gets the credit for passing down the temper that got me into this mess?"

Sam raised his hand. "Guilty." They all laughed.

Sally added, "I'm not sure I had anything to do with your trip to Earth. I was just a surrogate…"

"A what?" Danny asked.

She elbowed Sam in the ribs. "Go look it up on your 12-year-old boy's best friend."

"I wonder where Angel is?" Sally said to Sam. "I left her a message we'd be on the river and to take the late bus home after practice." She checked the answering machine. "No messages."

Sam shrugged as he poured himself a glass of wine at the counter. "She probably went home with Cindy."

Sally frowned and shook her head. "She would have called…"

She called the Palmers, and Cindy's mother, Ally, confirmed that Cindy had come home on the regular bus.

"Sam, I don't like this," Sally said as she began dialing Angel's cell number. She ran her hand through her hair as she waited for it to ring. He stepped beside her. "It went right to voicemail. I'm going to town." She tried to set the phone back into its caddy but missed and it rattled to the floor.

Sam leaned over to pick it up. Sally was already hurrying toward the front door. He followed her out to her car. She had the gearshift in reverse before she had even shut the door.

He shouted, "I'm sure it's nothing. Be careful, Hon!"

Sally took a left out of the driveway, her rear tires sending gravel flying.

Half a mile their side of Stone Creek, Angel was walking down the edge of the road, wearing her softball practice uniform and carrying her book bag. Sally pulled to a stop. "Whew! I was worried," she said out the passenger window.

Without a word, Angel tossed her book bag into the back seat and slid into the front. Staring straight ahead, she said, "My phone is dead."

"I'm sorry," Sally said. "We left a message. Went sucker spearing. Why didn't you call from another phone when I didn't show up after practice? And what happened to your shirt?"

The collar was ripped open several inches.

"Got tangled up with the fence going after a fly ball."

"Did you get hurt?"

Angel kept staring straight ahead without answering.

"I'm sorry, Angel, about the miscommunication. Don't you want to hear how we did spearing?"

"Nope. Just want to get home and take a shower."

CHAPTER 4

HE LIVES IN CHURCH

After the hearing, they dropped Danny off in front of the school. The judge had seemed very pleased with his handwritten apology to Billy. And he was even more pleased that he could just rubber-stamp Kellogg's plan, which the principal had revised to contain no mention of the circumstances that had led to the fight. On paper, it seemed like Danny had just snapped out of the blue. It was all cut and dried, just the way the good judge liked it.

He had put Danny on probation until the age of 18, and then, assuming there had been no further serious incidents, his record would be wiped clean. Also, the judge warned that if there was ever another incident involving violence, there would an expedited hearing, and Danny could face the possibility of being removed from his home and placed into either confinement or a foster home.

Hearing that made Sam's blood boil, but he kept a sober face and listened respectfully. He had a feeling those boys' shenanigans weren't over.

He leaned forward to ask the judge something, but Sally dug her fingernails into his thigh to stop him. He had wanted to ask, "What if these other boys continue to harass Danny? Or Angel?"

Despite Sally's warning, Sam kicked himself for rolling over and playing dead. He had a bad feeling about this whole situation.

Amy walked along the deserted school hallway. All the students were in class. Her path had crossed Danny's outside the school office, where he had to sign in. She glanced through the large plateglass window and saw Kellogg reading something at her desk.

"Danny," she whispered. "There is talk that those boys are going to try to get to you. Please keep your cool. And if anything happens, come to me, so somebody besides Ms. Kellogg has a record of it."

Before he could thank her, he felt a hand on his shoulder.

"Welcome back, Danny." Kellogg greeted him as if he were a long, lost friend. Addressing Amy icily, she added, "Don't you need to be somewhere, Ms. Wilson?"

Amy replied, "Oh, I was just telling Danny that the work he did from home and emailed to me—his theme on Abraham Lincoln—was the best of the class, and I am so proud of him."

Danny couldn't believe it. His teacher had just lied to the principal.

"Hello? Mrs. Ryan? This is Amy Wilson."

"Oh hello. Yes, Ms. Wilson?"

"Please, just call me Amy. The kids all do."

"Okay, Amy. What can I do for you?"

"You know that theme paper Danny did while he was suspended, on Abraham Lincoln?"

"I didn't know exactly what he was working on. But he did spend more time in his room than I imagined he would—you know, what with it being morel season and having his new puppy around."

"Well, he wrote the best seventh-grade paper on any subject that I've ever seen. What really impressed me is how he compared Lincoln's decision to free the slaves—knowing full-well the pain it would cause the country, and the agony Lincoln must have endured— he likened it to the pain Christ must have felt dying for us. Wow."

"I don't know what to say…"

"It's usually pretty easy to tell the Bible-types around here from those not so inclined. I didn't peg you all as… particularly religious."

"Umm, we're not…" Sally said. "But thanks. I think."

"Can I talk to you about Angel?"

"Sure, what's going on?"

"I think she's taking this thing about Danny pretty hard. And all her friends, except for Cindy, have abandoned her. It's just her and Cindy off by themselves."

"Around here, too. Overnight together here or at Palmers, every night since last week. And they were together all weekend. Didn't take time off from each other even on Mother's Day."

"I haven't seen her smile for several days," said Amy.

"Me either," said Sally. "I asked her last night if there was anything she wanted to talk to about. She said she's just worried about Danny."

"Did she tell you about the softball game in Park Rapids last night?"

"She just said they lost, didn't elaborate."

"Angel was running to second base. All she had to do was slide and she would have been safe. Instead, with a full head of steam, she bowled the shortstop over, and got kicked out of the game."

"WHAT? I'll have to have a talk with her!"

"Actually, I wouldn't mention it if I were you," Amy advised. "Let's just give her a chance to work through this on her own."

"Sam, come up here," Sally called from Danny's upstairs bedroom. "You gotta see this."

She was sitting at Danny's desk.

"Oh, no," Sam mumbled, imagining what his wife had found on their son's computer.

But the kids had the only two computers connected to the internet, and there was a house rule: Don't leave anything on your computer you don't want anyone else to know you've been looking at—especially your mother or father.

After Amy's call, Sally had scrolled through the browser history on Danny's computer. Besides dozens of searches for "Abraham Lincoln," she discovered that he had been researching Christ as well. There were four different sites accessed about Matthew 21:12.

And Jesus went into the temple of God, and cast out all them that sold and bought in the temple, and overthrew the tables of the moneychangers, and the seats of them that sold doves, and said unto them, It is written, My house shall be called the house of prayer; but ye have made it a den of thieves.

"Another site was accessed, too. It explained the temple incident—that Jesus's angry act led directly to his arrest and crucifixion, and then, as we all know, Jesus took his punishment without excuse." Sally pivoted to face Sam.

"He looked up this stuff after the incident. I don't think he had been plotting to stand up for his sister in that terrible way. He'd just had enough and it came out. Like Jesus in the temple. He needed to know that what he did was forgivable, maybe even the right thing."

Sam slapped both cheeks in mock horror. "Oh no! Do you think he's turned into...a Christian?"

Sally shrugged. "Well, kids have gone off on stranger tangents. But no, I don't think so. I think what he found on the internet..." She raised her eyes to the ceiling. "Somebody up there led him to it, to realize he's been forgiven. Maybe even Christ, himself!"

"This is getting pretty deep," Sam teased. "How about we roast some venison sausages at the fire ring and think about where we may have gone wrong. Shall I also bring a bottle of wild grape wine?"

"Yes. And definitely yes."

———

Sally had been raised Lutheran and had married Bill in the Streeter Evangelical Lutheran Church of America. She didn't set foot in the church for about a year after that, but then began privately attending a few times a month, seeking solace and guidance about her sorry marriage. Sometimes Pop, Bill's dad, went with her, seeking the same for his beloved daughter-in-law, although he didn't tell her that was the reason.

Sadly, things never improved. In fact, the marriage became worse by the day. Sally resigned herself to make the best of it, in spite of the beatings and Bill's serial philandering. She quit going to church altogether about three years before Bill's death—she had lost faith. She had last set foot in a church at Pop's funeral in 2003, except for the occasional wedding and funeral. But she never took Communion.

Sam had been raised Catholic. He went along with it while he was still in his parents' house—didn't really have a choice. If you skipped Mass and didn't get to confession before you died, the church said you were going straight to Hell. He didn't believe a word of that, but it was easier to placate his parents.

Even after he turned 16, got his driver's license, and found a weekend job at a gas station, he hauled his butt out of bed in time to attend 6 a.m. Sunday Mass every week, regardless of whatever foolishness he and his buddies had been up to the night before. The good news was that the priest seemed like he didn't want to be there either, skipping through the liturgy like a flat rock thrown across the surface of a calm pond. Sam was always on the road to his 7 a.m. job before 6:30—even when he stayed all the way to hear "The Mass is ended. Go in peace."

Several years after Sam quit going to church, it occurred to him: Why hadn't he just skipped church and gone right to the gas station and caught a little more sleep? Who would have known? Maybe the nuns, the priests, and his parents had gotten to him and instilled some of the proverbial fear of God into his DNA.

Yes, Sam believed there had been a person named Jesus Christ, and he had been a very good person—even someone whose life he should emulate. He agreed with the parts about loving unconditionally and having faith in something. Admittedly, those basic pretenses were often tough for Sam. He believed that Christ never intended to have a religion named after him, or for people to twist his message, and especially to harm others in his name.

Sam had figured out long ago that folks had invented a second God—the angry, demanding God who'd toss you straight into Hell for not following mortal men's frightful bastardization of who Christ was and his simple message. Sometime after the death of Sam's second wife in 1997, he had found his way to his version of the original god, which he called the Universe—the first and only real source of all that is good and wondrous. His personal god was the opposite of the one most Christians pray to, either for favors or to keep from getting on His bad side. Sam's god blesses, and that's all. The rest was up to us. There was nothing to be afraid of.

Sam had come to believe that becoming human and landing on Earth—it's our choice, with God's blessing. We volunteer to show up here, but in the process, we've forgotten who we really are. That's the way it's set up, on purpose. Life is about the journey, uncovering the layers, and remembering our divinity the best we can.

Like the ancient Sufi poet Rumi put it, so perfectly and simply: We search for Fana—recognizing God-The-Source in things earthly, and realize their incredible beauty is God, and when we make that connection, our spine flutters and our eyes tear, and we thank God. And we also revel in Baqa, which is God-Come-To-Earth through us, with us, to experience our experience—every experience, from the sublime to the opposite. For this, God thanks us.

Fana and Baqa, they are the perfect partnership— God and us, equal partners.

———————

The question "Why don't we go to church?" was bound to come up in the Ryan household at some point.

And it did, from the innocent lips of Angel. She had been five and her brother four. The family had been decorating the Christmas tree in the living room, complete with a tiny manger scene on the floor under the boughs.

"I want to sing at Christmas in church like my friends Gina and Susie," Angel said, more to herself than to her parents, as she carefully draped tinsel over a branch. "We sing Christmas carols in school. It's fun." She began humming "Silent Night" in perfect pitch.

Sam and Sally stopped arranging ornaments in the higher reaches of the tree and raised their eyebrows at each other.

"Ya, me too," chimed in Danny from the couch, which he had just climbed onto, to hug their Lab, Deja.

"Well, you're gonna have a Christmas program at school," said Sally. "And you get to sing then, ok?"

"But Jesus isn't there. He lives in church," Angel answered, quite sure of herself. "And under our tree." She dropped to her knees and gently touched the tiny baby Jesus on the top of his head. "Except our Jesus isn't real.

He's too small. I want to go see the real Jesus…in church. That's where Susie and Gina say he lives."

"Umm…" Sam stammered.

Angel stood and put her hands on her hips. "I wanna go see baby Jesus, and sing for him!" She tugged on her daddy's shirttail. "Babies like it when you sing to them. Nice songs."

Sam knelt down in front of his little girl, his hands on his thighs. Her brow was furrowed and she was expecting an answer—maybe even one she wouldn't like. How do you tell your baby girl that there is no such thing as the real baby Jesus?

He glanced up at Sally. She shrugged and mouthed, "I love you…good luck!"

"Actually, baby Jesus is in more places than churches at Christmas. The ones we see now are reminders of the real baby Jesus, so we'll remember to close our eyes and see him in our mind anytime we want. It's like the picture we have of my dad, your Grandpa Ryan, up there on the mantle. Do you remember how you loved to snuggle with each other in the big chair and he'd read you stories, and how he taught you to sing 'Lullaby and Good Night'?"

"Yeah!" Angel shouted, clapping her hands together. "That's what I want to sing to baby Jesus!"

"Well, Grandpa's gone now, and we can't see him with our real eyes anymore, right?" Angel nodded. "But we can look at his picture, and close our eyes, and we can feel him still loving us, even though we can't see him. Just the thought of Grandpa makes us happy. That's the way it is with all the baby Jesuses that aren't really him. They remind us about him."

As Angel turned her attention back to the tinsel and slowly pulled out a handful of strands, careful not to break or tangle them, she asked, "Did Jesus ever grow up?"

"Yup, and that's a whole other story. If you want, I'll tell it to you on Easter."

Sally rolled her eyes and turned away to hide her smile.

"Oh! I know already! Baby Jesus grew up and now he's the Easter Bunny! I'd like to eat a chocolate baby Jesus. Daddy, hide one in my stocking, pleeeeease?"

"Now what makes you think I put that stuff in your stocking?" Sam asked.

Sally laughed quietly to herself as she adjusted the treetop angel.

"Aw, come on, Daddy. I wasn't born yesterday."

CHAPTER 5

WATCHING HIS STEP

It was lunchtime. Students trickled into the courtyard to kill time, awaiting the bell. Only Angel and Cindy of the healing circle gang were by the big pine tree. They sat in the grass, visiting. The other five girls, who had all gone to school together since kindergarten, were hanging out near the courtyard doors.

Danny emerged with his friend, Nate. The two walked across to the far edge of the courtyard, where they would be out of earshot of anyone else. Danny glanced over at Kellogg's office window. She was watching them.

Nate was half a head shorter than Danny. He wore his dark hair buzzed, a style he had adopted when he'd joined the junior high wrestling team that winter. He had a stocky build and was strong for his age and size, from working on his parents' farm: haying, fencing, and picking rock. Nate's record for the wrestling season was 15–2. He had even been promoted to varsity the last three meets, and had won two of those three matches against kids four and five years older than him.

"Please," Danny begged, "don't do anything."

Nate said, "But they say they're gonna get revenge—Gavin, Dylan, and Mike."

"I'll take 'em out before they get a chance," vowed Nate. "In gym class wrestling, I pinned every one of them in about 15 seconds. Only took that long because I had to run them down first. They're chickenshit."

"Please, just let it go, okay?" Danny pleaded. "You're only gonna make it worse. If there's even a hint of anything going on that's remotely connected back to me, I'm sunk, I'm gone, either to juvie or a foster home. And I'll never be able to come back to Stone Creek School."

"Even if they start it?"

"Yep. I shouldn't have punched Billy like that."

"But he deserved it!" Nate growled.

Danny took another look at Kellogg's window. She was watching the courtyard doorway. Gavin, Dylan, and Mike had just come out and were looking around.

"Come on," Danny urged his pal. "Let's go talk to them."

"What? Are you NUTS?"

"It's part of my deal with the court—to apologize to all of them. I already wrote Billy a letter."

The five boys met up near the big pine, a couple of yards from Angel and Cindy. The girls stopped in mid-conversation to listen and watch.

"Hi, guys," Danny said, giving a little friendly wave.

Billy's friends stood shoulder to shoulder, faces rigid and feet apart. Nate took half a step toward Danny, prepared for the worst.

"Danny?" Angel asked.

"Everybody relax, please," Danny said. "I just want to apologize for what I did to Billy. I don't want anything like that to ever happen again. I'm sorry."

"Sorry, my ass," snarled Gavin. "You're going down... down the road. And so is your witch of a sister."

Angel leapt to her feet, but her brother waved her off. Nate took another step closer to the other three. Danny held his arms out to keep some distance between everyone. Angel glanced over at Kellogg, who was smirking and stroking her chin.

Out of nowhere, Amy appeared and stood in the middle of them.

"That's enough," she said. Pointing to the doorway, she ordered, "Gavin, Dylan, Mike—leave the courtyard. NOW."

Angel implored, "Danny, it's fine. I don't care what they say about me."

"Well, I care. But trust me, I won't do anything else dumb."

Amy said, "Let's just hope those boys get tired of this game. Danny, stop by my room. You'd better write down what just happened, word for word, and I'll keep it as a record."

"I can wait 'em out. Don't worry about me," said Danny.

"It's not just YOU I worry about," Amy said. She felt a hand on her shoulder. It was Kellogg.

Amy suggested, "The bell's gonna ring in a minute. Why don't you all head to class."

Kellogg waited until the kids were out of earshot then whispered, "I don't remember appointing you to be courtyard monitor."

"Why are you doing this to Danny and Angel? They're two of the nicest kids I know, and they're great students."

"It's my job," Kellogg said, with a fake smile across her wrinkled face. "It's why they pay me the big bucks—to make sure the students follow the rules, to keep order. And don't forget, I also direct staff. My advice is that you should just concentrate on your own business. Aren't you supposed to be in your classroom before the bell rings? Hmm…end-of-year staff reviews are coming up…"

Amy turned toward the door and began walking quickly, Kellogg marching right behind her. Just as Amy's hand touched the door handle, the bell rang.

———————

After Sam had dropped off Angel and Danny the next morning, he marched in to Kellogg's office without knocking. "I'm here to file a formal complaint against Gavin. He called Angel a witch."

"Mr. Ryan, unfortunately we have no such mechanism for a parent to file a complaint against a student. And what are you even talking about?"

"Out in the courtyard yesterday at lunch. Gavin said it, and eight others heard him say it. If that isn't provocation in an extremely delicate situation, I don't know what is. They said you watched the whole thing from your office window."

"Who did you hear that from?"

"A parent, but I'm not saying who, because then their kid would have a bullseye on their butt, too."

"Well, I'm afraid in that case," Kellogg said, "you'll have to get one of the students to come forward."

"You and I both know that's not going to happen. None of them trust you. They all know you're at the bottom of this."

"Oh, here we go again," Kellogg said, crossing her arms across her ample bosom. "Accusing me AGAIN of bias against your children. You see how far that got you with the disciplinary report. Two of the committee members didn't buy an ounce of it. And the judge loved it."

"Thanks for reminding me. As long as I'm here, I'll need copies of the complaints Danny filed against Billy and the others. And the ones about Angel's healing circle."

"Mr. Ryan, as I told you before, the complaints concerning Angel were rather informal. And, perhaps you've forgotten, I just informed you that the school doesn't have a mechanism for parents to make an official complaint about a student. As far as the complaints Danny filed, you are welcome to them, even though I considered them false claims. Turns out, a strong case could be made that Danny's complaints were filed with me, but he never mentioned them to you, because he was plotting the attack, which he knew you would certainly stop."

"Get them, please," Sam directed. "And if I were you, MS. Kellogg, I'd think back about those parents who complained about Angel, and make a list."

"For what purpose?"

"You never know…"

"One more thing," Sam added. "Trust me, Danny won't be going anywhere alone, where those boys can get at him."

"Or HE can get at THEM…" Kellogg said smugly. "Good thinking, Mr. Ryan."

Friday afternoon after school, Danny watched Angel and the rest of the junior high softball team practice. Amy was the assistant coach. While the girls were running a lap around the perimeter fence, the last thing they did at the end of practice, Amy walked over to Danny sitting in the bleachers alone.

She whispered, "You gotta watch yourself. Please."

"Thanks," Danny said, "but I learned my lesson. I don't care what anybody says, I'm never going there again. Trust me."

His instructions from his parents were to go nowhere alone, not even home on the bus. Gavin rode Danny and Angel's bus, too. That's why Danny was at practice.

"How about I give you and Angel a ride home? You can call your folks to let them know."

"Well, we're just going to the muni. Mom's working there and she gets off in a little while. She's bringing us home."

"Okay, then how about I give you a ride up there?" Amy offered.

"Naw, we'll be okay. But thanks."

––––––––––

Sally filled in for the day shift at the municipal liquor store two or three times a week. On those days, it was handy to bring the kids home with her. Her shift ended just 15 minutes after sports practice was over.

The muni paid minimum wage plus tips, which usually didn't amount to much, except when the deer hunters, snowmobilers, and fishermen were in town. It was a bonus when the out-of-towners hit it big on pull tabs. Then the tips would often roll in $10 and $20 at a time, sometimes even more than that.

Sally had a knack for keeping the tourists and the daytime regulars laughing. She'd join right in with them, trading jokes and barbs. Plus, it never hurt to have a female bartender who was as easy on the eyes as she was—especially in blue jeans and her muni-logo, button-front blouses and tees that flattered her figure. With her long blonde hair and Nordic features, men still did double takes when she entered a room, even at the age of 53. Some who didn't know her flirted, and who could blame them? But she had a way of deflecting their advances without hurting their feelings or putting a dent in their tip.

That little bit she made, plus the profits from the winery, giving folks trail rides in the wagon or the sleigh behind their team of Percherons, and having weddings at the winery or up at the fire ring all kept the Ryan family coffer stocked comfortably. But she tended bar more because it was a pleasant change of pace than for the money.

The Ryan kids headed uptown on foot. As they passed the alley between the bakery and old post office, they noticed Gavin, Dylan, and Mike surrounding another boy near the dumpster the far end of the bakery. Danny stopped in his tracks.

Angel whispered, "Come on!" She moved ahead of Danny a pace before he took a quick step to catch up.

"Hey!" one of the boys shouted. His voice was muffled.

Danny looked back. The other three boys parted. It was Billy on a dirt bike that looked brand new. He wore a heavy bandage across his nose, and both of his eyes were black. Billy hadn't been back to school yet, but he appeared to be getting around pretty well on the shiny bike. He began moving in toward Danny and Angel. The bike made only a whirring sound; it was battery-powered.

"Keep moving," Angel ordered in a loud whisper. "Just ignore them."

Billy accelerated and shot out of the alley. He circled in front of the Ryan kids, jumped the curb, and screeched to a stop three feet in front of them. The other three boys had rushed up behind them.

"Maybe if some asshole smashed YOUR ugly nose all to hell, your aunt would buy you some nice wheels like these for a get-well present," said Billy, his voice nasal and muffled.

Dylan shot a disapproving look at Billy and shook his head no. Angel saw it out of the corner of her eye, but Billy didn't seem to have noticed it.

Angel ordered through her clenched teeth, "Just leave us alone and get out of the way." She grabbed Danny by the elbow and stepped off the curb.

But Danny stiffened his arm and stood in his tracks. He looked back at the three boys standing an arm's length behind them and said softly, "We don't want any part of any trouble. Please just leave us alone."

"Hey," Dylan said with a smirk, "I hear your sister likes it when she gets grabbed by the pussy."

Danny's face began to flush and he sucked in a deep breath through his nose.

"Never mind, Danny." Angel pulled harder on his arm. He didn't budge. "I don't care what they say!"

He shook her loose, turned to face Dylan, and took a step toward him, stopping nose-to-nose.

Danny could smell Dylan's rotten breath. "And your mom loves it too when she gets her pussy grabbed in the muni!"

"Danny, NO!" Angel shouted in desperation, but his fist was already planted in Dylan's solar plexus.

Dylan dropped to his knees and began retching. Danny stood over him with his fist re-cocked. Angel was in shock, her hands over her face. She began crying. "NO, goddamnit…"

Billy mumbled as he twisted the accelerator on his bike and sped past them, "I guess you get the camera drone, Dilly. Good work!"

Gavin and Mike ran back to the alley and disappeared around the corner.

Angel whispered to Danny, "They got us—we can't ever tell anybody what they said. You know… Mom and the nightmares…"

Danny looked around, confused. He was shocked to see Kellogg across the street watching them from an SUV. As the driver's door window slid down, she held up a cell phone and snapped several photos. Then she made a call.

Dylan scrambled to his feet and lurched toward the alley, hunched over, still retching. "Over here!" they heard Mike shout.

Amy's truck approached from the direction of the school just as Dylan disappeared down the alley. She saw Angel sitting on the curb sobbing and Danny standing on the sidewalk, still bristling, his face red, rubbing the knuckles of his right hand. She screeched to a stop, her truck facing the wrong way next to the curb.

"What happened?" she asked as she bailed out the door.

"Danny…" Angel blubbered as she wiped her eyes with her sleeve. "He just slugged Dylan." She pointed across the street. "And Ms. Kellogg got pictures."

Amy looked over to where Angel was pointing. Kellogg was smiling widely and gave Amy a thumbs-up.

"Cops are on the way," she hollered. "I'll go get Mrs. Ryan from the bar. Maybe you should stay here until they arrive. It's probably best if you parked on the correct side of the street, though." The SUV pulled away from the curb.

———

Sally was shocked to see Kellogg come through the bar door. As far as she knew, the principal had never set foot in a Stone Creek watering hole. She had a smirk on her face and clearly was there to cause trouble. The dozen or so patrons scattered around the horseshoe bar looked up briefly, then went right back to their drinks and watching television.

"Ms. Kellogg!"

"Well, he did it again. Not surprised one bit."

Sally feared the worst. "Who? What?"

"Your Danny..." Kellogg wagged her finger, "just assaulted Dylan in front of the old post office." She pulled out her phone. "Got it right here!" She began tapping on the phone screen with her pointer finger. "Want to see?" she asked, smirking.

Sally's eyes grew wide, her mouth dropped open, and her heart started racing. "No..."

"You might want to be there when law enforcement arrives. Your friend Ms. Wilson is there with your delinquent children."

Sally looked around frantically. Some of the patrons were eyeing her with concern. She still had 10 minutes until the end of her shift. A county sheriff's car sped past.

She gasped and put a hand over her mouth, her eyes wide in disbelief.

"I got it. Just go," said Rusty as he slid off his barstool. He was also a fill-in bartender.

"Thanks!" Sally wiped her face and hands with a bar towel. She hurried toward the bottle shop and grabbed her purse from under the counter.

Halfway across the parking lot, she stopped and stammered into her cell phone, "Sam…Sam…come quick…"

Rounding the corner, she saw the deputy opening the back door of the patrol car, motioning Danny inside. Angel was sitting on the curb with her face in her hands. Amy had an arm around Angel's shoulders, doing her best to console her. Kellogg had parked in front of the bakery and stood outside her SUV, arms crossed, tapping her foot.

"STOP!" Sally yelled to the deputy. "Please don't take Danny away! There must be some mistake!"

The deputy, Sergeant Richard Roberts, smiled sympathetically and shook his head. He held his hands up. "Don't worry, ma'am." Sally reached for Danny. "Just need to get a statement and I'd rather do it in the car. Come on, sit up front with me, please."

The sight of her son in the back seat of a squad car tore at Sally's heart and made her light-headed. She hurried around to the passenger door and slid in, turning to look at Danny through the security fence.

"Oh my God. Why…what happened?" she asked.

"I'm so sorry, Mom, but the things they said…" Danny said.

Pen and pad ready, Sergeant Roberts said, "Let's start from the beginning, Danny."

Danny told them how the four boys had come out of the alley and surrounded them, and how Billy had taunted them with his new motorbike.

"What did they say exactly?" asked Roberts.

Danny hesitated and bit his lip. Tears ran down his cheeks. "I can't repeat it…it was terrible… And without thinking, yes, I punched Dylan in the gut, hard. That's all that matters."

"Well, let's get your sister in here," Roberts said.

Sally opened her door. "Angel, honey, come on in."

Angel's face was still red and splotchy. She wiped at her nose with her sleeve.

Amy stepped forward, "Sir? Umm, I didn't really see anything—just Danny and Angel sitting here on the curb, when I was driving past. But you gotta know there are no better kids in the world than these two. I'm not exactly sure what's going on, but I'm sure there's some reasonable explanation."

Just then, Kellogg walked up behind Amy. She was holding her phone up for Roberts. There was Danny standing over Dylan, who was on his knees bent over. "See for yourself, Officer," she said.

Roberts frowned and sighed heavily.

Kellogg said, "Danny is now indefinitely suspended from school, by court order—his second offense. The boys he's been harassing—if you'd like their statements, how about at school tomorrow?"

"Yes, that will work. I'll call ahead."

"Can I prepare a statement?" Amy asked. "I know about the circumstances leading up to this."

"That would be fine." Roberts nodded.

Kellogg shot Amy an icy glare.

Amy fixed her eyes on Kellogg's. "Danny, Angel, I got your backs. Officer, I'll have my statement ready for you tomorrow when you come to school. Ms. Kellogg knows where to find me."

He motioned for Angel to get into the back seat as Amy and Kellogg headed for their vehicles.

"Angel, what happened?" Roberts asked, almost whispering.

She told the exact same story, and like Danny, refused to tell what Dylan had said.

Sam pulled up behind the squad car just as they were all getting out of it.

"I'm not taking Danny into custody," Roberts said to Sam. "I could put him on a hold, but I won't. I'll stop by tomorrow and check in on him."

"So now what happens?" Sam asked.

"I turn my report in to the county attorney. He'll have the court schedule a hearing, if he thinks there should be charges. You'll be notified either way."

CHAPTER 6

STEVIE RAY AND PRINCE

Sally was at the kitchen sink, rinsing the fresh garden greens she and Danny had just harvested. Danny was at the kitchen range, browning two pounds of venison sausage. She asked Maureen and Joan, who were sitting at the kitchen table with Angel and Sam, "Can you stay? Spaghetti, with our homemade sausage and sauce…"

They had gathered to discuss Danny's predicament. Joan was staring off into space, her brow furrowed and wheels turning; Sally's question had gone right over her head.

"Thanks, but no thanks," Maureen said. "Our supper is in the crockpot."

Joan was still off in her own legal world. "We've got to really fight it this time."

Sam sat stone-faced, his jaw set. Sally and Danny both turned and nodded. Maureen was exasperated, shaking her head and rolling her eyes. Angel sat quietly, biting her lip, her hands folded on the table. She looked as if she was going to cry.

"This isn't your fault," Maureen assured Angel as she patted her hands. "It's not Danny's either."

Sally asked over her shoulder, "Let's get down to business. How does this work?"

"Just like for adults who are charged with a crime," Joan answered, "except there won't be a jury. But just like in adult court, a juvenile does get to face his accusers. It's a constitutional right. We can make them testify under oath. And before that, we can depose anyone connected, also under oath: the boys, others who have any information about the harassment, even Kellogg. It could get messy."

Angel spoke up. "I'm not sure if my friends will cooperate."

"Well," Joan said, "they'll have to if we go forward and subpoena them for their depositions. The county attorney can also depose them, and possibly require them to testify, even if we don't. In fact, I'm quite sure he will. He has to make his case."

Joan looked at the kids. "I know this is a touchy subject, but when the county attorney deposes you, he will no doubt ask what was said that set Danny off before he punched Dylan."

The brother and sister looked at each other and shook their heads.

"I'll never repeat what they said," Danny vowed as he quickly turned his attention back to the range.

"Me either," said Angel as she shook her head defiantly. "Danny and I made a pact. We'll never break it."

"That might be the key to getting this thrown out," Joan said. "The proverbial straw that breaks their backs. We know those boys will never admit they said anything terrible."

"Our word against theirs?" Danny said without looking up from the skillet. "Yeah, we've seen how far that gets us. They'll just say they came over to show us Billy's new dirt bike or something."

"The first order of business is to prepare for the initial hearing," Joan said. "That's when the judge will set the trial date, and also when the county attorney could ask for conditions of your release. Or he could even ask that you be held over until trial."

"Held OVER?" Sam leaned forward in his chair, his eyes wide. "What the hell does that mean?"

Sally shut the faucet off and turned to face Joan.

"It depends how much pressure the other parents are putting on the county attorney. They'll have a victim's advocate, too. She works out of that office. She could possibly make a recommendation for holding Danny over if they convince her that those boys are in danger. Whatever it is they're up to, they're holding most of the cards right now."

"Where would they hold Danny over?" asked Sally, her hands held wide.

"Two possibilities," Joan said. "Either juvenile hall or foster care—which are also Danny's possible outcomes if we go all the way to trial and they win. Kids, are you SURE you don't have anything to say in Danny's defense?"

Both shook their heads no.

Frustrated, Sally shook her head too and turned back to the sink.

"I've already notified the court that I'm representing Danny. Here's my plan for the initial hearing, which should be early next week," Joan said. "I'm going to talk to the county attorney and let him know there's evidence that you two were targeted. And second, in the event that the county attorney proposes to confine you, I'll counter that Danny should be put under house arrest, and promise you'll go no place off this farm without a parent present. Can you guys live with that?"

They all nodded.

"I'm pretty sure he'll go along with that. And then we start digging and find out what's really going on here. There's got to be a smokin' gun out there."

———————

Sam asked Joan under his breath, "What's SHE doing here?"

"Oh my God!" Joan whispered. "Chandler..."

She was still dressing like a drag queen with no fashion sense. Her hair was dyed dark black—too black—like a young girl who'd gone Goth, grossly accenting her pasty complexion. She wore a dowdy beige blouse buttoned up to her neck, with a black blazer over it, even though it was a 75-degree day. A long skirt hung to her ankles, paired with dark hose and clunky black shoes. Sam thought, *Yep, she still looks like the Grim Reaper.* She carried what looked to be the same briefcase from years ago. She waved across the way at them as if to say, "Oh yes, I'm back."

Danny leaned over to ask Joan, "Who's that?"

"It's a long story..."

She whispered to Danny and his parents. "Like I told you before, the judge will order a child protection worker. It never occurred to me we might get her."

"Can't we get her off the case?" Sally asked. "I doubt she'll like us any better now."

"I'll try."

As the door to the judge's chambers opened, the bailiff said, "All rise. The Honorable Judge Robert Belden presiding."

He was the same judge Danny had seen just seven days earlier—a gentleman in his sixties, with a large build and thick thatch of gray, wavy hair. He sat and, without looking up, said, "You may be seated."

He glanced up at Danny, then quickly cast his eyes down to the paperwork in front of him.

Joan couldn't read him. Was the judge exasperated? Feeling pity for Danny and wanting to give him another break? Or was he kicking himself for having gone too easy on him the first time around?

He addressed the county attorney. "I've got the file, your summons, and Ms. Adair's motion, but for the record, please state why we're here."

The county attorney, Greg Pearson, was thin and clean-cut, in his fifties, and groomed professionally. Joan knew him as a boring presenter. He was efficient though; he stuck strictly to the facts and always had them in perfect order. Pearson was rarely theatric like so many defense attorneys were when trying to impress a jury or judge. But he was effective, and the judges respected him for not turning their courtrooms into circuses.

"Your Honor, per your order from a week ago, if there were any future instances of alleged violence perpetrated by Daniel Ryan, I was to notify the court, thus this summons. Today I am asking to set this matter for trial in a month, and for the court to order whether Daniel should be held or released. I have met with counsel. In her motion, she is claiming extenuating circumstances—that Daniel Ryan was bullied into both of these offenses. It will take a trial to sort this out.

"In the meantime, I agree with counsel that neither juvenile hall nor a foster placement are in his or anyone's best interests. We have agreed to house arrest—Daniel will not be permitted to leave the Ryan farm without one of his parents present."

Sam leaned to whisper in Joan's ear and she nodded.

"Considering the end of the school year is less than two weeks away, and Daniel is an excellent student who has already proven he can keep up with his schoolwork from home—per the affidavit from his English teacher, Amy Wilson—I am asking you order the school NOT to expel him at this time, but to continue sending his schoolwork via email.

"And finally, I am asking you to assign a child protection worker to Daniel. It appears that the supervisor has appointed Ms. Dorothy Chandler to ensure Daniel's safety from any more of the alleged bullying, and to ensure that he complies with the court's order of house arrest. Ms. Chandler will also facilitate the standard psychological evaluation."

"Thank you," said Judge Belden. "Ms. Adair?"

Joan stood. "Yes, we've agreed to those conditions. However, I would like to amend the house arrest condition to allow Daniel to leave the property onto the trail system in the forest between the Ryans' farm and my place, and also to be allowed on the township road there. That's where Daniel works the new team of horses he's training. There's very little chance of him encountering the other boys back there. However, I think it would be prudent to include an order forbidding the other boys to travel that road, in the best interests of all concerned. One more thing. Danny is training his new Lab puppy. Part of their routine is to walk down the road adjacent to the Ryan property and swim at the bridge."

"That's reasonable, Ms. Adair. Thank you."

The judge addressed Danny directly, "What kind of horses, young man?"

"Percherons, sir," Danny replied.

"Tell me about your horses," the judge said.

"Stand up," his dad whispered.

"Sir," he began, then cleared his throat. "The new team we just got this spring are named Stevie Ray and Prince. Our old team—Elvis and Roy—we're retiring them, except for hitching one or the other with the newbies to teach them manners. I think I'm pretty close to hitching Stevie Ray and Prince together. Perches, even young ones, are pretty docile. They learn fast."

"Nice names," the judge said with a smile. "How long have you been driving horses?"

Danny finally relaxed and shrugged. "I can't remember ever NOT driving them, sir."

"Why do you have the teams?" the judge inquired. "Just for fun?"

"No, sir. We have a winery near Stone Creek. We give people rides on the trails and make bonfires for them. In winter, too, in a hay wagon we put skis on. And for parades. At the county fair, we shuttle folks from the parking lot for tips. They really like that."

"The people or the horses?" Belden asked.

"Both," Danny replied, smiling.

"Maybe I'll see you at the fair," the judge suggested. "I'll bring my granddaughters."

"Glad to oblige, sir." Joan nodded to Danny. He smiled again and sat down.

"And your puppy?"

Danny quickly stood back up. "We lost the Lab I grew up with, Deja, last fall. Misty's four months old—Deja's granddaughter. She's still a little spastic, but once you get her attention, she's a very fast learner. She already does 'sit,' 'stay,' and 'fetch' perfectly. But she needs some work on sitting still in the canoe and not jumping up on people."

Judge Belden smiled and nodded.

"I'd like to approach with counsel," Joan requested.

The judge waved her and Pearson forward.

In a whisper, Joan asked Pearson, "Did you know they were going to assign Ms. Chandler to this case?"

Pearson shrugged. "I just asked for a CP worker to be sent down. Why? What's the problem?"

"The Ryan family has a history with Ms. Chandler..."

"I think we need to discuss this in chambers," said Belden.

He stood and the bailiff said, "All rise."

———————

In chambers, the judge asked, "Ms. Adair, what's this all about?"

"Thirteen years ago, Ms. Chandler was guardian ad litem in Sally's divorce. Sally was pregnant, and Judge Friday ordered Ms. Chandler to perform a custody evaluation. The judge eventually questioned her impartiality, and not only removed her from the case, but relieved from any further guardian ad litem cases in this county."

Pearson asked, "Was that the case when the husband's attorney shot the husband in front of the courthouse, and then the bailiff had to shoot the attorney in self-defense?"

"I remember hearing about that," Judge Belden said. "But that was a long time ago."

"I can ask for a different worker," Pearson offered, "but don't hold your breath that they'll give us one. They are so understaffed and overworked up there."

The judge nodded.

"I tell you what," offered Belden. "Her duties are pretty simple, cut and dried. Let's allow her to file the report. If Daniel keeps his nose clean, I don't see how there could be any conflict of interest. But if you think there is, then file a motion and I'll consider it. Agreed?"

Joan and Pearson both nodded.

"Let's get back in there."

The trial was set for June 27th at 9 a.m.

CHAPTER 7

SPARE BARN BOOTS

Sam and the kids had whistled the horses up to the barn gate to give them grain. Six stout wooden posts with lead ropes tied on and rubber pails nailed to them. Elvis and Roy stood patiently by their usual posts nearest the barn. Sally's mare, Dolly, was at her spot next to Roy. Beyond the gate, Angel's mare, Sugar, stood quietly.

But Stevie Ray and Prince hadn't settled yet on who was in fifth place and who was in sixth. Stevie Ray, a year older, beat Prince to the fifth post. Prince tried to push his brother away, and both laid their ears back as Stevie Ray squealed.

"Knock it off, you two!" Sam warned as he grabbed a short whip leaning against the fence. Just the sight of the whip is all it took, and Prince begrudgingly sidestepped to the sixth post, his ears still pinned back when Sam snapped the lead rope to his halter. "I hope they figure this out soon. In the meantime, kids, always tie Prince first. Stevie Ray won't start anything."

A car turned into the gravel drive.

Under his breath, Sam muttered, "Chandler. Happy fucking birthday to me…"

"What?" asked Angel, as she tied Stevie Ray.

"It's a long story." Sam could feel the hairs on the back of his neck bristle.

Chandler pulled to a stop in front of the barn—right on time, exactly 9 a.m. Misty pranced toward the car. When the frumpy woman opened the door and swung her sausage legs out, she was greeted by a puppy jumping up to put its muddy, poopy paws on her lap.

"Get away!" she scolded, swatting at Misty's face with the back of her hand.

"Come on, girl!" Danny hollered to his puppy, as he snapped Sugar's lead rope on.

He trotted up to Chandler's sedan as she was brushing at the mud and poop on her ankle-length skirt. She frowned at the mess on the palm of her hand.

"I'm sorry. Trying to break her of that. Just a puppy, ya know."

"Every time I come here, I get attacked by some ill-mannered canine," Chandler said in disgust as she stood up, glaring daggers at Misty, who was peering suspiciously from behind Danny.

The Ryans hadn't told the kids about their previous experience with Chandler. Joan's advice was to not unearth any corpses. She had assured them that Judge Belden said Chandler's involvement would be minimal and cursory, so there was no need to tell the kids about her.

Another vehicle approached, coming from the direction of the bridge—Joan's SUV. It turned into the driveway and pulled to a stop near the house. She got out and waved to them.

"What's SHE doing here?" Chandler asked no one in particular, with obvious contempt.

"Auntie Joan!" Danny ran to her, Misty passing him halfway across the yard.

"Hey, guys!" Joan held her hand up to stop Misty, which had absolutely no effect. With his arms wide, Danny gathered Joan in, and gave her a bear hug as the puppy jumped and pawed at them.

Sam and Angel had walked up to Chandler. "Surprised?" Sam asked.

"Why would I be?" Chandler retorted haughtily. She continued sarcastically, "Doesn't everyone invite their attorney to the initial home visit in a child protection case?"

"Only in some cases," Sam said.

Angel narrowed her eyes and looked her dad in the eye, but didn't say anything. She knew he knew something she didn't. Sam sensed there was another Ryan family history session coming up.

"I've got several forms that need to be filled out," Chandler announced.

"Sorry. Got a bit of a late start with chores this morning. Birthday party last night." He turned toward the house. "Danny! C'mon, chores! The chickens and goats!" He shouted across the farmyard. "Angel, back to the horses, please…"

"Dad!" Angel barked. "I wasn't born yesterday! I know what I'm doing!"

"Okay, okay," Sam said, holding his up hands. "Sorry."

Angel turned and headed over to where the horses stood, waiting patiently. Halfway across the yard, she turned and looked back, her eyes narrowed again. Sam saw her steady gaze on Chandler.

He and Sally had noticed Angel had been uncharacteristically on guard and seemingly mad at the world the past couple of weeks. They reasoned she was like many kids teetering between childhood and growing into teenager. This was the angriest rebuke yet, though.

"Want to tag along and write as we go?" Sam suggested to Chandler. "I'll even let you keep all the eggs you find in the coop. Never mind the poop on 'em. It'll wash off. Not sure if your shoes will ever come clean again though. I'd offer you my spare barn boots, but I don't think they're big enough."

"No, thank you," Chandler said tersely as she opened the back door of her car.

"Well then, meet you at the picnic table when we're done." Sam yelled across the yard "Joan, get those two pygmy goat kids off the table! Have Sally bring the coffee out. And whatever's left of the cake from last night that Misty didn't get all the way into. Just cut away the parts with teeth marks."

"I'll pass on both," Chandler informed Sam icily, as she reached in for her briefcase.

"You might want to write down that we're so backward out here in the country that we eat out of the same cake pan as our shamelessly ill-behaved dog and fight the goats for it…"

"Hmmph." Chandler started walking toward the picnic table. "You haven't changed much in 13 years…"

"Neither have you."

———

"I don't like her one bit," Angel said as Chandler's car crunched away down the driveway. They were all sitting at the picnic table.

"Now, Angel," Sally began. "This isn't a big deal. Just formalities."

"That woman is surrounded by the darkest energy I've ever seen. She's up to something. It's the same thing Kellogg has following her around, too—dark, evil. What's the deal?"

Sam sighed heavily. "I'll just tell you flat out."

Angel and Danny looked their dad square in the eyes, waiting for his explanation.

"When your mom was getting divorced and Bill was letting everyone think you were his, Angel, the court assigned Chandler to make a recommendation about who got custody. She had been bought off by Bill's crooked attorney, and we knew she was going to recommend for Bill to get you. Judge Friday knew the whole thing stunk and threw her off the case and out of the guardian ad litem program, and here we are."

"Well," Sally said softly, "by the grace of God, or whatever you want to call Him, and the love of your father. We grew into a really good family. An almost normal one!"

Joan giggled. "Okay, back to business. Angel, any luck finding anything on Kellogg?"

"Not much. She's flown pretty much under the radar. Spent her early career teaching in three smallish schools in western Minnesota, went back to college part-time sometime during those years, and got her Master's in education in 2003. She got promoted to principal at her last school, down in the Ottertail County—Twin Lakes."

"How did you find this stuff out?" Sam asked.

"Easy," Angel replied with a shrug. "I just googled her."

Joan frowned. "But how did you find out about her previous employment?"

"Umm…it's complicated…"

"Spill it, please," Joan said.

Angel rolled her eyes and then directed her gaze away from the group. "Umm, I hacked into the Twin Lakes School computer system and looked up her employment record. No biggie."

"Oh my God. ANGEL!" Joan shrieked.

Sam slapped the table with both hands and tried to stifle a laugh. Joan shot him a wide-eyed look of disapproval.

Angel explained, "Hey, everything I found is a matter of public record. We could have driven down to Twin Lakes and asked for Kellogg's employment record. I just took a shortcut."

"Isn't there personal data in those records that isn't public, like marital status and social security number, that the school would certainly redact—you know, cross out— if we asked for the forms?" Joan asked.

Angel, looking innocent and angelic said, "I didn't pay attention to her social security number, but she IS married, if that helps. Her husband has a different last name—can't remember what it is, but I jotted it down on my desk calendar. And I wrote down her address. Far as I could tell, she still lives where she did when she was at Twin Lakes—in Perham."

"Well," Joan said, "at least that part was perfectly legal. You can get that kind of info on the internet from those people-searching outfits—for a price."

"Yeah, so I saved us a few bucks, right?" Angel nodded, looking around the table for approval.

Joan was thinking, drumming her fingers on the wooden table. "Anything else you'd like to share, young lady?"

"Next of kin and contact person were the same guy, her husband—David something. There was a phone number. I wrote that down, too."

"Probably a dead end anyway," Joan concluded.

Sam had a hunch. "Did you find out anything about Chandler?"

Angel bit her lower lip.

"Let's hear it," Joan ordered.

"I tried, but the county system's a lot more secure. I can try again, though!"

"NO!" Joan said. "Absolutely not. This isn't about Chandler anyway. She's just a stroke of very bad luck."

Danny muttered, "She's more like a festering pimple on your butt when you've got a day's horse ride ahead of you."

"Daniel Samuel!" Sally scolded. "Where did you ever hear such a phrase?"

Sam immediately began singing softly, "La la la la… la la la la…"

"However accurate that may be," Sally said, "don't you ever let anything out of your mouth like that again! Either of you!" She waggled a finger at Sam.

Together, in perfect concert, father and son made the zip-your-lips-shut-and-swallow-the-key sign and high fived each other while they convulsed to keep from laughing out loud.

CHAPTER 8

THE TRIAL

Nate and Cindy insisted on giving their depositions, against Angel's and Danny's wishes. Their other friends had evaporated into thin air. The Ryan kids didn't want to force them to make statements.

In a private settlement meeting after all the depositions had been conducted, Joan said to the attorney, "Greg, you have to know those boys were lying. Their stories are too exact. Clearly, they've been coached."

"I wish Danny and Angel would tell what they know," Pearson replied. "Belden might find the boys' stories suspect—he's no dummy. Angel and Danny were still pretty raw from the incident when Billy was punched and Elliot was called in, and therefore arguably believable. Not sure what he'll think of Cindy's and Nate's testimony—if he'll put any more stock into it. But without the Ryan kids' direct testimony about what actually precipitated the second incident, Belden may have no choice but to find Danny guilty."

"The kids won't budge," Joan said. "Danny's holding himself fully accountable for both assaults. Would be willing to compromise, so there's less of a chance the judge will send him away? Maybe house arrest again? That would just kill his family if he gets sent away. He's not the kind of kid that would survive something like that well."

"Of course I would, if the victim's advocate would go along with it. But she's only heard the other boys' side. Billy and Dylan are really playing the frightened-to-death-victim card, as you know. Mike and Gavin, too. So she has no choice but to present their concerns to the court, no matter what her inkling might be."

"Do you think Belden will put any weight on Kellogg's shenanigans with the complaint forms she pigeonholed?"

"Her reasoning, to an unbiased third party, could appear convincing, in light of very little evidence to the contrary. You do have Amy Wilson to possibly cancel out Kellogg. If you want a deal, you gotta work on Danny and Angel to come clean."

"Trust me, if I put any more screws to them, Angel won't even testify about the taunting by the other boys when Danny tried to make peace with them in the court-yard. She already said she may be losing her memory of that day..."

———

June 26, the Evening Before the Trial

"Goddamnit, kids!" Sally cried angrily, her fingers digging into her scalp. "Danny, you're no martyr. Say something!"

Both kids and Sam were taken aback by her language, their eyes widening as they held their breath.

"And goddamnit, Angel, I don't care what those boys said, if it will save your brother from going to juvie or someplace else and being expelled from Stone Creek, you have to help him...help us...our frickin' family!" Sally slumped onto the couch in frustration and threw her hands in the air. "What could they have said that was that terrible?"

"Please, kids...tell us," Sam pleaded. He squeezed the bridge of his nose with two fingers.

Danny set his jaw and vowed, "I'm sorry, but nobody's ever gonna hear those words again, at least not from us."

Angel put an arm around her brother's shoulders. "Mom, Dad, you gotta trust that this will work out for the best. Not sure exactly how, but it will. I know it."

Sally pleaded again, "Your best friends, Nate and Cindy, are trying to help you. But Joan says without your testimony about the fight with Dylan, the judge may not have any choice. Angel, are you gonna let them take Danny away?"

Angel said sternly, "If you're gonna drop that guilt trip on me, then yes. We're in this together—even if they take my brother away, which would be the worst day of my life. I'll never break my promise to Danny. We'll find a way."

"Don't put this on Angel," Danny snapped. "Family meeting over." He headed for the hallway, taking the stairs up to his bedroom two at a time.

The adults' biggest worry was the psychological evaluation and how Chandler had addressed it in her report. She had taken all the minor concerns of the psychologist and expanded on them, while ignoring Danny's positive qualities. Her final analysis suggested that he was highly impulsive and idealistic.

Joan's plan in court was to expand upon all of Danny's positive attributes, and make Chandler justify her conclusion. In Chandler's opinion, Danny was at risk to reoffend, although nowhere in the report did the psychologist indicate that. She also recommended that he undergo therapy, although the psychologist hadn't suggested that either.

It was a closed courtroom. The judge was up on the bench. The jury box to the right of the judge was occupied by the victims' advocate, a woman who appeared to be in her twenties. A lectern was in the front of the judge.

The bailiff, a young woman fresh out of law enforcement school, stood by the door to the jury room, where the prosecution's witnesses—the four boys with their parents, Kellogg, the two deputies, and Chandler—were waiting to be called. The witnesses Joan would call after Pearson had rested his case were out in the lobby—Angel, who had Maureen with her, Amy, and Cindy and Nate with their parents.

Witnesses were the only other people allowed in the courtroom, and only during their testimony, except for the victim's advocate. Not even the parents were allowed in as their children were sworn in and testified just like adults.

"Your Honor," Pearson began, "we are here in the case of Daniel Samuel Ryan versus the State of Minnesota. I have charged him with two counts of fifth degree assault: intentionally inflicting bodily harm on another—one victim being Billy Anderson, and the other, Dylan Karl. These are two incidents that took place nine days apart. I am trying these two cases together because of ongoing issues between the parties, and I believe the incidents are related. If found guilty, I am not asking for a specific disposition. I will leave that to the discretion of the court. Thank you."

Joan approached the lectern. "Your Honor, we do not dispute that the altercations took place. However, there are extenuating circumstances that led Daniel Ryan to act out in this unfortunate manner. Some witnesses asked not to get involved. My client asked that we not force anyone to testify if they choose not to. Also, Daniel and his sister, Angel, refuse to testify to what was said by the other parties in question that precipitated the second incident. This entire matter has holes in it, and we may never know the complete truth. I would ask the court, due to the widely differing testimony you are going to hear, for an exoneration of my client. Thank you."

The judge said, "Your first witness, Mr. Pearson."

"The State calls Billy Anderson."

Billy proceeded directly to the witness box and remained standing, as if he'd been there many times before. The victim's advocate had given the four boys a run-through of the courtroom and schooled the boys about how court works. Billy was sworn in by the bailiff. The judge asked him to be seated. If Billy was nervous, it wasn't showing. In fact, he seemed smug.

Pearson asked, "Billy, what were you doing immediately before being tackled by Daniel Ryan and punched in the nose?"

Billy shrugged. "Just goofing around. I was riding a broom like a hobby horse out in the courtyard."

"Did you call Angel Ryan a name?"

Billy hung his head. "Yes, and for that I'm sorry. I called her a witch. I was just teasing, didn't mean anything by it. It was very, umm, insensitive of me." He hung his head and brushed across the bottom of his nose with his pointer finger.

Danny closed his eyes and shook his head at Billy's pathetic attempt at acting. His mother put a hand on his shoulder.

"Next thing I knew, Danny was on top of me, and then everything went black."

"That's all, Your Honor. Your witness, Ms. Adair."

From the defense table, Joan asked, "Billy, how many times did you and your friends harass or tease Danny and Angel?"

"Well, it went both ways—just a couple of times. That's all it took. But Danny, he wouldn't leave us alone."

"What do you mean?"

"There was like six times he threatened me and my friends, before he finally attacked me. We'd be in the bathroom or in gym class, and Danny would say something like, 'You're gonna GET IT for teasing my sister.' "

His testimony was nothing new to Joan and Pearson. Billy was testifying verbatim from his deposition. He still hadn't looked at Danny.

"Did you ever fill out a report with the principal?"

"No, by then I was already afraid of him. I thought it would make Danny madder if he got hauled into the office by Ms. Kellogg, and then I'd REALLY get it…"

"If you were so afraid of Danny, why did you ride the broom past his sister and call her those names?"

"It was a dare. We didn't think he'd do anything about it in front of 50 people."

"Just one more thing," Joan said. "What was said just before Danny punched Dylan Karl in the stomach that day in front of the old post office?"

"By us or by him?"

"Both. Whatever you can remember."

"We were just telling Danny, 'No hard feelings,' then WHAM, Dylie got it in the gut."

"Did Danny say anything before or after that?"

He looked sheepishly at the judge. "I'm not sure if I can say it in court without getting in trouble."

"Go ahead," Judge Belden said.

"Well, after Dylan dropped to the sidewalk, he called us 'motherfuckers,' and then he said, 'Two down, two to go.'"

"You realize you ARE testifying under oath?" Joan asked.

"Objection," Pearson said. "Badgering the witness."

"Please, Ms. Adair," Belden said, "confine your questions to the incidents in question."

"Excuse me, Your Honor. No further questions."

Having been advised beforehand by Joan, Danny and his parents sat stone-faced, but were no less frustrated by the lies spewing out of Billy's mouth. Sam had scribbled on a legal pad and showed it to Joan. "Who would talk these boys into lying under oath?"

"I've got my suspicions…" Joan whispered.

"So do I. But why?"

———

The other three boys' testimony matched Billy's, almost to the word. Joan did not question them further. But she did cross-examine Kellogg.

"I want to get this straight," Joan said. "Even now, do you truly believe that not sharing Danny's concerns about being harassed with his parents was the right thing to do, considering what has happened since?"

"That is correct."

"But isn't it your job to follow up on these things? To sort them out?"

"I only notify the parents when I find there is any substance to the complaint. In this case, I didn't want to lend any credence to what Danny was doing."

"Assuming for a moment that Danny was harassing the other boys, did any of them ever file a formal complaint against him?"

Kellogg gave the impression that this was a giant waste of her time. She raised her eyes to the ceiling before answering, took in an audible breath, and then spoke in a monotone. "Dylan and Mike did come in, and I offered them the opportunity to file, but they declined, fearing retribution from Danny. Why are we going through all this again? I've already shared this with you in my sworn deposition."

"Please just answer the questions, Ms. Kellogg. On the day of the most recent incident, why were you parked across the street?"

"I was picking up some takeout from the restaurant. Just happened to be there. I stop there all the time, you can ask anyone."

"How much of the altercation did you see?"

"I put my food in the car, then I noticed Angel and Daniel walking in front of the bakery. I saw Daniel pause in front of the alley, but didn't think anything of it. I decided to take the salad out of the bag to keep it from getting warm from the chicken. I leaned over and fumbled with the salad carton and it opened, made a mess. When I straightened back up, there were Danny, Angel, and the other three boys, plus Billy on a scooter of some sort."

"Did it occur to you that there might be trouble? That you should intervene?"

"Well, no. It just happened so fast. Suddenly, poor Dylan was on the sidewalk, beaten. Gracious…"

"But not so fast you that you couldn't get your cell phone up and take several pictures?"

"I had it in my hand already and was about to make a call. With all the issues between those boys, I figured a few pictures would help sort it out. And then Amy Wilson pulled up, and I offered to go notify the Ryan kids' mother."

"Oh, just one more thing. Why did you come out of retirement to take the principal's position at Stone Creek?"

Pearson stood abruptly. "I object! Relevance, Your Honor?"

Belden contemplated for a few seconds. "Objection sustained."

"No further questions, Your Honor," Joan said, staring at Ms. Kellogg for a few moments longer.

Pearson called Chandler next.

"I have your report. It seems you have some concerns about Daniel's behaviors, past and potentially in the future. Would you please share them with the court?"

"I'd be pleased to," Chandler said. "For starters, I was treated rather poorly by Mr. Ryan when I went to their farm to conduct the initial interview. First of all, their dirty dog attacked me while I was getting out of my car and ruined my clothes. Disgusting! Then he forced me to wait for them to finish chores, even though we had an appointment set for precisely 9:00 a.m. It seems he got a late start with chores because he had been—in his words—'partying' the night before."

"Objection, Your Honor." Joan stood.

"On what grounds?" Belden asked.

"This is the first I'm hearing about this particular accusation. And it's not relevant."

"Nobody asked me during deposition," Chandler retorted.

The judge said, "Ms. Chandler, please confine your remarks to the psychological evaluation and your observations of Daniel."

Pearson chimed in, "Your Honor, I would ask the court to allow it, because it does lend to parenting style, which can be reflected in a child's actions."

Chandler shot a look of satisfaction at Sam that the judge couldn't see.

"But respectfully, Your Honor," Joan pled, "Ms. Chandler has way overstepped her bounds here as a child protection worker."

"In what way?" Belden asked, leaning forward and clasping his hands.

"She is attempting to get sympathy for herself. Please, I ask the court to compel her to confine her testimony to the regular duties of her appointment as a child protection caseworker, which were to simply ensure Daniel's and others' safety between her assignment to this case and your eventual disposition."

Belden ordered, "Please strike the testimony concerning Mr. Ryan the day of the home visit from the record."

Joan won that skirmish. But the horse had already left the barn.

"Let's move on to the psychologist's report," Pearson said. Chandler shuffled the papers she had brought with her to the witness box. "What are the psychologist's points of concern?"

Chandler began, "Daniel is highly, even overly, idealistic in his view of right and wrong, and is likely to act out on his own when he perceives injustice has been perpetrated on those he is closest to." She stabbed her finger at the report. "It's right here—verbatim."

"Your witness," Pearson said to Joan.

"Ms. Chandler," Joan asked, "had you had any prior interactions with the Ryans before you were assigned to this case?"

Chandler hesitated and looked to Pearson for an escape. After a few seconds of silence in the courtroom, even the court reporter had stopped typing and was looking at Pearson. He finally asked, "Relevance?"

Joan answered, "Your Honor, it needs to be of record, to ensure there is no bias on Ms. Chandler's part. I ask that she testify as to her previous dealings with the Ryans."

"Allowed," said Belden.

For a change, Chandler was flustered. Her face turned crimson and she held her hands together tightly as she straightened up stiffly. Joan took her time having Chandler testify about her botched attempt to take Angel away from Sally in 2004. Chandler's hands shook as she took several sips of water between questions.

Joan asked, "Were you the guardian ad litem assigned to perform a custody evaluation in Sally and Bill Hunter's divorce in 2004?"

Chandler nodded.

"Please speak up so the court can hear you," Belden said.

"Umm, yes I was."

"Did you see that case to its conclusion?"

"No," Chandler admitted.

"Please tell the court why you did not."

"I was removed by Judge Friday."

"Why?"

"You'd have to ask him," Chandler said, wringing her hands.

"I will, if I have to," Joan warned. "Why don't you just tell the court."

"He accused me of being partial to Bill Hunter."

"Was there any other fallout from that case?"

Chandler's eyes narrowed in anger. "Yes, Friday—"

"Excuse me," Belden said, "that would be JUDGE Friday."

"I apologize, Your Honor. Judge Friday had me terminated from the guardian ad litem program in this court district."

"How did you get into Social Services?" Joan asked.

"The two departments aren't related. About two years after Judge Friday retired, they came looking for me. I already had a Bachelor's degree in social work, and other than that one glitch as guardian ad litem, not that I'm admitting I had shown any bias in the Hunters' case, I had a very good reputation with everyone else having anything to do with this county."

"No further questions," Joan concluded.

After lunch, it was Joan's turn to defend her client. She called Amy Wilson first.

Joan asked, "Did you hear from other students that the four boys—Billy, Dylan, Mike, and Gavin—were out to bait Danny into an altercation?"

"Yes, several students—five or six—came to me and said they heard the other boys plotting their next move to get to Danny. I didn't know about Danny's complaints against the other boys until the disciplinary committee meeting. I'm the teacher representative for the committee. Ms. Kellogg had disregarded those complaints, which to me doesn't make sense."

"Did you talk to Danny about this?"

"Yes. I figured somebody besides Ms. Kellogg needed to keep a record."

"Would you say that Ms. Kellogg was unhappy when you got into the middle of the boys in the courtyard?"

"She let it be known that I hadn't been appointed as courtyard monitor, and said I should stick to my own duties, seeing as end-of-year performance evaluations were coming up."

"The day that Daniel and Dylan and the others met in front of the old post office—can you explain what you saw and did?"

"I had heard from several students that the other three boys were more determined to get Danny into a fight before the end of the school year, and make it look like he started it. It sounded like it was a game to them."

Amy looked down at the table and sighed. "When I drove up the hill, Dylan was ducking into the alley, hunched over, and Angel was sitting on the curb, crying. I didn't notice at first, but Ms. Kellogg was parked across the street."

———

Joan hoped that Cindy's and Nate's testimony might add some weight to Danny's case. Pearson declined to cross-examine them, nor had he questioned Amy Wilson.

It was finally Angel's turn to testify. She was the last defense witness before Danny was to take the stand. She told her story from the beginning, when she and her girl-friends had formed the healing circle. She said the only students who had objected or bothered them were the four boys. In fact, some of the older students and a couple of teachers came to her with requests that she and the girls send their own friends and relatives healing light.

Joan walked up to the witness box and put a hand on the rail. "Please, Angel, tell the court what was said just before Danny hit Dylan."

Angel looked up at Judge Belden, tears threatening to spill. "Your Honor, I...I could say I don't remember, but that would be a lie. I do remember, but I'll never say those words, even if I'm charged with contempt of court." She sat up straight and looked forward, her hands folded in front of her.

The judge sat back in his chair and looked upward, as if seeking divine guidance.

"That's okay, Angel," he said. "I'm not going to find you in contempt, but I do want to see you after your brother has testified."

Belden looked to Pearson. "Counsel?"

"No questions, Your Honor."

"You may step down, Angel."

She burst into tears as she ran to the defense table, where she met her family for a long hug.

She leaned her forehead against her brother's and, looking into his eyes, they hooked their little fingers of both hands. She whispered, "We're gonna do this...find the truth, right? Without hurting anybody we love." Danny nodded. Angel was escorted out of the room.

"Your Honor," Joan began. "The only thing left to hear from Daniel is what was said just before he hit Dylan. Daniel, please tell the court."

Looking straight ahead and stone-faced, Danny shook his head.

Judge Belden said softly, "Danny, this is so important. I wish I could take you and your sister into chambers and you could tell me there—just the three of us, and it would never leave my office—but it doesn't work that way."

"Judge, please do what you have to do. Let's get it over with, sir," Danny said without expression in his voice or on his face.

"Bailiff, please have Angel Ryan come back in here."

After Angel was seated next to her father, Judge Belden took in a long breath and let it out. He folded his hands on his desk and looked toward the ceiling again. He took another breath and looked across the room at the Ryans and Joan.

"You are all so lucky to have each other. You're a good family. These children are models of what most people want theirs to be, except for the...recent unfortunate events. Daniel, I admire your resolve and your courage, and wish I'd had it when I was 12 years old, or even now, at 68. But I have to follow the law. Daniel and Angel, have you anything else to say?"

All five at the table were holding hands tightly. Angel shook her head no. Danny looked right at the judge and said, "No, sir, Your Honor."

"Clerk," Belden said, "would you call juvenile corrections and have her come down here? And bailiff, please have Ms. Chandler come back into court." The bailiff quickly stuffed a tissue into her pocket and opened the jury room door.

Chandler strode in confidently and stood in front of the closest jury chair.

"Daniel Ryan, please stand…" The judge paused for several seconds. "In the interests of insuring safety for all the children concerned, I'm ordering you to serve 30 days in juvenile detention, and 6 months of probation after that."

Sally was crying, convulsing, leaning on Sam's shoulder. Sam stood with his head down, tears dripping onto the table. Angel had one arm around her brother and the other around Auntie Joan.

"I cannot order Stone Creek School to reinstate Daniel, so it will be up to you, Mr. and Mrs. Ryan, to make arrangements for Daniel's further schooling."

Joan looked across the courtroom at Chandler, who was having difficulty hiding her smug look of satisfaction.

"Ms. Chandler, I am leaving you assigned to Daniel's case, per protocol, until he has served out his sentence and probation."

The courtroom door opened and the corrections caseworker walked in—a sandy-haired woman with glasses stuck on top of her head. She looked to be around 40 and was dressed casually in slacks and blouse.

"Thank you for hurrying down," Belden said. "Daniel, this is your probation officer, Holly Gibbons. After court, you'll go up with her to complete the intake procedure. Ms. Gibbons, I am ordering you not to take Daniel into custody until after the holiday weekend."

Gibbons looked confused but nodded. Chandler coughed to get the judge's attention and raised her hand.

"Yes?" Belden asked.

"I'm not questioning Your Honor's judgment, but in my opinion, sending Daniel home for a week is not in his best interests. I consider him to be a flight risk."

"Oh good grief!" Sam shouted.

"Please, Mr. Ryan," Belden said. "If you and Mrs. Ryan can assure the court you will not let Daniel out of your sight until next Wednesday, July 5th, my order will stand."

"Understood, Your Honor," Sam said.

"Yes, sir," Sally concurred.

"Your Honor," Danny said, "thank you for not finding my sister in contempt, and thank you for not making me repeat those words."

Belden nodded at Danny. "Court's in recess." He stood and hurried down off the bench toward his chambers.

Chandler said across the courtroom, "Mr. and Mrs. Ryan, I will be dropping in on you unannounced between now and then."

"Oh, geez," Sam said. "We've got two weddings at the winery this weekend, and we don't need you snooping around. Except Judge Friday will be officiating at the Sunday wedding. Maybe you two can catch up on old times…"

"Hmmph." Chandler turned smartly and clomped ungracefully out of the courtroom.

———

"I'm keeping my fingers crossed that this temporary reprieve goes well," said Gibbons to Joan and the Ryans as they signed the required paperwork. "This is highly unusual. Daniel, please don't let the judge down. I'll be at your place 8:30 Wednesday morning." As they stood to leave, she added, "See you Sunday."

Sam asked, "Oh? You coming out with Chandler to check on Danny?"

Gibbons smiled. "No, my sister's wedding is at your winery. Judge Friday is an old family friend. Looking forward to it. Officially not on duty then, so no shop talk. Just want to get my sissy hitched, smell working horses like our grandpa had, and tip back some of your wonderful wine. I really need that week of vacation after the wedding, except I'll see you Wednesday morning."

CHAPTER 9

THE WINERY

The Ryans' Stone Creek Winery and Vineyard had come a long way since Sam had begun building the 24 x 36 stone tasting room back in 2003. He had also tried his hand at transplanting wild vines and had bought a few varietals.

Sally had invested in the winery, as she knew Pop would have loved. She had inherited two-thirds of Pop's estate—the third he had willed her directly and the third that had been Bill's. Bill's brother, Robert, had inherited the rest.

Pop's old attorney friend had been the trustee of the estate and, per Pop's instructions, had set up Robert's share in a trust that he could draw from to accommodate his basic needs. Sally hadn't heard from him since they'd had to liquidate Pop's farm back in 2004. Last she'd heard, Robert was still living in his ramshackle house on the edge of Streeter, unloading bags of seed and corn and the like at the co-op.

Sally's money from Pop had financed the building of the winery and vineyard at an accelerated pace, beyond what Sam had expected. In the summer of 2004, he and his son Matt had finished the four stone outside walls of the tasting room and the huge stone fireplace inside. Sam knew just enough about carpentry to install windows and doors, and to set the pitched roof and cover it with cedar shakes.

The following summer, he and Matt had put in plumbing and electricity, covered the inside framed walls and ceiling with rough-sawn pine boards, and poured the concrete floor. They had framed up the wooden wine-tasting bar, which Sam had finished that winter with a thick coat of resin.

In 2005, with Matt and wife Marsha home from Walla Walla for the summer, they had a contractor build them a production building, attached to the back of the tasting room and twice its size. It wasn't as charming as the stone building—made of metal wall panels, inside and out—but it wasn't supposed to be. It was strictly utilitarian, for crushing, fermenting, and storage. But when all the equipment had been set up in there, it had its own charm.

Sam and Matt built the first of two small log houses that summer, to serve as lodging when Matt and his family came to work with Sally and Sam. It was agreed that Matt and Marsha wouldn't move up from the city until Sam retired around age 70, then Matt would take over. They'd reverse roles, so Sam would become the "hired hand," and he and Sally would live in the cabin.

The second log cabin had been built in 2006, off the edge of the yard and into the woods about half a block. It would be used by other family members and friends, and also rented out as a honeymoon cabin. By the summer of 2012, the younger Ryan offspring, in various combinations, had taken it over as one big clubhouse or slumber party. The other adults had to either bunk with Matt and Marsha or in the farmhouse.

Back then, Sam's oldest grandson, Josh—son of his daughter, Ellen, and her husband, Keith, from Boise—was 11 and the ringleader. Second in command was his little brother, Sammy Bob, who was 9, followed by Angel, who was 8, as was her nephew, Sam Anthony, who had been born two minutes after her. Danny was 7 that summer. Finally, Matt and Marsha's second was little Maggie, who was not yet 5 but insisted on attending the slumber parties with the older kids. They doted over her like mother hens.

These kids were cousins, brothers, sisters, nieces, nephews, aunts, and uncles to each other. It didn't matter to them which branch of the family tree they were perched on. There was never a dull moment among the Ryan tribe.

Growing grapes was a slow process that had been taken a steady baby step at a time beyond Sam's fledgling start. Obviously, they needed enough grapes under cultivation to transform the operation from its original hobby status into a business.

In the late winter of 2004–2005, Matt coached Sam from Walla Walla about how to take cuttings from his favorite wild vines that winter and store them until he could start them in pots in the spring. They ordered 100 cuttings of Frontenac vines from a vineyard in the St. Croix River Valley near St. Paul. Matt had figured that along with Sam's first vines he had been nursing along, they would have enough from their one acre of producing vines to open the winery on a limited basis by the fall of 2007.

He estimated they'd produce around 150 cases that first year, just from their homegrown grapes. And he was very close. Only trouble was, once word got out in February 2008 when they began bottling, even though they hadn't set business hours to open the tasting or sales room, folks were beating down either the farmhouse or the winery door and asking for more!

Setting aside a mere 25 cases for family use, they sold out the 2007 harvest in a month, just by word of mouth. When the 2008 harvest was ready in February 2009, it had grown by 240 cases. That year, they had held back enough wine to supply a dozen small weddings, held at the fire ring under the arbor by the vineyard, or in the tasting room in front of the stone fireplace. That allowed for two cases per wedding, with a limit of 40 people, which is all they had room for. It was small, simple, and homey, and folks loved it.

Matt did the math and figured by 2019, when he'd likely take over, they'd produce nearly a thousand cases. He planned to build a new, bigger venue to hold events, seating up to 100 people, and would design it to look like a converted horse barn.

Weather permitting, Danny or his dad handled the team of horses during the weddings, driving guests 20 at a time to either of the outdoor locations, while Sally, Matt, and Marsha served the others wine in the tasting room. They had retired Pop's old dray wagon, which they had only been able to pack 8 or 10 people into, and not all that comfortably. Except they did hitch the team to it for funerals and parades, and the occasional family outing. The new wagon was built lower to the ground and had bench seating along both sides and the front. Danny's buddy, Nate, helped out hitching the team, and then usually rode in the back. During loading or unloading, he stood next to the stairs and politely assisted the folks.

Angel and Cindy were Sally's helpers, setting up the reception area, pouring coffee and water, and cleaning up afterwards. Matt and Marsha filled in wherever they were needed and available, by bartending and pouring wine at the tables, setting up, tearing down, and cleaning up.

The food was catered and served by the popular restaurant in Stone Creek, The Smoky Hills Bar & Grill, which had grown famous for their family-friendly fare—especially the smoked brisket, ribs, cheese, turkey, and chicken. If beer and liquor were ordered, they supplied that too.

The entire crew wore smart, long-sleeved Western shirts—red wine-colored, of course—with the Stone Creek Winery logo on the back, the stone fireplace in the background, and two crossed wine glasses in the foreground. Each worker's first name was embroidered above the front left pocket, and gold initials S.H. pinned to the right one. Sam and the boys wore matching black Stetsons, with gold pins worn on the sides of their hats. S.H. was in honor of Samuel Hunter, their beloved and much-missed Pop.

Danny especially liked to tell the story of Pop and his team of Percherons, how it had been Pop's idea to have weddings there, and how the first one up at the fire ring had been big brother Matt and Marsha's, and the second one his folks'. Danny loved it when people asked him something like, "Matt is your BROTHER?" or "Sam is your FATHER?" He'd chuckle and say, "It's a long story, but a pretty good one…"

One time, Danny pondered aloud to a guest, "If I have to get married someday, it'll be up here at the fire ring. It's a family tradition."

The guest, a little tipsy on wine, assumed Danny was joking. "Which part is the family tradition—getting married at the fire ring, or HAVING to get married?"

"Both, I guess!"

Sally overheard the exchange, closed her eyes, slapped her forehead with the palm of her hand, and turned away. Sam walked over and said, "Now what?"

"Our son, the math genius…apparently knows babies take nine months, and he only took eight, and I bet he figured out Sam Anthony got here in a record six and a half. The family tree Ellen put together for Christmas—I saw him engrossed in it and counting on his fingers…"

———————

Cindy and Nate stayed overnight that Friday, saying they might as well get a jump on the preparations, what with the Saturday wedding being at 11 a.m. The four kids retreated to the guest cabin right after supper. That was unusual. The farthest they usually ever went before dark, which was still three hours away, was the tasting room, where they listened to music, watched movies on the flat-screen TV, or played board games.

Sally, at the kitchen sink window, leaned forward and looked toward the guest cabin. "Hmm. I wonder what they're up to."

Sam dried as she washed. "Oh, just trying to make the most of their time until Danny goes away would be my guess. At least I hope that's it…"

"Remember the theory you shared with the kids when all this began? That there's a reason for everything?"

"Ya. If something doesn't make sense, we're usually missing something…or we haven't gotten to the bottom of it."

Sally stole another look out the window. "Well, Angel told me again yesterday that she thinks this is all too crazy. You know, Kellogg making such a big deal about the healing circle in the spring? Heck, they were doing it last fall, and Kellogg never said a word. Nor did those boys bother them. Angel says she's gonna keep turning over rocks until she finds the reason. This detective work and Cindy and Nate around so much seems to have helped her out of the funk she's been in."

"Yup, they must be brainstorming up there."

"Angel told me it's going to be hell for Danny among those thugs and delinquents in juvie. Even in detention, they have a pecking order and dangerous gangs. And if they provoke Danny, it could get ugly."

Sam said, "I still don't get why neither kid will tell the court what was said that day. They certainly would have been more believable than the boys, and even Kellogg. And Danny knew if he didn't tell, he'd be going away."

"And to that place…" Sally lamented.

Sam sighed. "Oh, something's going on alright. I just pray they aren't planning anything dumb."

———

Chandler arrived unannounced Monday morning, at 8:00 a.m. sharp. The wedding reception Sunday hadn't broken up until after 2:00 a.m., so Sam and Sally were sleeping in. She pounded on the door four or five times, waited five seconds, and repeated the barrage.

As she raised her fist to pound a third time, she heard Sam mumbling, "Just a minute…just a MINUTE! Oh, super. It's you."

"Just checking in, per my orders. I'd like to see Daniel."

"He's not here…I mean, not in the house."

Her eyes narrowed.

"He and the other kids are in the guest house, up there." Sam pointed over his shoulder.

"Hmm, is that so?" Chandler said. "Weren't we in the same courtroom Tuesday, when Judge Belden ordered you not to take your eye off Daniel during his temporary release?"

Sam shot back, "Geez, woman, were we supposed to sleep in the same bed with him? Is that what you think the judge meant? Maybe where you came from, but not around these parts."

Just then Danny walked from around the back of the house to the front porch.

"Well, hello, Ms. Chandler. How are you?"

She demanded, "Who's up there in that cabin with you?"

Sam said, "None of your fucking business. You've got two seconds to make sure this is the real Daniel Ryan and not some imposter—then hit the goddamn road."

Chandler tossed her head back and strode toward her car, stopping halfway to scribble furiously on her notepad. "This will NOT look good in my next report," she threatened, and then turned back toward her car.

"Oh!" Sam shouted. "Almost forgot. Judge Friday said to give you his best."

As her car turned with a spray of rocks onto the gravel road, Angel came from behind the house.

"Can I stay with Cindy tonight?"

"Don't you want to spend some more time with your brother, before they...?"

"It's okay, Dad," Danny said, grinning. "We've been practically joined at the hip all weekend. I could use a break from her anyway."

Sally opened the door, yawning. "What's going on?"

"Dad just ran Chandler off the place," Danny said. "And Angel wants to stay overnight at Cindy's. Nate has to go home and help with haying. I'll be fine. How about us three and Misty canoe the river? I'd like to give her one more lesson before I leave—learning how to sit still in the boat. And how to stay there!"

Sally shook her head as she looked out the driveway at the dust left behind from Chandler's hasty exit. Angel leaving her brother for a day, two days before he goes to juvie? Just didn't seem right.

"You guys riding your horse double to Cindy's?" Sally asked.

"No. You remember Cindy's sister, Carrie, who's gonna be a senior? She'll pick us up."

Sam thought, *Those girls never go anywhere together without their horses, except to school.*

"Thanks, Mom and Dad!" Angel shouted over her shoulder, as the Ryan kids dashed back behind the house.

Sally's brow was furrowed. She was thinking the same thing Sam was: *Something's up.* "Oh, shit..." she whispered.

CHAPTER 10

A NOTE

Wednesday, Early Morning

Sally woke up and squinted at the alarm clock. The numbers glowed a rosy red—5:27—an hour before it was set to go off, just in time to get chores done and breakfast into the four of them before Danny's probation officer was to arrive at 8:30. The morning birds were chirping, and it was light enough in the house that she didn't need to use the little flashlight she kept in her nightstand. She slipped out of bed without waking Sam, wanting just one more look at her boy and his puppy blissfully curled up together in bed.

She treaded carefully and quietly up the stairs. Halfway up, she paused and heard Misty's gentle snoring. She let out a sigh and peered around the corner into his room. Misty must have heard her, because the puppy was staring at the doorway, her tail whipping the bed lightly.

"SAM!" she yelled. "Danny's gone!"

"WHAT?" Sam leapt from bed and yanked the bedroom door open. "Are you sure?"

"Check Angel's bedroom!" She closed her eyes and prayed, awaiting Sam's response. Misty jumped down from the bed and wriggled up to sit in front of her, head cocked to the side.

"Gone, too!" Sam yelled toward the stairway, shaking his head.

Sally descended the stairs, hanging onto the railing, her footfalls heavy. Misty sat on her butt up at the landing. Sam met Sally at the bottom step. She leaned down onto his shoulders.

"Fuck," she whispered. "What do we do now?" Sally was the only one of the family who typically chose her words carefully, except in the direst situations.

"Coffee, let's think..." Sam mumbled as he led her down the hallway with his arm tight around her. He beckoned to Danny's pup. "Come on, girl."

He had set up the coffeemaker the evening before. Their ceramic cups, Christmas gifts from 2003 with the words *Sweeten My Coffee with a Morning Kiss*, sat neatly alongside it as always. Sam pushed the start button. Misty wasn't done with her nightly snooze yet, so she jumped up onto the living room couch and curled into a cozy ball.

"Look..." Sally said softly. "A note."

Sam reached for the light switch and the room brightened. "What does it say?"

Her hands shook as she unfolded it. "Here." She handed it across the table. "I can't. You read it."

The coffeemaker gurgled and released its first steamy aroma. Sam slid a chair back and sat down across from her. She stood with her hands on the back of a chair, biting her lip, prepared for the worst. He set the note back on the table without opening it and rose from the chair.

"Come on, honey." He approached his wife with open arms. "You know our rule: Coffee first, life second. Let's go out to the porch swing, okay? But first, I should probably put on my sweats. You, however, are dressed just fine." He hurried toward their bedroom.

He could always get a grin out of her, no matter how serious the circumstances. She looked down at herself and self-consciously crossed her arms across her breasts. She was wearing her sheer, satiny pajama top and the short matching bottoms, with nothing underneath—Sam's favorite. She didn't want to start anything, especially out on the porch.

"It's a little chilly," she called out.

"Ya, I saw that!"

"Umm, grab my robe, please, will you?"

The immediate heart-pounding shock of their kids having run away from home—and the law—was starting to wear off. She tried to believe in the trust they'd always had in their kids.

Sam came out to the porch with her robe over his arm. He hugged her tight, then they kissed lightly. He swung her robe behind her and held it open so she could slide her arms into the sleeves, pulling it shut and carefully tying the belt. He sat first, and then Sally settled in next to him, pulling her legs up onto the swing seat and adjusting her robe to cover her legs. She leaned her head on Sam's shoulder.

"Yup," she said, with a big heavy sigh. "We knew they were up to something."

"I never would have guessed this, though. Then again, Angel was so afraid for Danny being in that place."

"This is not gonna be good. Judge Belden isn't gonna like this one bit."

"They must have it all figured out, don't you think?"

Sally sat up. "Coffee must be ready." She disappeared through the front door.

When she returned a minute later, she had the letter in her teeth and both their coffee mugs. She handed Sam hers. They kissed each other's mugs, clinking them together lightly on the rim, and exchanged them.

Sally took a sip. "I'll do the honors." She shook the note open with one hand. "Probably just kid stuff, right? They're scared. Maybe if we can get them to come home, Judge Belden will go easy on them."

Dear Mom and Dad,

The night after Danny got sentenced to 30 days in juvie, I got down on my knees next to my bed and prayed. I didn't know what else to do. I asked for guidance, for wisdom, even just a clue about what's going on. And then that night I had a dream—it felt like a premonition. Actually, it was more of a nightmare.

When I woke up, I asked my Spirit Guide if I should even share it with you, because I was afraid it would trigger another nightmare for you, Mom. She said, "Your mom will be fine, tell them." I saw a young boy. I couldn't see his face exactly, but I knew him—a bigger kid was molesting him. And the little boy cried and begged for him to stop. I woke up with chills and I sat straight up in bed. I held my hands together and gave thanks.

Sally's hand began to shake and she couldn't hold the paper still enough to keep reading. Sam took it from her and continued aloud.

> I knew I could never let Danny go to that place, even before the dream. I didn't tell him about the dream, or Cindy or Nate. And Danny doesn't know about this note either. But we all agreed to keep him out of juvie, and to keep searching for why this whole damn thing is happening.
>
> Please trust that we're safe. And help Nate and Cindy find out the truth before the cops find Danny and me and put us both in that terrible place.
>
> Love, Angel

"Whew…" Sam said.

"We'd better call Joan and Maureen." Sally gazed out at nothing across the gravel road, and her eyes became moist. "Let's wait until 6:30 or so."

"Might as well get busy with chores," Sam said. He took another sip of coffee and leaned forward, his elbows on his knees. "I suppose we're gonna have plenty of company this morning."

"Any idea where they might have gone?" Joan asked.

"Not a clue," Sally said, shaking her head. "They both took their cell phones though, and near as I can tell, a couple changes of clothes."

Maureen said, "Holly Gibbons, as congenial as she is when you're on her good side, is a pit bull when it comes to tracking down runaways. I remember hearing she had a case similar to this years ago. She was a new agent and said to give him a day or two before calling out the hounds. Two days later, he was found, overdosed on drugs and alcohol. He died."

Sally drew in a sharp breath and looked at Sam.

Joan continued, "Trust me, when she finds out Danny is gone, her first stop will be at the county sheriff's investigator's office, and the second will be at judge's chambers to get a subpoena signed to begin gathering evidence. You need to help me get some idea about what's going on first. Did they spend a lot of time with Cindy and Nate over the weekend?"

Sam replied, "Yup, they were pretty much here all weekend, working the weddings with us. All four stayed in the guest house."

"No doubt, planning this," Joan concluded. "It's probably a pretty solid plan."

Sally pushed Angel's letter cross the table, and Joan and Maureen read it silently to themselves.

"Okay, so we need a plan, too," Joan said. "As you know, I'm not big on lying to law enforcement or corrections, but as your attorney and Danny's, I can advise you not to offer any information. My advice right now is to burn this letter. I'm sure sooner or later somebody will ask if they left a note. This letter implicates Nate and Cindy as co-conspirators. And if there's a smoking gun out there for us to discover, we don't want them to know somebody's on their trail."

Sam balled up the letter and walked to the woodstove.

Sally said, "Angel is absolutely convinced this is more about Kellogg than Chandler. The principal was about as harmless as a kitten for the entire school year until this spring. It was like flipping a light switch."

"UGH. Chandler." Sam rolled his eyes as he held a match to the letter. "What a pain in the ass. Obviously, she's not gonna be any help. In fact, as we've already seen, she's out to get revenge for what happened back in 2004. Are you sure we can't get rid of her?"

Joan shook her head. "Believe me, I tried. Talked to the social services director, but his hands are tied. They just don't have the resources to shuffle CP workers around once a case has been assigned. However, he did admit that Chandler came to him just before Danny's second hearing, offering to 'squeeze in' another case."

"Yup. That can't be a coincidence," Sam said.

Sally suggested, "I might be tempted to say we're being just a little paranoid, even though Chandler is after us and we all know why, but Angel sure believes there's more going on here than is obvious."

A vehicle crunched over the gravel driveway and stopped next to Joan's car. Sam went to the front door. As Holly Gibbons was getting out of her county car, a second vehicle pulled in and parked just beyond it— speak of the devil.

Sam, Sally, Maureen, and Joan met them on the porch.

"What's SHE doing here," Chandler demanded, pointing to Joan.

Joan crossed her arms in annoyance. "Danny's missing."

Chandler rolled her eyes. "Why am I NOT surprised?"

"Any idea where he went?" Gibbons asked, exchanging a glance with Chandler.

Sally shrugged. "No, we got up this morning and he and Angel were both gone. We have no idea when they left, where they went, or how."

Sam glanced over to the barn. "I see their bikes are gone."

"What can we do to help?" Joan asked.

"For starters, let's see which way the bike tracks go," Gibbons said.

As they approached the barn, Gibbons paused to look out over the pasture at the four Perches and two quarter horses, "This weekend was really fun—a lot of memories made that day…"

"Memories?" Chandler asked.

"Yes," Gibbons responded, with a contended smile across her face. "My sister had her wedding here Sunday. Danny really knows how to handle a team of horses and treat wedding guests. A fine young gentleman. I can't believe he did this. He must have a reason, but I have a job to do."

They turned their attention back to the place where the bikes had been leaning against the barn and walked over to look for clues. The knobby tire marks went toward the road instead of up into the woods on the trail, where Sam thought they would. They followed the tracks out to the gravel road, where they took a right, heading for the asphalt county road half a mile away.

As Joan predicted, Holly Gibbons wasn't going to cut the kids any slack. "Sorry, I need to be right on this."

"Anything I can do to help?" asked a smug Chandler.

"No, nothing from you at this time. But if you hear anything, give me a call." Gibbons pulled a business card from the back pouch of a small notebook. "The second number is my cell."

"What I need for now," she said to the Ryans, "is their height, weight, and school pictures. I'll be stopping by the sheriff's office. Also, is there anybody who might have helped them, who I can talk to?"

"They've got a lot of friends..." Sally said.

Chandler said, "The smart money would be on Angel's best friend, Cindy. The day of Daniel's trial, the victims and witnesses mentioned her. I don't know what her last name is, but I can find out."

"It's Palmer," said Sam. "Take a left out of the drive-way, cross the river—down there about three miles. Horse pasture out to the road, wooden rail fence, painted white."

Gibbons said, "I'll check in after I get the paperwork going."

Chandler added, "Better also check with Daniel's best friend. I think his name is Nate. I heard the boys say they wouldn't want to run into him in a dark alley..."

"Skogquist," Sam said blankly. "Lives the other side of Stone Creek. When you get just about to Cindy's, take a right at the old broken-down one-room school-house, head west out to the tar that goes to Stone Creek. Dairy farm with two big, blue silos, about a mile south of town."

"Thank you, Sam," Gibbons said as she scribbled into her notebook. "As you know, I was supposed to be on vacation this week, and only came back on duty this morning to pick Danny up. I better get on this." She pulled out another business card and handed it to Sam. "If he does show up, call me immediately."

Gibbons looked at her watch. "Can we go inside for the info I need, and the kids' pictures?"

Sally nodded in the direction of the front door and they all headed toward the house, Chandler bringing up the rear with her awkward lumbering steps.

Gibbons stopped short and turned to face Chandler. "I won't be needing to talk to you until Daniel shows up or is found. Have a good day."

"Hmmph," Chandler retorted. She turned quickly and headed to her SUV, immediately stepping in a pile left by Misty, then cursing under her breath as she attempted to scrape it off her shoe with a stick.

Pretending not to notice, and stifling a smile, Joan said, "I better get to the office. You guys have it under control. Thank you, Holly." She hugged Sally tight. "It's gonna be okay."

The others turned to go inside, but Sam waited to watch Chandler leave. Instead of taking a right out of the driveway—the quickest way to anywhere beyond the hills and state forest—she turned left toward Cindy's house.

Once inside, Gibbons said, "You know, Chandler's only a few months from retirement. The other cases I've had with her the past several months, she's been acting like she's already out the door—just going through the motions and cashing her paycheck. CP workers don't personally go looking for missing clients. But in Danny's case, she's being awfully HELPFUL…"

After Gibbons left, Sam hurried back inside. He went to the kitchen phone and traced his finger down a list of names and numbers on a sheet of paper taped alongside it.

"CINDY—I need to talk to your mom or dad. I mean right now."

"Mom! It's Sam…"

"Ally, you probably haven't heard," Sam informed her. "Angel and Danny took off last night. I think his child protection worker is on her way to your house to question Cindy. She thinks she's goddamn Telly Savalas."

"Who?" Ally asked.

"Oh, never mind. Probation needs to notify law enforcement to find the kids. Trust me, fat-ass Chandler will be snooping around. You can't miss her—she's a huge, angry old woman who'll kick your dog in the throat with her clodhoppers if it gets within range. She has a vendetta against anyone who's friends with Angel and Danny, so if I were you, I wouldn't let her anywhere near Cindy for now. We need to talk—with Nate and his parents, too."

Sally entered the kitchen just as Sam hung up and began searching for Nate's phone number. "What's up?"

"Chandler's headed to Cindy's. I just gave Ally a heads-up. I'm sure her next stop after that will be Nate's." He punched in Nate's number.

Nathan Sr. answered. "Yup, Junior told us about this. This is bullshit. Set up a meeting. Let's all get together. I won't let Chandler onto the sidewalk if she gets here before we leave, don't worry."

"What time are you done with milking tonight? I'm thinking we'll need my sister-in-law to be there."

"Joan, right? Sure, we can be cleaned up and wherever you want by eight tonight. Junior and I will be hauling some bull calves to the sale barn in a few minutes, with our older son Dale. Do you remember him? If I can get his sorry butt out of bed. Out late last night with his girlfriend."

"His girlfriend?" Sam asked.

"Yeah, Carrie Palmer. I have no idea what those two were up to until two in the morning, and I don't want to know. Shirley's gone to Fargo for the day, shopping. How about meeting here? You bring the wine."

"We'll be there at eight." Sam hung up.

Sally asked, "What are you smiling about?"

"Oh, nothing. I'm just glad Danny's got Nate as a friend."

"You're not a very good liar, you know."

He confessed his hunch about Carrie and Dale. They decided not to say anything to the other parents, Joan, or Maureen, and to just see how it unfolded.

"Let's go for a ride," Sam said, then whistled to Misty. "Hop in the truck, girl!"

"Where we goin'?"

"Got another hunch…"

They drove to the dam. Sam helped the puppy down from the back. But instead of immediately running as hard as she could, hell-bent down the trail and baling off the bank into the river, Misty began sniffing furiously at the edge of the road across from the path to the canoe launch. Sally was confused as she watched the intently busy pup. She hurried over, ready to scold the pup, who acted like she was about to find the most delicious rotted fish to roll in.

"Sam, come here!"

Scratched with a stick into the damp, sandy edge of the road was a message: "We ♥ you." There was also an arrow drawn in the dirt, pointing into the cattails. They could see the handlebars of one of the kids' bikes poking up through the swamp grass. Misty pounced on the three-foot length of willow one of the kids had broken off to use to write in the sand. She held it down with one paw while she frantically nibbled at it on the big end, trying to pick it up with her teeth. Finally she had it, darted across the road, and ran for the river, most of the branch hanging out the right side of her mouth, whipping the brush, poison ivy, and lady slippers that lined the path.

"You think Dale and Carrie picked them up last night?" Sally crossed the road, following Misty.

Sam was hanging onto a willow sapling and reaching for one of the bikes. "That's my guess." He dragged it up onto the road shoulder.

Sally urged Misty, "Here's a better stick! Come on!"

By the time Sam had pulled the second bike from the cattails, Misty was at his heels with the better stick. She dropped it at his feet and whined for him to toss it.

"You know what I want to do today?" Sally asked.

"What?"

Her shoulders sagged, her head hung, and the tears began to stream down onto her sweatshirt. Sam was struck with how helpless Sally must have been feeling—her young and innocent children suddenly gone from her, to who knows where. Misty loped across the road. Instead of jumping up on her with both muddy feet, she reached out with one paw and gently touched her on the shoe.

Sally knelt on one knee. "You're such a good girl…" Misty licked at her tears. When her eyes were finally dry enough to see Sam across the road, he was rubbing his eyes with the palms of both hands.

"Sam Ryan," Sally said tenderly. "Who was it that told me, 'When the Earth has seemingly spun off its axis, and you feel like you've been hurtled into outer space all by yourself forever, to just let go, let the river'?"

He crossed the road, she stood, and he embraced her, whispering through his tears, "You are the most amazing person…mother…partner…wife…"

Sally leaned back and held Sam gently by his shoulders, her eyes looking into his. "A picnic on the high sand bank?"

"Should we bring Misty?" he asked.

"I don't think so. You know how cold her nose is…"

———————

"This is my fault," Judge Belden said to Pearson, Gibbons, and the newly appointed county sheriff's investigator, Shawn Elliot. "I wish Danny and Angel had opened up just a tiny bit. God, they're really good kids—to a fault, when it comes to standing up for their own. I can't imagine what they were hiding about Daniel's second assault."

"I know the family pretty well," Elliot said. "Sam and I go back to grade school days. I just saw him in The Smoky last week, at the going-away party the city threw for me. He's sure there has to be something else going on. Even if there is, I can't go there on a hunch, even my own."

"What's important right now is to find those kids and make sure they're safe," Gibbons said.

Belden added, "I'm not so sure sending him up to juvie is safe. He would not do well up there, in with all those others I've sent there."

"When we do find him, then what?" Pearson asked. "We can't put him in shackles."

"All I can say is," Belden said, "when Danny's caught, somebody needs to bring me an order so he doesn't have to go up there."

"The subpoena." Pearson slid a form across the judge's desk. "For now, we want Angel's and Danny's cell phone numbers. Ms. Chandler said she believes their best friends, Nate Skogquist and Cindy Palmer, most likely aided them in running away. And there has to be an adult component to this, or at least someone with a driver's license, so we've named their older siblings, Carrie Palmer and Dale Skogquist, as well."

"Are you sure that basing this subpoena on a child protection worker's hunch is sufficient?"

"It's not just Chandler," Gibbons said. "The school principal, Esther Kellogg, also believes these four are all working together. She suggested that if we name the school in the subpoena to provide those phone numbers, it will expedite matters."

"It says here you want the cell tower pings for a 60-mile radius of Stone Creek within 48 hours. How have the cell tower companies been getting you that information lately?" the judge asked Elliot.

"This is my first case asking for that information, but my boss, Frank Davis, says the tower company attorneys usually give the okay within 24 hours. We could start looking before dark. But as you know, those pings, if we find any, can only get us in the general neighborhood. The kids might have disabled their phones anyway."

The judge sat back in his chair, closed his eyes, inhaling and exhaling loudly. He leaned forward and put his cheater glasses on, taking another deep breath. "I want Daniel found more than anything I've ever wanted from the bench, but not so I can send him up there. Find him, and let me know when you do."

CHAPTER 11

PLAN B

The three families sat around the Skogquists' huge, oblong wooden dining room table. Carrie and Dale sat at the center island in the kitchen, snacking and visiting, as if this hadn't a thing to do with them.

The Palmers were young enough to be Sam's children. Dave worked in the hospital lab in Detroit Lakes. Ally worked from home—a sewing business. Cindy and Carrie had inherited their mother's red hair, although Ally's and Carrie's locks weren't nearly as fiery as Cindy's. Carrie was tall and slender like her dad, pretty, with straight hair falling halfway down her back—athletic too, excelling in both basketball and volleyball.

The Skogquists were closer in age to Sally. They were both a little rotund—by design, Nathan claimed, for their Christmastime gigs as Mr. and Mrs. Santa Claus. They were perpetually cheerful, welcoming, and friendly. Dale wore a few extra pounds too, which slowed him down on the football field, so he plugged the middle of the line on both offense and defense, where size and strength were more valuable than speed. They obviously ate well around the Skogquist table. "Little Nate," Shirley had once told Sally, "was a happy accident!"

"So Chandler is convinced," Sam began, "that Danny and Angel had help, at least in planning their run, and I'm sure it's safe to assume that Gibbons suspects the same." He glanced beyond Ally's shoulder and saw that Dale and Carrie had quit visiting and were eavesdropping on the conversation. "And it's pretty obvious that they did. We found evidence that somebody picked them up at the dam."

Nate looked down at the counter and Cindy stared absently at a napkin that she shredded piece by piece.

"Now, Cindy and Nate—don't get me wrong. We're not here to point fingers, not at all. What we need to do is, number one, make sure Danny and Angel are safe, and number two, find out what's really going on here."

Joan said, "I'd advise any client of mine not to talk to Chandler, for sure. Holly Gibbons, Danny's probation officer, is a reasonable person, but she's also got a job to do. You might want to put my number in your phones in case they try to pin you down."

Dale spoke up from the kitchen. "Is Chandler the sasquatch who was pounding the front door off its hinges when I was trying to sleep this morning?"

Shirley had heard enough about Chandler to get the idea, and she was on her second glass of Stone Creek wine already. "Now Dale!" she scolded. "Watch your mouth! We don't want to offend Sasquatch!"

That broke the ice, and the ideas and plans darted around the table like tadpoles swimming in a pond.

Cindy spoke up. "Angel and I tried to dig deeper into Ms. Kellogg, but couldn't find anything new. A dead end. As far as Chandler goes, it sure looks like it's revenge."

"What doesn't make sense though," Sally said, "is that if Kellogg was out to get Angel and Danny all along, why did she wait until the last few weeks of school?"

Dave suggested, "Maybe she was waiting for maximum effect and minimum fallout? I mean, she's out of there now, scot-free."

"No, she's not gone," Cindy corrected. "She stayed on for summer school."

Nate said, "Those boys—Billy, Dylan, Mike, and Gavin—it was like a contest to them, a competition. There was nothing directed at Angel and Danny until this spring. They were never the brightest bulbs, but they weren't so mean before. Why would they lie in court like that? Why would Kellogg keep coming up with 'alternative facts' about Danny filing reports against the boys? There's gotta be a connection."

"Angel and I thought of that," Cindy said. "Dylan, Mike, and Gavin have lived their entire lives here. So if there's a wild card, it's Billy. He didn't come to Stone Creek until the beginning of this school year."

Nathan suggested, "Might be interesting to find out where Billy came from."

Joan said, "That's not gonna be easy without his parents' cooperation…unless we can find out their names. Then, I suppose you could search the internet for info about them, Cindy."

"It all seems like dead ends," said Ally. "I wish somebody could do a little more digging on Kellogg."

"What about Amy Wilson?" Sally suggested. "She's teaching remedial English during the second summer session. Could she maybe check the school records?"

"Whoa!" Joan said. "I would not advise that. Too risky, not to mention illegal."

Maureen reminded, "But in the meantime, we've got Danny and Angel out there, who knows where, on the run. We don't even know if they're safe."

Sam looked at Cindy, "Are they?"

Cindy gazed into her folded hands. "How much do you wanna know?"

"Nate?" asked his father.

Sam faced Nate but glanced into the kitchen. Carrie and Dale sat perfectly still, as if waiting for the other shoe to fall.

"I don't think we need all the details," Sam said. "Just the general plan."

"In fact," Joan said, "the less detail we adults have, maybe the better?" Several of the others nodded in agreement.

Carrie caught Sam's gaze. She was biting her lip and squirming a bit on her stool.

Nate confessed, "They're in a hunting shack, with plenty of food and water. Not here in the Smokies, though. I can't tell you where. I can't tell you who told us about it, either. It wasn't officially offered to us. It was just sort of mentioned. There's one bar of cell phone signal up there, in case of emergency. I called Danny last night to make sure they're okay and that their phones work."

"Oh, cripes," Joan exclaimed. "First thing Gibbons will do, and probably already has done, is get a subpoena to secure cell phone numbers and search warrants for the cell companies to turn over phone numbers and ping data."

Cindy asked, "Could she get the school to give her phone numbers? When Carrie and I drove past there this afternoon, I saw a large, older woman with jet-black hair exiting."

From the kitchen, Carrie added, "And a blondish woman and Officer Elliot were also leaving at the same time."

Carrie quickly slid off her barstool and Sam could see that her face was flushed. "Hey, Cindy. Got a second? Dale and I are really late for the movie. Picked up a new wrap and some salve for that cut on your horse's leg, like you asked. Should probably put it on tonight..."

Cindy pushed her chair back quickly, then obediently followed her sister and Dale out to the porch.

Out by Dale's truck, Carrie turned to her little sister. "Crap—their cell phones! I forgot they can be tracked, even if they're turned off."

Cindy's eyes began to fill with tears.

"Please don't cry. I'm sorry. It'll be okay." Carrie said.

Inside, Ally said, "We need to find those kids! Nate, can't you call and tell them to come home?"

"Sorry," he said, "they can call anytime, but we set it up so we can only call them at exactly noon, to report in. Otherwise, their phones are shut off to save on the batteries."

Cindy returned to the table. "Let's be patient," she said. "We're into Plan B, and Dale and Carrie are in on this."

"To our advantage," Joan said, "locating someone by cell phone ping isn't an exact science, not like GPS."

Nathan asked, "Isn't there something we can do in the meantime?"

Cindy said, "We think our Plan B is pretty solid, that is if we get into it before they find Danny and Angel."

Sally asked, "Joan, can you get a subpoena so we can investigate Chandler, Kellogg, and Billy?"

"Doesn't work that way," Joan said, shaking her head. "Law enforcement can get a subpoena based on probable cause, even on sound evidence brought to them by a civilian, but the court won't give one to us regular joes just to go fishing for dirt on another civilian."

Ally's cell phone rang on the table in front of her. She looked down then closed her eyes. "Sorry, I better take this." She walked into the living room. "Hello. Yes, this is Ally Palmer." She listened for a few seconds, then began to sob.

Dave hurried to his wife. "What?" But he knew, even though they thought they still had a few weeks, that it was about his grandmother.

"We'll be right there," Ally said as she fumbled to disconnect the call.

Cindy walked to her parents and put her skinny, freckled arms around them both. "Gram's gone?"

Her mother nodded and kissed Cindy on the top of her head. "It's for the best. She was really suffering. It's a blessing she went sooner. Now we can relax."

Sally said, "Oh…I'm so sorry. You could have been there, except for this…us."

"Nope," Cindy said authoritatively as she turned to Sally. "I think this meeting is what she would have wanted. You gotta hear about my Gram. Actually, she's my dad's Gram. I've been recording conversations of her life the past two years, and someday I'm gonna turn it into a book. You all would have loved her. I've already written the teaser for the back cover of my book, and Gram approved it!"

"The colorful wife of a logger/pig farmer, who suddenly found herself a widow with 5 kids at the age of 27, after a giant white pine fell on her husband. She made her own whisky, and as she said, 'I castrated every damn piglet on the place that was stupid enough to be born with nuts, all by myself!' "

"Oh, Cindy," her mother implored, "please clean it up!"

"I already did!" said an aggravated Cindy in her own defense. "Back to what I'm getting at—Gram just loved Angel and Danny, and she wished she'd been able to help. Since this crap began, every time I went to see her, she'd shake a bony fist and say something like, 'Those sonsabitches, Kellogg and Chandler, I'd like to show them two some whoop-ass! What a buncha bullshit!'

"And then she'd say, in a sweet voice, like any little old grandma in a rocking chair, 'Even though I can't get the hell outta bed—and if by the goddamn grace of God I somehow managed to, and then lit on my feet instead of my ass, I friggin' wouldn't be able to walk or see where the hell I'm going, and I'd have to stop to get my stinkin' diaper changed every goddamn four hours of the trip anyway—is there anything I can do to help?' "

The looks on the adults' faces ranged from dropped jaws to hands hiding eyes that were laughing or embarrassed.

Cindy continued, "Talk about timing, I bet Gram's finally helping out now like she wanted to. Come on, everybody. A toast to Gram. This is exactly the way she would want it to be, except maybe you'd be sipping her moonshine instead of wine."

Ally smiled through her tears as she raised her glass. "To our Gram…and these goddamn special kids!"

Dave pushed his chair back. "I'd better call Carrie with the news, and we should get to the hospital."

The others began clearing the table. Retreating to the fireplace in the living room, Dave called Carrie to give her the sad news.

Shaking his head and grinning, he announced, "Carrie says Gram's already on the job. Dale was doing 80 down Highway 34, and Carrie swears she heard Gram say, *Slow down, goddamnit!* Actually, that was an edited version. Carrie got Dale to cut it back to 65. Sure enough, a state cop had a speed trap set up just past the wayside rest. All he did was blink his Christmas lights and shake a finger at Dale."

When Dale and Carrie arrived at the gate, it was a half hour past sunset. The thick clouds streaming in from the west blotted out the nearly full moon in the east. Carrie stepped out of the truck. "Can't get any darker than this."

They were in the middle of the south unit of the Paul Bunyan State Forest, where the closest artificial light was four miles south—glowing from yard lights and cabins on a lake halfway to Nevis. From a hilltop on a cloudless night, you would be able to see the line of lights down there, and even the red lights atop the Nevis and Akeley water towers, and a handful of communication towers dotted across the horizon. But not that night. The sky was threatening thunderstorms.

The truck lights shined past the gate far enough for Carrie to find the tree with the plaster rock at its base with the key inside. The lock connected two ends of a stout chain, which was wrapped around a rusting, yellow cattle gate and a 6 x 8 fencepost.

Dale stood waiting by the truck as Carrie unlocked the gate, saying, "Feels like rain. I don't like this one bit. It feels like it's going to be nasty. I'll shut the gate behind you." A distant rumble of thunder echoed across the countryside.

After Dale drove through, she hooked the lock back onto the chain ends but didn't click it shut.

The hunting shack sat at the far end of a clover-covered, two-track trail that wove its way over half a mile back through the privately owned 80 acres of steep forested hills. This section of the state forest covered almost 100 square miles, much more if you counted the odd private parcels like this one within its boundaries.

It wasn't exactly untracked wilderness. The forest service had long since turned the railroad spurs, built during the logging boom in early the early 1900s, into decent gravel roads and had maintained them well. Crossing the gravel roads were a variety of recreational trails: walk-in hunting trails, rutted dirt bike paths over the rocks and through the mud holes, hiking trails almost indiscernible except for the blue splotches of spray paint on the tree trunks, two-track trails for four-wheelers and smaller side-by-sides, and side roads that had been bulldozed wide enough to accommodate logging trucks. After the logging was complete, those were closed off with a line of boulders or a berm of dirt three or four feet high. Set yourself a compass heading, and it wouldn't be more than a mile or two before you'd encounter a trail of some sort.

The hardest part was that there were some places so steep you'd have to claw your way to the top, like a miniature Alps.

Dale stopped the truck at the last bend in the trail, 150 yards before the shack. He signaled with the car horn like they had arranged: three short honks one second apart, wait 10 seconds, then do it again. Then they waited two minutes before driving up to the shack. It looked deserted, dark inside and out. Dale shut off the headlights and they waited.

In a minute, a flashlight blinked on and was pointed into Dale's face.

"Whew, it's you guys," Angel said. "What's up?"

"Quick," Carried implored, hopping down from the truck. "Let's get inside and light a couple candles while you pack. We need to use Plan B."

Danny walked up behind Angel. "What? Are they already on our trail? Shit!"

The kids hurried to load up what little they could fit into the two backpacks, which were already nearly full— two bottles of water each, a short chunk of salami, and a block of cheese.

Carrie said, "Oh, and take out your cell batteries right now, and don't put them back in unless somebody breaks a leg. Better yet, give me your phone, Angel. I'll put the battery back in when I get to town, and hide it in a truck that looks like it's just passing through."

They did as instructed. Danny stuffed his disabled phone and its battery into opposite pockets.

"How much time do we have?" Angel asked, as she handed her phone parts to Dale.

"Don't know," Carrie said. "But we're pretty sure Danny's probation officer and Shawn Elliot have all our phone numbers. Shit! I forgot to take my own battery out. Well, it's a little late for that."

"Better dig out your rain ponchos," Dale said. "It's gonna be a very wet night." He checked the weather app on his phone. "Don't think you'll be able to get far enough away and set up camp before it hits."

As Plan B, the six of them had pre-packed two escape backpacks with camping equipment: a lightweight two-person tent, folding saw, two jackknives, matches in a waterproof container, energy bars and trail mix, insect repellent, a first aid kit, space blankets and waterproof ground pads, and spare batteries. Danny's .177 caliber BB air pistol was in the top of his pack. He undid his belt and slid the holster slot onto it.

Most importantly, in the front pouch of Danny's larger pack were the GPS and spare batteries, plus a map of the state forest that showed coordinates of trail inter-sections. In Angel's front pouch were a pen and a small notepad listing an escape route where they would meet up with their crew, or at least have food and other sup-plies dropped off nearby.

Navigating via GPS was nothing new to the Ryan kids. Years ago, their dad had taught them to read one when they'd explored state forests in search of mush-rooms or grouse. Sam would purposefully lead them a couple of miles off the beaten path, then make them use the GPS to guide themselves back to the truck. Getting out of the woods that way became so second nature, it was no longer a challenge. The last couple of years, the kids chose instead to read the wind, the trees, the clouds, the sun, listen for distant traffic or other manufactured noise, and let their common sense and intuition be their guide.

Sometimes Danny cheated, secretly bending or breaking off twigs and brush that he could follow later.

The Ryan kids were as comfortable in the woods as most bears. They had insisted on sleeping in a tent in the yard when they were four and five. By the time they were eight and nine, they had spent several nights each summer up at the fire ring.

The July before, they packed their backpacks with everything they'd need for supper and an overnight and breakfast. They talked their folks into helping them put the canoe in at the dam, and camped out on the high sand bank all by themselves.

Just before midnight, Angel had called her mother to fill her in on their adventure. "We saw Mercury right after sunset! And Venus, too! We had to wade across the river and climb a couple of trees to get a good view. When we got back to camp, a bear had gotten into the cooler. We know it was a bear 'cause it made a lot more noise than a coon when it ran away. And it took a huge crap right in front of the tent door. That bear should chew its corn better! I got a picture of the pile. I already made it the screen saver on my phone."

———————

"You guys better get going," Carrie said. "Dale and I will clean up the rest of your stuff, just in case they do find this place. We've got enough drop-off points marked for five days, right? Be careful when you're walking the trails. I've got a few folks I know I can trust to make the drops and pick up the notes. Dale and I better not come back up here, in case they're tracking us too.

"Remember, we're gonna have the helpers use your trick, Danny, with the bent twigs, and hide the things under them, within 100 feet of the signs. You're gonna do that too, for the notes. Just to make sure we're all clear, somebody will go to Point A between 11:00 and noon tomorrow to pick up your note—let us know how it's going and if you need anything. Do you think you have enough to eat and drink to get you through tomorrow and into Friday?"

Carrie quickly looked around the shack. She grabbed a six-pack of bottled water. "Here, Danny. Angel, you take the other one. Don't trust the water from any springs. Okay, scoot!"

"No, wait," Carrie said as she squeezed her eyes shut and sucked in a breath. "One more thing. Gram died this evening." Carrie hadn't taken the time to digest the loss herself; she was too busy figuring out how to save Danny's and Angel's hides.

"I'm so sorry," Angel said. "Tell your mom and dad and Cindy how sorry I am."

"Me, too," said Danny.

Angel, with her arms open, approached Carrie, who had slumped down into a chair and was squeezing the bridge of nose and fighting back tears. Angel was trying to squeeze in her own tears, when they heard Danny say, "Uh oh." He was looking out the window toward the bend in the trail a block away. "Headlights!"

"Come on!" Angel implored. They flew out the door, backpacks in one hand and bottled water in the other.

Carrie grabbed her phone. "Oh shit, I wonder if we're in trouble. Come on, Joan..."

"Hey, Carrie. How's Plan B going?"

"The kids just left in a big hurry. They're gonna be fine, but somebody just drove up. It's gotta be the cops."

"I'll stay on the line," Joan said. "Put me on speaker and I'll listen."

Carrie set her phone on the table and there was a sharp knock on the door. "Who...who is it?" she asked, her voice trembling. Dale stood like a deer in headlights, his mouth half open.

"Sheriff's Investigator Shawn Elliot. Can we come in?"

Carrie leaned toward her phone. "Joan?"

"Yes, it's okay. Let him in."

Dale opened the door slowly. Elliot had a penlight in one hand and shined it back and forth between the two kids. "Dale, Carrie, you two here alone?"

"Yes," Carrie answered quietly.

"What are you doing up here?"

"Don't answer that," said Joan through the speaker. "Sorry, Shawn—Joan Adair here. Just need to know what's going on here first."

"Uhh, okay. No problem, Joan."

Someone behind Elliot stepped inside. "Holly's with me. We traced the kids' cell phones to this general area last night. In case you don't know, we're up in the Paul Bunyan State Forest, north of Nevis."

"You and I know you can't track someone that precisely with GPS. How did you decide this might be the place?"

Elliot replied, "Chandler was following us around like a rabid pit bull all day. When she heard about the general location of the pings, she said she had a hunch. Gotta hand it to her—she went through the property records in this area and came up with this shack owned by an Edward Wilson, said she knew of a possible connection."

Just then, another vehicle pulled in. As the driver got out, a bolt of lightning sizzled as it hit a tree less than a block away, followed by a deafening boom. She clomped to the shack.

"Did ya get those little fugitives?" Chandler pushed her way past Gibbons into the shack.

"Ms. Chandler, fancy meeting you here…" Joan said.

Chandler jumped, as if it were a ghost talking to her.

"Huh! The Wilson connection—just what I thought! Where are Angel and Daniel?"

"Don't know," said Elliot, shrugging. "Just these two here."

"Well, they're obviously accomplices. This can't be a coincidence they're up here 50 miles from home!"

Joan asked, "Ms. Chandler, who suggested to you that Amy Wilson could be involved?"

"Th…that's really none of your concern. It's police business." She tilted her chin upward in defiance, although Joan couldn't see her.

"Never mind," Joan said. "I'm pretty sure I know."

Chandler piped up. "Mr. Elliot, aren't you going to take these two obvious accomplices into custody, for harboring fugitives?"

"Don't forget to read them their Miranda rights first," Joan advised, "and exactly what they may be charged with…"

"Not tonight," Elliot said.

There was another flash and, two seconds later, a thunderclap. The sky opened up like a dam bursting. The huge raindrops and nickel-sized hail pounding on the shack's metal roof was deafening.

Gibbons picked up the phone so she and Joan could hear each other. "But we will be continuing our search. However, I suspect further checking for cell phone pings will be useless. You know, Joan, I'm just doing my job."

"Don't they have tracking dogs around here?" Chandler screamed through the roar of the deluge. "Why didn't you call them in? The trail's going to be washed away soon. It's dangerous for Daniel to be out there on the loose!"

Frustrated and shaking her head, Chandler pushed her way past Gibbons and out onto the stoop, where she paused, contemplating a hail-pummeling and rain-soaking dash to her SUV. "Do I have to do that for you, too?"

After Chandler descended the two steps to the ground, she turned and shrieked, "You call yourself an investigator?"

She clomped to her SUV, hauled herself inside, and backed away, spinning her tires and sending mud flying as she headed down the trail toward the gravel road.

"Sorry, kids!" Elliot yelled. "Not to sound unprofessional, but if Angel and Danny were in here and ran off, it was because of Chandler. She said she'd come up here herself if we didn't. We were fine letting the kids sit until tomorrow, and then were gonna start checking cabins in this part of the Bunyan. I'll shut the gate. Do you want me to lock it?"

"No," Carrie hollered. "Just leave it open. We'll be right behind you."

After Gibbons and Elliot left, Carrie shut the door and held the phone close to her face. "Joan, now what?"

"First of all, are the kids gonna be okay?"

"They're fine—maybe getting a little wet—but to those two little woods rats, it's just like they're on a camping trip. We've got it all planned out. They could stay out here the rest of the summer if they had to. We've got points set up to drop off supplies and communicate as we need to."

Joan replied, "Doesn't seem like Holly and Shawn are hell-bent to find Danny and Angel just yet. But we can't take any chances. And I have a feeling Chandler won't be standing around twiddling her big fat thumbs."

"I wonder if maybe we should bring the kids closer to home, but make Shawn and the others think they're still up here? And maybe also let Sam and Sally in on it?"

"The trouble with that," Joan explained, "is that if they are perceived as harboring their fugitive son, they could end up in jail. Ironically, it's best to keep them in the dark as to Angel and Danny's exact whereabouts. But I WILL let them know the kids are okay."

"Okay, I guess that makes sense. But I'm still gonna work on getting them closer to home. Dammit! This hunting shack was so handy, so perfect. Oh well. Tomorrow, my friend Linda is gonna pick up a note they'll leave, right after 11. And I'll have her leave a note from me. We'll figure out something. I just know Chandler's gonna be watching us."

"Probably Kellogg, too," Joan added.

CHAPTER 12

ONE SOGGY SOCK

First thing in the morning, Ally and Cindy stopped at the winery to fill in the Ryans. The yard was dotted with puddles and scattered leaves from the previous night's storm.

Sally was dressed in her muni bartending clothes. "Whew, we must have gotten three inches of rain. I hope the kids weren't out in that mess."

"How much can you tell us now?" Sam asked. "I can hardly sleep…"

"Well I hate to tell you, but they were out in that weather," Cindy said. "We had them holed up in a nice, dry little shack over in the Bunyan. But Chandler tracked them down and made Shawn and the probation officer go up there to find them. The kids had to make a run for it. With Chandler's lucky sleuthing, she discovered that the land and shack are owned by Amy Wilson's father."

Cindy filled them in on the remaining details.

"Oh shit," Sam said. "This isn't gonna be good for Amy…"

Cindy continued, "But we have a solid Plan B—had their camping packs all ready just in case."

"Yup," Sam said, "we noticed all that gear was missing."

"We're thinking about hiding them closer to home," Cindy said.

"So where?" Sally asked.

"Still working out those details."

Sam held up a handful of letters. "Better get these in the mailbox…"

Halfway down the driveway, he heard a vehicle approaching slowly from the direction of the bridge. He stood near the road, waiting for it to pass. It slowed to a stop as it approached the end of the driveway. A dark blue Grand Cherokee Jeep—Chandler. The passenger window rolled down. She held up her phone to snap a picture.

"Picture this," Sam yelled as he gave her the finger from about 10 feet away.

Chandler grinned and chirped, "Have a nice day, Mr. Ryan!" She rolled away slowly, sticking her chin in the air.

Back by the porch, Sally said, "This is insane."

"At least she's not up in the Bunyan snooping around," Cindy said.

Sam crossed the road and put the letters in the mailbox. He noticed another vehicle approaching, from the direction Chandler was heading. Amy Wilson pulled up next to him.

"Looks like I got some time on my hands," she said with a frown.

"WHAT?"

"I'll fill you in," Amy said as she turned into the driveway.

They met on the porch. "Guess who was just fired. By Kellogg. Says I 'broke school rules' by helping Angel and

Danny run away and hide. How the heck did she even figure out they were up there?"

Cindy explained, "We overheard you telling somebody about the place, and then we figured it out ourselves! That's my story and I'm stickin' to it!"

"Technically, that's true, Cindy," Amy said. "But they're still assuming it was all my doing. Either way, if I want my job back, I'm gonna need an attorney."

"Seriously?" Sally asked. "Let me call Joan. She'll take care of it."

Sally walked toward the house with the phone to her ear. She nodded and turned back to the group. "Amy, you're covered."

Sam said, "Listen, Amy, we're meeting with Shawn Elliot at the muni before Sally starts her shift. Why don't you come with us? You know Angel and Danny as well as anyone."

"With this hanging over my head?"

"Shawn is a very reasonable man," Sally said, putting her hand on Amy's arm. "And it sounds like he feels awful for scaring the kids away into the storm. Have you met him?"

Amy shook her head. "Seen him around school a few times, but we never talked."

"Is that so? Hmm, well maybe you should meet him."

———

"Nice to officially meet you." Amy shook Shawn's hand. *Strong grip*, she thought.

"Yes, I noticed you, too," said Shawn. "I can tell the kids really like you." He glanced at his khaki shirt sleeve and nervously ran his fingers through his hair. "No more uniforms for now—just got moved into the sheriff's investigator position."

Absently, he was still hanging onto Amy's hand. Sally and Sam glanced at each other and waggled their eyebrows.

Shawn noticed the gesture and quickly let go.

"I've known Shawn since around sixth grade, wasn't it?" Sam said. "Drove him on the school bus occasionally."

Shawn laughed. "Oh man… One day after school, I was getting on the bus and a pack of cigarettes fell out of my jacket pocket, right in front of Sam. They landed right by the shifter stick. What was I—a ninth grader? He picked it up and put into in his shirt pocket without even looking at me."

Sam shrugged and smiled.

"I figured I was busted. I was no stranger to trouble back then, but I didn't really want any that day. I was the last one off the bus and was dreading walking past the Jammer. That's what we called him because of how, umm, EFFICIENT he was getting us to places—especially on long trips, like to the cities or Fargo. When we got to my stop, Sam didn't open the door right away. He just handed the cigarettes back to me and said—and I'll never forget it—'No thanks, I'm trying to quit!' "

The others laughed.

"True story," Sam said as he nodded. "But back to business, Shawn. Let me tell you why they ran. Angel's a very special girl, in ways that a lot of folks can't understand."

Sally continued. "She sure is. I was a little skeptical at first, about the things she sees…knows…dreams. She had a dream that her brother would get molested up in juvie. They are truly soul twins. She would do anything to keep her brother from getting hurt like that. Essentially, you're up against a mother bear...one who's also quite psychic."

Shawn said, "I wish I'd had a mother bear for a sister...or even for a mother."

Just then there was a furious pounding on the locked muni front door. A large figure loomed, blocking out the sunlight, hands cupped around her face, peering into the dark bar.

"What the fu—?" Sam mumbled.

"I'll take care of this," Shawn said.

Sally handed him the key.

"Did I miss anything?" Chandler asked as she squeezed through the door. "Mr. Elliot, I called your office and they said you'd be here."

Her eyes adjusted to the dim light. She pointed at Amy. "What's SHE doing here? She's an accomplice! I hope you're questioning her!"

"Ms. Chandler," Shawn said in an even, authoritative voice, "I'm asking you to leave."

"What? Daniel Ryan is my client. It is in his best interests that I know everything that's transpiring in the quest to bring him to justice."

Shawn shook his head and closed his eyes. "Our only quest right now is to get him back safely, and that has nothing to do with you. Please, just let us handle this."

She planted herself firmly and stuck her beefy hands onto her ample hips. "Who was it who figured out where they were hiding? Without me, you wouldn't even BEGIN to know where to look for those kids!"

"Without you, if they'd been in that cabin, at least they would've been safe overnight." He approached the door and held it open. "Now please, we've got work to do."

Chandler turned and grunted her patented, "Hmmph!" She clomped across the wooden deck, her head tossed back.

Shawn returned to the table. Amy spoke up. "Just to clear the air...yes, the kids knew about my dad's hunting shack, and I—"

Shawn held his hand up. "Please, I know all I need to know about that. What I need to find out today is how capable are Danny and Angel out there by themselves?"

Sam and Sally filled in the blanks, about how the other kids would meet up with them and keep them supplied. Shawn smiled. "I'm sure they've got the cell phone thing figured out. The list of possible helpers could be into the dozens. I'm certainly not gonna form a posse to stake them all out. But when Holly gets back from vacation Monday, she may put some pressure on, and I don't blame her. They'll come back sooner or later, right?"

They both nodded. Sam said, "I wouldn't hold your breath though. It could be a while."

"What I think might work in Danny's favor is that Judge Belden..." Shawn said, "This doesn't leave this table, okay? He suspects there's something fishy going on with Chandler and Kellogg. He said that if Danny's apprehended, let him know and he'll figure out something else so Danny doesn't have to go right to juvie. My sense is that the judge, as much as any of us, wants to find the truth."

Sam asked, "In the meantime, can you help us do some digging on Chandler and Kellogg? This just doesn't make any sense, at least about the principal. Those two sure seem to be teamed up. How else would Kellogg know that Chandler figured out the cabin belongs to Amy's dad?"

"I can't go there," Shawn said. "Unless somebody brings me some real evidence that suggests they're committing some sort of crime."

"Can I do some digging on my own?" Amy asked.

"Maybe," said Shawn. "What have you got in mind?"

"I've noticed the four boys around town and at the city beach. I'll ask around about whether they've said anything."

"No harm in that, I guess. In the meantime, I'll keep checking cell phone pings so I'll have something to show Holly. As I said, my first and foremost duty is their safety. And I feel pretty good about that for the time being. Thanks for sharing."

"We'll keep you posted," Sam said. "Thanks, Shawn."

"Anytime, Jammer."

Shawn fished three business cards out of his notebook. "Amy, you keep in touch too, if you hear anything. Call me anytime."

"Do you have another card?" Amy asked. "In case you need to call me?"

Shawn quickly found one and slid it across the table. He handed Amy a pen from his shirt pocket.

Sam and Sally each wore a sly smile.

"Question for you, Amy," Sam said, a knowing look crossing his features. He named 10 different dates in various months. "Which one's your birthday?"

Surprised, Amy answered, "Umm...October 17th. How did you know?"

Sam confessed, "Your birth card—it's sort of like astrology. You're the Five of Clubs, the Seeker of Truth. It takes one to know one—I'm May 27th. Except, at my age I complain about the truth more than I go looking for it.

Our kids could not have a better friend right now. You'll find the truth. I know it."

Shawn piped up, "How about May 31st?"

Sam grinned. "Ace of Clubs—Desire for Knowledge. You two will make quite a team!"

Amy and Shawn looked at each other, not sure what to make of Sam's statement.

"So, uh...call me if you come up with anything," Shawn repeated to Amy, with a hopeful look.

"I better get this place ready," Sally said as she stood up. "The *Price is Right* gang will be pounding on the door in about five minutes."

Amy and Shawn headed for the door. He opened it for her, and then they stood on the deck, facing each other and making what appeared to be small talk. Sam watched Amy tuck her hair behind her ear. Shawn, smiling, said something and she nodded. They waved as they headed for the vehicles.

"Anything I can do, honey?" Sam asked as he slid out of his chair.

"I think you've done enough already," Sally answered. "Except you forgot to kiss your own old girlfriend goodbye..."

"Gladly."

———

Linda Carlisle, Carrie's linemate and bookend on the volleyball and basketball teams, drove up into the Bunyan, arriving half an hour early, and found the trail crossing. She drove on past it half a mile, as instructed, turned around, and drove back past it again to make sure she wasn't being followed. A block beyond the trail crossing, she found an abandoned logging trail and drove her truck up to where the trail ended at a dirt berm, a little over a hundred yards from the gravel road.

The trail was wide at the berm like a small cul-de-sac. She parked off to the side where she couldn't be seen by traffic on the road below. She scanned the woods. It was a mature forest, almost park-like. It would be an easy enough walk to the drop-off area, but she'd have to be careful to stay out of sight. Carrie had warned her that the road was probably used as a shortcut between Nevis and Bemidji, and there likely would be some traffic.

Knuckles rapping on the back window jolted Linda out of her reverie.

It was Angel and Danny.

Linda, wide-eyed, gasped as she turned and saw the two kids, their shirts and pants still wet from the night's thunderstorm. She quickly opened the door and slid out. "What the f….?"

Angel's eyes were narrowed and Danny stood a step behind her, holding his hands out and shaking his head, as if warning Linda not to get too close.

Angel growled, "In our frickin' hurry to get out of the hunting shack, we forgot toilet paper. Between that little oversight and the fact that overnight I joined the ranks of womanhood, we're down to one soggy sock between the two of us." She looked like she'd bite the head off a rattlesnake that dared stick its tongue out at her.

"Oh my gawd!" cried Linda. "You poor thing!" She leaned into her truck to open the glove box. "I've got a couple pads in here."

"Plan C," Angel said through gritted teeth. "Point B— before dark. You pick a time—any fuckin' time. Socks for both of us. Panties for me, plus pads, and GODDAMN toilet paper. Please."

Linda blurted out, "But what about BEARS? I heard they attack women who are having their period!"

"Trust me," Danny said as took another careful step backward, "any bear that shows up in our camp will wish he'd never let go of his mother's tit."

Angel turned and demanded, "REALLY? Am I THAT bad?"

He took another step backward, not daring to respond.

"Here's the thing," said Linda. "We're getting you out of here this evening. That was Shawn Elliot and the proba- tion officer last night, with Chandler close behind—she's the one who figured out about Amy's father's hunting shack."

"Where are you gonna take us?" Danny asked.

"Carrie and the others are figuring that out as we speak. They're planning on somewhere closer to home, hopefully somewhere a lot drier. But we still have to be real careful. Chandler's been busy, that's for sure. And other strange vehicles have been hanging around. In the meantime, Cindy and Nate are still digging."

"Tell them this," Angel said. "What little I slept last night, I saw Gram at Fox Lake Beach, sitting on a yellow, wooden deck chair, with a huge umbrella shading her. She was drinking her moonshine from a silver flask as she gazed out over the gentle waves, smiling. Gram looked right into my eyes, and held the flask up toward me like a toast. She said, 'A Frenchman, Georges Braque, said this a hundred years ago: The truth exists; lies are invented.' What do you think of that?"

That was the kind of detail from Angel's dreams that either made a person a believer or compelled them to pound a stake in the ground and gather firewood.

Danny added, "And tell Mom and Dad we're okay, and we love them and miss them. Where do you want us to meet somebody tonight? And when? The moon's just about full. It's gonna be bright all night until just before dawn."

Linda looked around. "How about meet me right here? Ten o'clock will be fine. We'll have Carrie and Dale both take them on wild goose chases about eight. We'll send out so many drones, they won't know which one is the real thing. Will you guys be okay until then?"

Danny looked up beyond the treetops. "The sun's out. It's gonna hit 88 degrees or so. I guess we'll dry pretty quick. Hey, you got any salt and pepper in the glove box?"

He patted his holster. Angel grinned and licked her lips.

"Why? What?" Linda asked. "Ya, there might be some little packets from the drive-through. Oh! Almost forgot—sandwiches…" She reached to open a small cooler on the floor in front of the passenger seat.

Angel said, "One more thing. I had a lot of time to think last night when I couldn't sleep. Tell Cindy I remembered something from when Danny punched Dylan. Billy said his aunt bought him that dirt bike as a get-well present. That's an awfully loving aunt for the likes of that little creep to have. And then, after Dylan got punched, Billy said something like, 'Good job, now you get the camera drone.' Maybe they can look into that?"

That afternoon, Angel and Danny sat still as statues in a blind of limbs and branches at the base of a huge red pine, their faces smeared with mud as camouflage.

Danny prayed softly. "Dear God, forgive me for shooting a turkey poult out of season, but after what you did to us, and especially Angel last night…and to me as collateral damage…" Angel elbowed her brother hard in the ribs. "Ouch! We'll call it even if we don't have to eat those sandwiches made of discount white bread slathered with margarine and generic peanut butter and jelly for supper…"

A hen and her dozen poults wandered out in the meadow a hundred yards away, picking off insects from the grass and low brush. Just like his dad had taught him, using only his mouth, Danny cut loose with a raucous *kee-kee-run* wild turkey call, compelling the flock to instantly and unanimously believe one of theirs was lost and crying for help.

He had always thought it was odd that instead of the flock calling the lost turkey back to it, they'd all hurry to the rescue in one big frantic stampede. Then again, his dad had told him, turkeys' tiny brains don't exactly make them Rhodes Scholars. The whole flock ran, flopped, and wobbled up to six feet from the blind, their necks all craning as they paced anxiously, as if their scaly little feet were on hot coals, while frantically peeping and squawking the same *kee-kee-run* to see which of their brood was so pathetically lost.

"Nice shot, Danny!" The rest of the flock stood around the stricken poult, still calling but with less angst, watching it flop its life away. In half a minute, when it finally lay still and was dead, the rest just wandered off toward the meadow, chirping softly, pecking at insects along their path, as if saying, "Oh well. It sucks to be him."

"*Wope la*," Danny recited with his eyes closed, as his father had taught him, giving thanks for taking a wild animal's life for his own use.

"Yes," Angel said. "Thanks to the Creator."

They rubbed it with salt and pepper and slowly roasted it to a perfect brown on a green willow spit over a small oak fire. They finished it off with a technique their mother had taught them: a couple of handfuls of dry oak twigs tossed onto the glowing coals, causing the flames to rise and lick at the bird and sear in the freshly rubbed-on wild raspberry glaze. It wasn't much bigger than a grouse, but was a meal fit for a French gourmand—or two kids from northern Minnesota who spent more time in the woods than most bears did.

CHAPTER 13

LITTLE PERVERTS

After lunch, Carrie took Cindy to town and dropped her off in the beach parking lot. Cindy wore her bathing suit under a loose top and cutoffs, and had a towel over her arm.

Through the open passenger window, Carrie asked, "You don't really think those boys will talk to you, do you?"

"I'm just gonna snoop around," Cindy answered, as she surveyed the area. "If they aren't here, they're in one of the church parking lots, I bet."

"I'll pick you up at two o'clock, right here. In the meantime, I'm gonna track down Amy Wilson. I hope she'll take Angel and Danny. No reason she wouldn't, now that she's fired from school, right?"

Cindy shrugged. "I think I hear them coming across the trail. You better scoot. I'm gonna run down to the beach and get wet." She disappeared down the steps.

Sure enough, around the corner at the west end of the parking lot came two remote control battery-powered monster trucks, weaving and swerving. One flipped over onto its top. The boys were laughing. Gavin ran ahead and set his truck back on its wheels. "You're gonna die, Mike!" he yelled.

Mike trotted over, holding the controller out in front of him. He fiddled with the knobs and buttons, and smashed his truck into Gavin's. Both veered wildly. Gavin's ended up on its top again, Mike's on its side, its fat wheels churning, causing the truck to spin in a tight circle.

Billy was cruising along behind them on his electric dirt bike, so slowly he had to steady himself with his feet brushing the pavement. Dylan walked beside him, carrying a camera drone. He told Billy, "Saving the batteries for the beach. Hope those two senior high girls are working on their tans today!"

Billy parked his bike and took the key out. The four of them headed up the parking lot and onto the steps leading to the beach, two hundred feet down a gentle slope. Gavin and Mike drove their trucks slowly next to them, like they were walking electronic dogs. Halfway down, the boys took a right, walking past the deserted picnic shelter, on their way to the far edge of the park, to launch the drone unseen.

Mike decided he wanted to surf the internet on his phone and sat at a picnic table. "You guys go ahead," he said as he poked his finger at the screen.

Gavin set his truck on a table for Mike to keep an eye on, then followed the other two boys down the slope.

Cindy approached from behind. "Hi, Mike. Whatcha doin'?"

He jerked his head around at the mention of his name, but quickly resumed looking at his phone.

Cindy and Angel had always felt that Mike was a fish out of water compared to the other three, who were poor students and screw-ups. He had been pretty much a loner until he'd joined with the others that spring—a bookworm and a techie, with his pimply face usually a few inches from a computer or a phone screen.

Just then, the drone went airborne and the three boys chuckled and pointed. Cindy walked past Mike and sat on a nearby bench. They both watched the drone head out over the water, rise up to treetop height, then bank left toward the main beach.

"Pretty nice present from Billy's aunt," said Cindy. "Was your truck a gift, too?"

Mike didn't look up from his phone. He shrugged and continued poking at the screen. "Who told you that?"

"The day Danny punched Dylie, Billy bragged about it. So I assumed she also bought the remote control trucks, right? And the drone?"

"Don't want to talk about it," Mike mumbled.

"Did you ever meet this nice aunt of Billy? You know, so you could at least thank her?"

"Nope."

"I guess I could see her giving Billy that bike as a get-well present, but why give Dylie that drone? He's not even related."

"We're all best friends. Guess she didn't want us to feel left out."

Cindy decided to change the subject. "You hear about Angel and Danny running away?"

Mike nodded, keeping his eyes glued to the phone screen.

"Oh yeah? How'd you hear about it? Oh, I suppose maybe the cop or probation officer let it slip. That's the kind of news that's hard to keep a lid on and travels pretty fast."

"Ya, something like that…"

Suddenly there was a commotion on the beach. "You little perverts!" A senior high girl was pointing at the drone hovering overhead.

Without saying a word, Mike scooped a truck under each arm and took off at a clumsy run up the hill toward the parking lot. Dylan backpedaled down the narrow beach to the far edge of the park, his drone following overhead. When he reached a neighboring house, he lowered his drone to the ground, waited a couple of seconds for the blades to quit spinning, and then disappeared with it behind a privacy fence. Billy and Gavin scrambled up the bank and ran to the parking lot. Billy shot Cindy a suspicious glance as he passed by her.

———————

At two o'clock on the dot, Carrie pulled into the beach lot to pick up Cindy. "We're heading over to Amy's house to talk about changing the plan. Linda hooked up with Angel and Danny just like we arranged, but things didn't go very well last night. Nate and Dale are meeting us over there. You find out anything?"

Cindy said, "Got a chance to talk with Mike alone. He didn't say much, but he all but came right out and admitted that Billy's aunt bought all four of them the gifts. And he knew that Angel and Danny are on the run."

———————

Amy lived in a little country house, a genuine fixer-upper, about five miles south of Stone Creek. She had happened across it early the summer before while driving around the countryside, after she had been hired to teach

English at Stone Creek. The breakup with her boyfriend had been difficult, but not totally unexpected. After college, she had longed for open, quiet space, not so much because she was one-eighth Ojibway from her mother's side, but because that's the way her family had brought her up. She loved it all—hunting, fishing, campfires, and most of all the starlit and moonlit nights, far from city lights.

She met her college boyfriend, Phillip, an art history student at St. Cloud State, during her junior year. He was quite the opposite, which is what had attracted her to him. He was worldly and knew every nook and cranny of not just St. Cloud but also Minneapolis and St. Paul, where they spent just about every weekend with his friends.

Phillip knew that side of life like she knew every duck slough and Department of Natural Resources wildlife management area. Or the farmers who would let her, her dad, and brother hunt pheasants in the rolling countryside where she had grown up, halfway between Alexandria and Fergus Falls.

During those two years with Phillip, she had delved into his bohemian world—tattoos, piercings, indie bands, and all-night parties. But two years was enough for Amy, and just before graduation she told him that she liked her old life better, and wished him good luck. Phillip had called her a hick and a squaw for choosing the job in Stone Creek over several offers in the cities for almost twice as much pay. Her degree and teaching certificate in hand, and her curiosity about love and life in the bustling city satisfied, she was looking forward to really being alone for the first time in her life.

Two blocks back from the Fox River, the house was tucked tightly into a tangle of untrimmed trees and overgrown brush. She had noticed just a corner of the white house with green trim from the road, a thick stand of volunteer spruce blocking the rest of the view. What was left of the rotting wooden gate was off two of its four hinges and resting on the ground, held shut with a piece of rusty wire. The yard was overgrown with thigh-high grass and weeds and poplar shoots, some as big around as the end of a pool cue, and towering over her head by a yard.

She stepped over the sagging, wire fence. Paint was peeling off the wooden lap siding, and curled like potato chips on the green faux shutters. The windows were shuttered with fiberboard framed with 1 x 4s, with only a shadow of pale green paint remaining. One shutter on what looked like a porch was loose. She pulled the corner of it open and peered inside. An old International Harvester refrigerator and a bumper pool table was all she could make out in the room, lit only by the shaft of light she had let in.

A little tool shed stood next to the house, five steps away. Alongside the shed sat a ringer washer with a galvanized laundry tub over the top to keep the rain and snow out. Farther back was another much bigger shed, with a slanted corrugated roof and a lean-to whose timber purlins and vertical supports had rotted, caving it in over the rightmost half of its length.

Despite its appearance, there was a certain charm and potential to this neglected home and yard. She stopped at a house up the road a quarter mile when she saw a middle-aged woman weeding her flower garden.

"Hi! I'm new to town. Just found a deserted house a little ways back. White with green shutters, set back a bit. Do you know it?"

The woman smiled and brushed dirt off her cheek. "Well, welcome! You know, some schoolteacher from Chicago used to spend summers up here. Haven't seen him in close to 10 years. But was a busy place back then. He must have had something to do with the church. All summer, there were these young men in long, black robes, walking up and down the road. Looked like priests or monks maybe."

Amy found the owner's name and address in the county assessor's office and wrote him a letter, explaining she was a schoolteacher, too. She apologized for snooping, writing, "It was like a voice was calling to me. I can't really explain it."

It was a long month before she heard back—a frustrating month, because she had to find someplace to spend the winter, and there were no affordable rentals around. Her folks' camper at the resort for the summer was fine, even fun. But renting a cabin there over winter would have strained her budget to the breaking point.

Her phone rang as she basked in the sun on a lounge chair. She didn't recognize the area code, and said a silent prayer before she answered. "This...this...is Amy Wilson."

"Yes, Ms. Wilson. This is Don Hill. I'd LOVE to have someone in my house!"

He told her how it had sat there empty far too long, and he worried it would fall down in on itself if nobody lived there. He said he'd be up the next week, on Wednesday, if that worked for her.

"We'll see what needs to be done, ok?" Don asked with a hint of excitement in his voice, "Say, do you have one of those four-wheel ATVs? I'd love to see it all again, but I'm not doing too well on my feet these days."

––––––––––

When he arrived, they hit it off famously. Don Hill, in his 80s, drove an old, rusting minivan. He had easily been a six-footer-plus in his younger days, but was now quite hunched over. Still, he moved with purpose and confidence, although slowly. His bald head was tan and blotchy from decades of sun, the rim of gray hair bushy and unruly. His forehead was deeply wrinkled, his gray eyebrows also bushy, matching his plentiful ear hair. His blue eyes sparkled from inside his roundish face.

As she shook his hand, Amy got tingles up and down her spine, a feeling that somehow he had been waiting for her, specifically her, to write to him. At first glance, he acted as if the place was already hers, asking permission to walk around, and insisting that Amy stay there right from the get-go. He showed her how to take the porch shutters off, turn the electricity on, and start the water. There was a steel army bed with a sagging, thin mattress on the porch for her until she got the bedroom ready. In the meantime, he'd take a room at the Stone Creek Inn. She accepted and told Don she needed a few things from the camper.

That night, she found her way in the dark to the middle of the meadow and sat in a mesh folding chair, crickets chirping and lightning bugs flickering gently around her. She started to tear up, asking the Universe above, "Am I home?" A coyote howling from the northwest caught her attention. Then another straight north of her, followed by a raucous chorus of yipping and chirping from the northeast—a mother and her pups. She smiled into the darkness. Suddenly, out of the corner of her eye, a shaft of pale green northern light burst from the horizon and rolled in waves to the zenith of the inky night sky.

———————

Amy had seen on the county parcel map that Don's land with the house encompassed 120 acres and sat along half a mile of the Fox River. He owned another adjacent 400 acres as well, also along the river. She had the county print out two aerial photos of the expanse in color, one for her and one for Don, and pored over her copy.

Over Don's three-day visit, during short jaunts on the ATV, from the seat behind Amy, he shared his life story, how a Korean War army vet from Chicago turned Latin language high school teacher had amassed 520 acres of northern Minnesota.

He spoke about his separation pay from the army, and the train ride soon after to Wadena. A realtor had picked him and his rucksack up at the station. His first 40 acres were just woods and swamp. He camped there for a week and hitchhiked back to Wadena. A year later, the same realtor hooked him up with the 40 acres across the river that had the shack on it, which had been built in the 40s right after World War II.

From that second year on, he drove his car up and stayed all summer. Another 80 acres here, another 40 there, every few years, bought from neighbors who didn't see much value in paying taxes on woods, swamp, and sand under the thin grasses—nothing like real soil you could grow a decent crop in.

"Never married or went on big vacations, other than to the Vatican twice. Lived with my folks my entire life, until they passed on. Matter of fact, I still live in their house. My Latin professor from college talked me into turning this place into a summer camp for seminarians who were falling behind in their Latin studies, with me as their tutor. It was great."

Don reminisced fondly, recalling details as if it had been only last week. "My retired army buddy, Sarge, hooked us up with big tents, and the students dug latrines and bathed in the river. We had a huge garden that the students hand-pumped water to through a series of pipes and roof gutters. Priests from the seminary in Winona took turns coming up a week or two at a time to say Mass every morning and to fish all afternoon. And, of course, to enjoy Gallo wine with me by the gallon every evening— you'll find hundreds of empties in the barn!

"We re-sided the outside walls right over the tarpaper, and installed paneling inside on the walls and ceiling over the rough-sawn boards. Pounded in a well, added the bathroom addition…oh, and the porch. Put in electricity and had the students hand-dig a septic system. It occurred to us we should probably insulate, but to be honest we spent that part of the budget on wine. Heh, heh.

"Only came up once during a winter in all those years—over Christmas break—and almost burned the place down, building too hot of a fire. It was 30 below, you see, and we sent the smoke and flame into a plain brick chimney that was hardly fit to carry away a puff of cigar smoke. First thing, Amy, you gotta get rid of that stove, cover the hole in the wall so the bats don't get in, and put in a propane space heater. Ah, those were the days..."

The third morning, he sat at the dining table and made a list in a small notebook of various improvements that would make the house livable year-round.

"So you really like it here, right?"

Amy's eyes lit up. "Yup, I sure do. It needs a little work, but then again, so do I! We're a pretty good fit, I'd say. I can't afford to buy it, though. You know, just starting out on my own. Could I maybe work for rent? I'm pretty handy."

"Well, here's the thing. The thieving tax assessor says it's worth $95,500, which is a bunch of baloney. But let's use that as a starting point anyway."

"Starting point?"

Don was deep in thought and didn't hear her question. He continued, "All the repairs—the biggie being tearing off the siding, insulating, and re-siding—plus the space heater, attic insulation, new shingles—by my estimates, will add up to around $50,000, with maybe half that cost as labor.

"It's yours. I'm discounting it to $45,000, contract for deed at 1%. How does $200 a month sound? I'll buy the materials. It's stuff I should have been taking care of all along anyway. I just didn't think I'd live this long! Think you can get it ready for winter?"

Amy was dumbfounded. She opened her mouth and nothing came out. But her eyes were leaking. She rubbed at them with her wrists. "I'll sure try!"

Don continued excitedly, "Now once I'm covered with six feet of terra firma, the seminary in Winona is getting the other 400 acres. My hope is that they'll build a camp here like we had in the old days, complete with nature trails, and let the Boy Scouts use it too. I know how they're strapped for cash to operate the college. They'll just dump this beautiful land to the first bloke with a fistful of Franklins."

"But that still doesn't add up!" Amy said. "Even with the so-so condition of the house and buildings, this land alone is worth a lot more than $45,000. And you're kicking in another $25,000 of your own money?"

"Hey," Don teased, "I was a Latin teacher, not a mathematician. I'll have my old attorney's son in Detroit Lakes draw up the papers this afternoon, and I'm cutting you a check on the spot."

His eyes glistened. "I'm just so happy someone will love this place like I did...and still do."

"One more thing I suppose I should tell you, in the interest of full disclosure." Don chuckled. "The rocking chair over there—that's Sarge's. He helped me a lot with this place. He's been dead for over 20 years, but after he left, he still came back and rocked in it once in a while. He smells like he needs a bath and he strums a ukulele, like he's announcing his presence. It's badly out of tune, and he never did know how to play it anyway. Just tell him to go away if he gets too annoying."

Don's sister called in December to inform Amy that he had died. That afternoon, she filled the chainsaw with gas and oil, and commenced upon the brush and blowdowns in the north woods, clearing a path wide enough for an ATV.

It was almost dark when she broke through the brush on the other side of the forty. She held up her chainsaw with one weary arm as a salute. "I dub thee the Don Hill Trail, the first of many I'll carve out of these woods, and share with the kids from school. I'll tell them of you and your love and dedication to these wild lands, and of your generosity."

Amy sniffled then stifled a laugh. "But I won't tell them about the three pickup loads of Gallo wine jugs in the barn that I hauled away."

CHAPTER 14

LISTENING FOR WOLVES

"Here's the deal," Linda told the others seated around Amy's picnic table. "I'll go back and pick them up at 10:00 tonight. We decided to use the same spot where I met them this morning. Nobody saw me."

Amy added, "Shawn Elliot isn't going to look for them for a while—at least not until Holly Gibbons gets back to work on Monday. I met with him, Sam, and Sally this morning."

"It's Chandler I worry about," Carrie said. "She's got a sixth sense. It's creepy. No doubt, she's gone over Shawn's head and put Hubbard County on alert."

Amy said, "Shawn told me this morning he did alert them about Angel and Danny possibly being up there, but asked them to make it low priority. Said if they run across the kids, yes pick them up, but don't bother to go out of your way to look for them otherwise. He also told them to expect Chandler to come knocking, and said to refer her back to him."

"Even if Chandler's off the scent," Linda said, "we need to get them out of there. They're down to one sock, no toilet paper, and haven't bathed in a couple of days."

Carrie pleaded, "Actually, Amy...we were kind of hoping YOU might take them in..."

Amy squeezed her temples and closed her eyes for a couple of seconds. "Yes, bring them here, at least for tonight. We have to get them cleaned up. Oh wait...shoot."

"Is there a problem?" asked Cindy. "I mean, we can take them to my house, or even home and have them go stay in the guest house. But my place and the Ryans' are just too easy to watch just by driving by. Are you worried about getting caught?"

"Well, yes and no... Not what will happen if I get caught. Shawn Elliot and I are meeting for a burger at The Smoky tonight."

"To talk about Angel and Danny?" Nate asked.

"I suppose that too," Amy admitted.

"You mean a DATE?" Carrie asked. She and the others had their eyes glued on Amy, who was looking down at the picnic table.

Amy exhaled loudly. "I swore I wasn't even gonna look at a guy for two years. It's a long story. I certainly don't want to lie to him, or make it seem like I'm using him. Maybe I should just cancel tonight..."

"Angel and Danny wouldn't want you to cancel your date," Cindy assured Amy. "But do you think you can have him out of here by 11:00?"

"Geez, Cindy! This isn't even a date! I'm certainly not bringing him home with me!"

The kids burst into laughter, slapping their thighs. Amy shook her head and rolled her eyes. "You guys..."

With the authority of a football coach during a time-out, Cindy summarized the plan. "Okay, a couple of things for tonight's meetup, Linda. Fresh undies...and stuff...for

Angel. Pick them up at my house. Have Danny put his cell phone battery in and call Nate, so the pings make the cops think they're still up there. Dale and Carrie, you get here to Amy's around ten o'clock and park out of sight. Watch for snoopers instead of making out, if you can manage. If something looks suspicious, call Linda.

"Linda, if you have to, take Angel and Danny home to the guest house and tell them someone will pick them up at the bridge at dawn. I'll let their parents know there's a slight chance you'll be driving in. And Amy, thanks. Considering we need to get them out of the woods, this really is the best option, at least for now."

———

After Linda pulled into the meeting place and parked, she worried that it was too bright out, that someone in a passing vehicle might notice the glint off a window. The moon, nearly full, hung above the treetops. Nervously, she checked her phone for the time. She was 10 minutes early. She had an uneasy feeling in her gut.

Fifteen minutes after Angel and Danny should have been there, Linda got out of her truck. She leaned against the tailgate and listened. A twig snapped, and she heard leaves rustling alongside the grassy trail beyond the berm. She whispered, "Over here, you guys."

A flashlight beam shined in her face, almost blinding her. "Hey, cut it out! C'mon, let's get outta here before somebody comes along."

A large black dog ran up to Linda and sniffed at her feet. "What the…?"

A woman's voice she didn't recognize said, "What are you doing here?"

"WHAT? Who are you?"

"DNR Conservation Officer. I need to see your driver's license."

Linda, still blinded by the strong beam, could only make out a dark form outlined against the berm.

"Simba, heel!" said the woman.

"It's in my phone case." Linda pointed to the cab of her pickup. "Can I get it?"

"Go ahead."

The interior light cast a yellow glow out the truck door. When Linda turned around, she saw the CO was in uniform and decked out like any patrol cop, a heavy belt with several attachments, including a service pistol, plus a bulky bulletproof vest under her shirt. The dog was a black Lab, and sat next to its master, its long, pink tongue hanging out the side of its mouth, like a family pet.

Linda, shaking, held out the case, and the CO stepped into the arc of light. She appeared to be around 35 years old. Her brown hair was pulled back into a ponytail. She seemed too petite to be out in the middle of the night in a state forest busting poachers and partiers.

"I'm Pamela Reese." She shined the light on Linda's license. "What exactly are you doing way out here in the middle of the night?"

"Umm…umm…I love to hear the wolves howl. I was told this is a good place for that, right?"

"You got plenty of wolves over in the Smokies, a lot closer to home," Reese said. "Who were you looking for when I came walking up?"

"N…nobody." Linda instantly wished she had considered her answer more carefully.

"Let's take a look in your truck," Reese said, her voice steady and commanding. She warned, "Simba here might look like a big puppy dog, but I suggest you just stand still over here for a minute." Reese pointed to a spot 10 feet away at the edge of the arc of light.

The CO clicked the button on the radio speaker attached to her left epaulet. "I'm out on an 11–54 with one female. Gulch Road, quarter mile north of the Blueberry Lakes crossing, a grassy side trail going west."

A female voice crackled from the speaker, "Do you need backup?"

"Negative. I'll let you know when I'm clear."

"10–4."

Reese began her search, shining her light under the front seat on the driver's side. She slid the seat forward and peered into the half-cab behind it. Satisfied, she went around to the passenger door and did the same. She barely looked into the bag that was for Angel. Nothing in the glove box interested her either.

Reese walked back around to the driver's side. "Huh, this is a first."

"Huh?" said Linda, in a bewildered voice.

"First time I ever checked a kid in one of these party spots and come up empty-handed. Or haven't found a couple…you know…getting it on. But I still need to know who you were looking for."

Linda's mind whirred and she spoke without thinking. "I'm sorry, I lied about the wolves, although we do often hear them. We have an orienteering club. I'm just a driver and a runner. You wouldn't catch me dead in the woods after dark. Too creepy. I just dropped off my friends Nate and Dale back there on another road." She pointed to the west. "Must be taking them longer than they thought…"

"Sorry," Reese said. "I was parked, backed up into the ATV trail a little ways." She pointed to the north. "Let Simba out to pee. Was just gonna have coffee and a sandwich and saw your lights coming, thinking you'd be going past in a few seconds. And you pulled in here. Hope I didn't scare you too bad."

"Oh, that's okay." Linda laughed nervously. "Can I pet Simba? She won't bite me, will she?"

Reese laughed. "I'll tell you a little secret if you promise not to tell the bad guys."

Linda nodded, knelt down on one knee, and clapped her hands. Simba wiggled up to her and gave her a sloppy lick on the cheek.

"If somebody's trying to hide a duck in their hubcap or too many grouse behind the shed or a deer in the garage, Simba will find them for sure. But the closest she comes to being an attack dog is licking faces."

Reese's radio crackled. "Pam, somebody hit a bear cub at Inner Forest Road and Spur 1. It needs to be put down and they don't have a gun. Can you take it, or should I call County?"

"I'm clear here," Pam said into the microphone. "Be there in 15."

As the CO hurried down the trail toward the gravel road, Linda called out, "Thanks, Officer Reese!"

"You're welcome," Reese hollered over her shoulder. "Just call 911 if your friends don't show up. I'll be in the neighborhood until three o'clock. Stay safe."

When Angel and Danny still hadn't shown up at eleven, Linda called Carrie.

"They're not here! Things got screwed up, I think. A conservation officer saw me pull in here and she had a dog. She was nice enough, it turns out, and hadn't a clue what I'm really doing here because I'm apparently such a goddamn good liar that I didn't know I had in me—and I've never even said *goddamn* before—but I think the kids saw her and got spooked. Now what?"

"Thanks, Gram," Carrie said softly.

"What?"

"Nothing. Just wait until midnight, in case they were nearby and watching. I'm hoping, praying, they're just being careful, and they'll show up soon."

"Me, too," said Linda through her tears.

Carrie said, "Call me right away if they show up. If they don't, call when you leave. I better call and tell Amy what's going on."

"At least it's real pretty and quiet up here," Linda said. "There must be a million frogs—their chirping's almost deafening. Oh, a wolf just howled! Wow, and the frogs stopped, just like flipping a light switch."

"Wait a minute—the signal!"

"What signal?"

"The one we used when we drove into the hunting shack to let the kids know it was us. Try it! If they aren't too far away, they'll hear it. Then they'll know it's safe and come back."

"What is it?"

"Three short beeps a second apart. Wait 10 seconds, and repeat."

"Okay, I guess it's worth a shot."

"Yes! Then do it again in 10 minutes. And again. And again. Keep trying all night if you have to, please…"

———————

Angel sat with her back against a tree, cradling her knees. They were on a hilltop above an old railroad grade. Danny had one arm around her shoulder. He could hear her choke back a sniffle. That made him teary, too.

"Danny, I'm never going camping again. Or into the woods at night ever again. This is a nightmare. Now what?"

"Come on, sis. You gotta trust that something good will happen. And believe that this isn't a nightmare. We're making a memory—a helluva memory. I can hardly wait to tell your kids, my kids about this. They're gonna think we were nuts!"

"And they'll be right," Angel said, as she snuggled tighter against her brother.

Just then a wolf howled, and the frog chorus stopped instantly. It was hard to tell which direction the haunting howl came from, as it echoed off the hills and through the valleys.

"I'll take that as a sign," Danny whispered. "Something good is about to happen, you'll see." He hugged his sister tighter.

Soon a few frogs dared to chirp again, slowly picking up the pace.

"I'm waiting…" Angel teased as she turned her head to look into her brother's eyes, the flames from the little fire flickering off them.

Beep…beep…beep

Stunned, Danny sat up and tried to gauge where the sound was coming from.

Beep...beep...beep

It seemed to be coming from the east, where they were supposed to have met up with Linda, but got scared away by the game warden's truck. Both their mouths dropped open.

"The safe signal!" they blurted to each other.

Angel leapt to her feet and began stomping on the little fire. Then she poured the water from a bottle on it. "Good call, little brother! Clean panties, here I come!"

"Eww, TMI…"

Angel grabbed her pack, tossed it down the hill, and slid 20 feet down the bank after it to the old railroad bed. "Come on!"

"Thank you, Jesus!" Danny yelled into the moonlight, causing the frogs to go instantly quiet again. "And thank you, too, wolf. Aaaah-woooo!" He jumped off the ridge, his feet hitting the sandy bank halfway down, sliding on his butt the rest of the way.

After hanging up the bedside phone, Sally fell into Sam's arms and laid her head on his shoulder. "Thank God, Linda found them and they're safe—going to Amy's. Why couldn't we have had NORMAL kids?"

He laughed softly onto her shoulder. "They're probably saying, 'Why couldn't we have had normal parents?' "

She snuggled against him. He wiped a tear from her cheek with a gentle touch of his fingertip. She kissed his hand. "I want your arms around me…all night."

Carrie advised Amy and Dale, "We better take a quick look to make sure nobody's hanging out nearby. Better do it on foot, though."

"There's only one possible hiding spot on my place—the Pine Grove Trail down by the bridge," said Amy. "It's easy enough for someone to back in there and not be seen. It hooks up to my meadow trail, off the edge of the yard where your truck is parked. I'll walk it. Going toward town the other way, on the other side of the road up by the property line, the neighbors have an access road into their woods—another good spot to park and snoop from. We're probably just being paranoid."

"Yeah, Dale and I know the spot, but don't ask how. We got an hour. And it's a gorgeous night. We'll take the ditch up toward the property line."

"Meet you back here in 20 minutes."

For almost a year, Amy had been driving, walking, skiing, ATV-ing, or snowshoeing the two connecting trails on her land, often in the dark. The moon was approaching its zenith. It cast almost enough light to make out the bright green of the pines and grasses, and the pinkish blooms of the wild roses. She rounded a bend in the final block of the trail, where deer hunters used to camp in a swale surrounded by the huge red pines.

Moonlight glinted off a vehicle parked up the rise from the road, just inside the gate she never bothered to close.

She stopped dead in her tracks, heart thumping wildly. Instinctively, she stepped off the tire track into the thick, stunted spruce.

Lovers? Partiers? After the place had been neglected for 10 years, she'd found ample evidence of both—a pickup load's worth scattered around a makeshift rock fire ring—cans, bottles, broken lawn chairs, a rotting sleeping bag, even an empty beer keg. So she had stapled a Private Property sign to a plywood board and nailed it to the gate post. But apparently, a few folks believed it didn't apply to them.

Her first autumn there, some deer hunters who had been using the land without Don Hill's knowledge claimed that she should honor their deer camp tradition if she was any kind of sportswoman. Besides, one hunter claimed, after so many years of unfettered use, they could lay legal claim to the land.

"Go ahead and try that in court," Amy had threatened. "In the meantime, this land is in MY name and I pay the taxes on it, and the insurance. I'm calling the cops, and you're getting charged for trespassing." She had taken down license plate numbers as they took their time leaving, and never heard from them again. Amy was a real pit bull when it came to things like this.

Suspicious that this vehicle had nothing to do with deer hunting or partying, she called Carrie. She whispered, "Somebody's parked by the gate. I'm gonna circle through the woods to the road and sneak up the edge of the trail."

Carrie whispered back, "It's a good thing I remembered to put my phone on vibrate, or the person in the car we're sneaking up on would've heard it ring. We backtracked and cut up into the woods and are about 100 feet uphill behind it. Whoever it is, I can see the glow from a phone. Can see only one head, so it's safe to assume... What? Oh, Dale, gross! He can't keep his mind out of the gutter."

"Get out of sight and hang tight," Amy ordered.

"You be careful, too!" Carrie replied. "As long our suspect is talking on the phone and can't see out very good, I know we can sneak up and get the plate number. Your cop boyfriend might come in handy…"

"Shush! He's not my boyfriend. Be careful now."

Carrie whispered. "He's getting out. Bye."

Amy backtracked halfway around the pine grove trail, putting a couple hundred yards between herself and the vehicle. She dialed Shawn.

"Shawn, I'm so sorry to bother you."

"Huh? Oh…Amy? That's okay, I couldn't sleep anyway. What's up?"

"There are two vehicles parked in the woods either side of my driveway a couple of blocks. We have no idea who they are or how many. One vehicle's on my land on the trail near the bridge. I'm thinking it's gotta be more of Chandler or Kellogg snooping. The other's across the road toward town on the neighbor's property. Dale and Carrie are up there. I'm circling through the woods on foot, and I'm gonna come up to this one from the road."

"Oh god, be careful! No, wait…I can be there in 10 minutes."

"I'm afraid they might be gone by then," Amy lamented. "I'll be okay."

"I'm on the way anyway," Shawn said.

"One more thing, Shawn." Amy began to stammer. "Tonight was nice, running into Frank and Marla. Very nice…"

She returned to the business at hand. "Angel and Danny are on their way to my place right now. They should be here in 15 or 20 minutes."

"Don't worry. I'm not going to do anything about them tonight. Trust me?"

"Yup. Thanks. I'm just about out to the road, and I'll be heading back in along the trail. I better hang up. I'll call you when I find out who this is. Three minutes, maybe."

"I'm on my way…"

The driver of the SUV in front of Carrie and Dale pushed the door open a crack and the dome light went on. It was an older man with gray hair. The kids ducked behind a big oak tree.

Once out of the vehicle, he stood back and faced into it. "Well, come on," he said in a loud whisper, "do your business."

A large dog jumped out and trotted past him into the dark, behind the SUV.

"Oh, shit," Dale whispered.

The dog paused and stiffened, staring in their direction. It began a low, throaty growl. "What, girl?" the man said to his dog. "Who's back there?"

The kids stayed still and quiet. He ordered, "Get in the car." But the dog stood its ground. "Come on, GET IN." When the dog didn't obey, he hurried to it and grabbed it by the collar. The man peered in Dale and Carrie's direction as the dog barked angrily and tried to break free. Carrie was shaking. She dropped her phone and it clunked against an exposed tree root.

The man pulled his phone from his shirt pocket and dragged the dog back to the SUV. "Get the fuck in there!" He shoved the dog across to the passenger seat, then flopped into his seat. His phone to his ear, he slammed the door with his free hand. In an instant, he had the vehicle started and in gear, and was spinning the tires.

Dale and Carrie ran after him, but he was down onto the road and squealing his tires on the asphalt before they could get a good look. As they reached the road, he finally turned his lights on, but it was too far to see any details other than a broken left taillight.

Then tires screeched down the road in the direction of the pine grove where Amy had gone. Carrie punched at the phone screen.

"Come on, Amy...PICK UP!"

After six rings, it went to voicemail.

"DAMMIT!" She dialed again, with the same result. "Oh fuck! Come on, Dale. We've gotta get down there!"

Carrie took off down the moonlit road at a sprint. Dale, not exactly built for running, followed a couple of paces behind. He kept losing ground. At Amy's driveway, with Carrie out of sight in front of him, he bent forward, his hands on his knees, and gasped for air.

A car, driving faster than it should have been, suddenly came around the big bend in the road from the direction of Stone Creek. The driver, upon seeing Dale bent over, screeched to a stop right next to him.

"Dale! What's going on?" Shawn yelled through the window.

Dale attempted to catch his breath. "The car we were watching took off...toward Stone Creek. The one Amy was gonna check out must have taken off, too! We heard it squeal its tires. It went the other way. Amy's not answering her phone. Carrie ran down there." He pointed and wheezed another breath in. "The gate. On the left... just another block..."

Before Shawn could get his foot off the brake, they heard a scream through the darkness. "OH GOD! NO…"

Shawn sped away in the direction of Carrie's cries. Within seconds, his headlights shined up the trail. Carrie was kneeling down, her hands slid gently under Amy's bloodied head. Amy lay still, her head a foot from the heavy, railroad-tie gate post with the Private Property sign. Her right leg was bent grotesquely between the knee and hip. Carrie was sobbing uncontrollably.

"HELP! HELP! Whoever you are, goddamnit, help!"

Shawn bailed from the car and sprinted over. He felt for a pulse through the fresh blood running down from a three-inch gash on top of Amy's head.

"She's alive. Don't move her head, though." He scrambled to his feet and ran to the car, grabbing the radio microphone. "This is Shawn Elliot! I need first responders and an ambulance, maybe even a Life Flight. Five miles south of Stone Creek on County Road 27. They'll see my car. Severe head injury. Unconscious. Hit by a vehicle. A broken femur, and who knows what else. Hurry… PLEASE!"

When Dale arrived a minute later, puffing and red-faced, Shawn was kneeling across from Carrie. He had his fingers on Amy's throat again, checking for a pulse. He nodded quickly.

Carrie could see that the blood had drained from Dale's face. "Don't be a pussy, Dale! Get back to Amy's house! The kids'll be there any minute. Don't let them come down here!"

All Dale had left in him was a shuffling, clumsy jog. Halfway to the driveway a long block away, he bent forward and retched. He wiped his face and bent over again, resting with his hands on his knees. A squad car, lights flashing and siren blaring came around the big bend. The driver skidded to a stop past him. Dale limped to the car and waved his arm in the direction of Shawn's car.

"See the taillights?" Dale shouted.

The deputy roared away, and Dale turned back toward Amy's house. A stone's throw from the driveway, the first responders' rescue truck roared around the bend and past him. Another squad was crossing the bridge from the other direction. The entire countryside was suddenly flashing red, blue, and white. Voices crackled from the squad car speakers. "Ambulance four minutes out..."

He bent over, hands on his knees again. A pickup truck approached and slowed to a stop. Danny rolled down the window. "What the heck is going on?"

Still winded, Dale could barely get the words out. "A...Amy...hit by a car. Somebody parked on that trail down there. She went to check. Somebody else up here, too." He pointed up the road.

"That fuckin' Chandler!" Danny growled.

The passenger door flew open so hard it knocked Dale off his feet and onto his butt. "No!" he shouted. "Don't go down there! Carrie said..."

But Angel and Danny were already sprinting down the road.

"I better call Sam and Sally," Linda said to herself. She put her truck in gear and let it crunch down the gravel driveway. Dale stumbled along behind her.

———

Angel beat Danny to the scene. When she got there, Carrie was still cradling Amy's head, and tears were running down her cheeks. Two deputies and three first responders were all kneeling around Amy. Shawn stood behind Carrie, his face creased with anguish, and jaw clenched. He had a bloody smudge under one eye.

Angel stopped in her tracks. A young woman carrying a cervical collar knelt across from Carrie. "You're doing great, hon. Here, let me slip this on, okay? Lift very gently and pull back with just a tiny bit of pressure. You got it?"

Carrie nodded and bit her lip.

Danny ran up and stood by Shawn's car, his face a mixture of grief and fear. He and Shawn exchanged desperate glances.

A first responder knelt down. "Let me take her, please." He slid his hands underneath while Carrie pulled hers back slowly. They were covered in Amy's blood. She leaned back on her heels and took in a heavy, shuddering breath. A deputy handed her a white towel. Shawn and the cop helped Carrie to her feet and she stumbled a few steps back. Shawn put his hands on her shoulders to steady her. Angel ran to her and grabbed onto Carrie so tightly it took her breath away.

The ambulance arrived, and the attendants hopped out and rushed to Amy. One listened for heart sounds while the other tapped the back of her hand to find a vein for an IV. The first paramedic wrapped a blood pressure cuff around her arm. Angel let go of Carrie, stepped toward Amy alongside the paramedic searching for the vein, and knelt next to her. A first responder with a leg splint got down on the ground. The deputy lifted her broken leg gently into the splint and the paramedic strapped it securely. Amy still hadn't moved a muscle, nor had she made a sound.

A second ambulance arrived. A paramedic unbuttoned Amy's blouse and stuck the heart monitor electrodes to her skin. It was deathly quiet as she turned the monitor on. After just a few seconds, Angel piped up. "What is it?"

"Thready," the paramedic said. "She's shocky." She shouted to the driver from the second ambulance. "Make sure they have a neuro available…and a helicopter. I'm taking your partner with me."

"Ten–four." He reached in for the microphone.

A first responder had a backboard ready. Another had the gurney on the ground at the back of the ambulance. "Let's get her to town. Come on." Six of them gently tipped Amy onto her left side—the side with the leg that wasn't broken—and then back down onto the board. They strapped her on. On the count of three, they lifted her off the ground and began walking Amy toward the ambulance.

Angel grabbed a handhold on the backboard and helped them walk to the gurney. "I'm going with," she informed a paramedic. "I gotta help…"

"I'm sorry, but you can't ride along," said the woman sympathetically.

The first responders tripped the wheels of the gurney and slid it into the back of the ambulance. Angel became pale and unsteady. When the ambulance pulled away, lights twirling and siren blaring, she took a step back and her knees started to buckle. Danny caught her, and they both slumped to the ground.

"Let's just get her up to the house, Dave," Shawn said to the deputy, who had come from the direction of Stone Creek. "It's been a tough couple of days for her." They helped her into the squad car.

The other deputy, Sergeant Rich Roberts, asked, "You want me to do the report, Shawn?"

"No, thanks. Well yes, help with it would be great." Shawn seemed unable to focus, turning his attention quickly from the road to the trail to the spot where Amy had lain. He touched the palm of his hand to his forehead and looked down at the ground. "Yup, in your notes, please, the tire tracks—looks like the vehicle went south. Check for evidence up here—maybe car parts. Police tape it, please. Sorry. You've been doing this since I was in grade school getting in trouble."

Rich patted him on the shoulder. "Not to worry."

Shawn said, "I'll come back in the daylight and look around again. Then I'll put the final report together. Thanks, Rich."

He leaned back against the hood of his car, exhausted and covered in Amy's blood, and watched Rich search the area with his flashlight. Dave pulled up in the squad car, having dropped off the kids at the house.

"Got something here!" Rich shouted. "Dave, bring the numbers and your camera."

"What is it?" Dave asked.

"I know this woman. She's the kids' favorite teacher," Shawn said, and then took in another deep breath.

Dave asked quietly, "Are those the two kids…?"

"Yup."

"Shawn," Dave said, "I'm off at three, but I can be back here whenever you want. Rich, is that okay?"

"Ya. Go ahead. I'll get your shift covered for tomorrow night. But first, take a look at this…"

Rich shined his flashlight on three shards of clear plastic. The larger piece was about six inches long, an inch wide at one end and tapered to a sharp point at the other. The other two pieces were similarly shaped but about an inch shorter. All three chunks had a lip on the wide, flat end.

"Somebody's missing part of their headlight cover," Rich surmised. "This has to be the point of impact—or maybe a couple of feet farther along this trail."

Shawn turned and shined his light on the gate post five or six yards away. The thought of Amy flying through the air made him close his eyes and hang his head. "Dave, get some pictures."

After Dave was finished photographing the evidence, Rich picked up the shards. Like a puzzle, they fit together perfectly in the palm of his hand. He examined them more closely. "No numbers, dang it. One in a million to find out what kind of vehicle they came from—just about anything from the past 20, 25 years."

Shawn said, "Thanks, both of you. I appreciate the help."

Dave dropped the shards into the bag he was holding.

"How about seven, Dave, at my house?" Shawn asked.

Rich hollered to Dave, "Why don't you clock out right now? I got it here. I'll take pictures and tape it off out by the road and back up the trail a ways."

Shawn called Sally. "You'll want to come down to Amy's place. That's where they brought Angel and Danny. You can go ahead and take them home."

"We're already on our way—the kids called. How... how's Amy?" she asked.

"Not good, I'm afraid. Not good at all. I'll meet you at Amy's house."

"That was Jeremy, from the ambulance." All eyes were glued to Shawn, as the Ryan family, Carrie, Dale, and Linda sat awaiting news. "He said they lost her once on the way to Detroit Lakes, but were able to revive her. She's lost a lot of blood from her head wound, and some is pooling inside her thigh from the broken femur. They just did a CT scan and will need to drain the bleeding, which is causing pressure on her brain. I hate to say this, but they don't know if she'll make it to Fargo…"

Shawn stared up at the ceiling, tears forming at the corners of his eyes. He reached up with the side of his hand and wiped one away. "Sorry. I've been to a hundred of these. I never get like this."

Sally went to the sink to dampen a dishcloth. She dabbed at the dried blood under his eye. When she was finished, she leaned forward and put her arms around him.

"It's okay," she whispered. "Tell you what. Come to our place tonight."

"We just met. Not sure why this is hitting me so hard."

Angel stepped up beside him and held his hand in both of hers. "Please…you shouldn't be alone tonight. But first things first. We need to send Amy our love and ask the Universe to send her healing. Everybody, please form a circle around the table and join hands. You don't need to do anything but picture Amy in your mind. Put a smile on her face. It's your intention that counts. The Universe will do the rest."

They shuffled around the dining table to form a circle. If Shawn wasn't a believer, he was certainly a good actor.

Angel started. "First thing, I need to ask Amy's Guide and Protector whether she wants our help, because Amy can't tell us herself at the moment. Close your eyes, everyone. Whoever you are, is it the Universe's will—Amy's will—for us to intervene on our dear friend's behalf?"

"Whoa!" Sam and Angel shouted in unison, making everyone jump and drop hands. Again in unison, Angel and Sam spoke excitedly, "Mother Mary!"

Shawn's mouth hung open. "That thing about the pearly halos in religious paintings. It's true? Hers was blue, though."

"That's the color of healing," Angel said. "You saw her?"

"I saw something…"

"Let's get back to business," Angel advised. They joined hands again. "Wait—special request. Mother Mary wants to join the circle, between Mom and Shawn."

The group allowed an empty space between them.

"Just imagine she's holding your hands," Angel said.

Shawn rubbed his fingers together, then opened his hand. "Now what?"

"Imagine gentle, blue light, like the northern lights, streaming around Amy as a force field that's protecting her. Imagine us surrounding her, and all of our hands holding hers. That's what I'm seeing. And Mother Mary standing at the head of Amy's bed, her hands outstretched, her palms emanating a shimmering light. It flows around and into all of us. *We are all one*, Mother Mary says. *Trust in the Creator…*"

The circle was quiet for a minute as each participant did their best to feel and experience what Angel described.

"That's it. It's out of our hands now."

They dropped hands. Most took in a deep breath. When Shawn inhaled, his face screwed into a knot. "Not to change the subject, but I smell something rotten. We should find Amy's garbage and get it out of here." He glanced around the kitchen.

"Umm…" Danny said as he sniffed his armpit, "I think that's coming from me and Angel."

Angel shouted, "Dibs on the shower!"

"You won't get any argument from me! Eww." Danny pinched his nose and backed away.

Linda offered, "My truck already smells like a stock-yard from you guys. I'll drive ya home."

"Dale and Carrie," Sam said, "thanks so much. You guys go on home. We'll keep you posted if we hear anything about Amy, okay?"

"Thanks, Sam," Carrie said as she took Dale's hand and they headed for the door. "Any time of day or night."

"And tomorrow, we all need to get our heads together."

"Oh, I forgot," Shawn said, shaking his head, his eyes closed. "Her folks. I need to call them. I don't know the number."

Danny plucked the landline phone out of its charger. He had a hunch and punched a button and scrolled through a screen, checking outgoing calls. "Last evening at 10:02, a call to an Edward Wilson?"

"Yup, that's her dad's name," Shawn said. He took the phone with him as he headed for the door. "I'll take care of this from my car."

First he called Jeremy, who was on the Life Flight. Shawn could barely make out what he was saying through the roar of the helicopter engine and propellers.

"Shawn, you're not gonna believe this! A couple of minutes ago, Amy's vitals shot up back to almost normal, and she's breathing much better. Almost seemed like she was gonna regain consciousness. She mumbled something, sounded like 'Mary.' Now she seems to be fairly stable."

"I'm gonna call Amy's folks now. You going to Prairie to Pine Hospital as usual? What's your ETA?"

"Yup," Jer shouted. "Fifteen minutes."

Sam and Sally walked out to Shawn's car as he was ending the call. He gave them the good news, leaving out the part about her mumbling. "Tell that Angel of yours thanks."

"You tell her yourself. Coming?" Sam said. "She'll shrug you off, though. To Angel, what we did around the table tonight is just the way things should be done."

"I'd better call Amy's parents. I'll be along shortly."

After they drove away, Shawn sucked in a deep, slow breath. "Mother Mary, I need a hand, please." Instantly, a calm began to flow into him, like a glow building inside a streetlight that had just blinked awake. He took another deep breath and dialed.

"Hello," said the groggy voice of a woman.

"This is Shawn Elliot."

"Oh! Yes, Amy called tonight and mentioned you. I'm her mother, Vivian."

"Did she mention that I'm the investigator for the Becker County Sheriff's Department?"

"No, just that you had dinner. Why?" Vivian's voice turned questioning, afraid.

"I'm afraid Amy's been in an accident."

"ED! Come quick! Amy's been in an accident! OH NO!" she cried. "It's her new friend Shawn on the phone. He works for the sheriff's department!"

Shawn could hear Ed shout in the background, "Put the phone on speaker! Put it on speaker!"

Shawn explained the situation as calmly as he could. Vivian couldn't stop sobbing, "Oh no...my baby! NO!"

Ed tried to remain calm, but his mind was racing. "Where IS she? Has this got anything to do with those two kids who ran away?"

"Amy's on a Life Flight to Fargo. Doing as well as can be expected. My friend Jer is attending. He said to give you his number. They're taking her to Prairie to Pine Hospital."

"Amy told us about those horrible people stalking the kids. And getting fired. Do you think it was them?" He covered the receiver and shouted, "Vivian, go get dressed. Hurry!"

"Honestly, sir, I don't know what to think right now, but I will get to the bottom of this," Shawn vowed. "For now, my best advice is to drive carefully. Let me give you my number and Jeremy's. Ready?"

CHAPTER 15

A NICE, FIRM HANDSHAKE

Angel came out from the bathroom wearing a night-gown, her hair combed back and still wet. "It's all yours, Danny."

He got up from the kitchen table where Sam, Sally, and Shawn were sipping wine, trying to dull the edge from the night's events.

"Come here, Sweetie," Sally said, as she pushed her chair back from the table. Angel sat on her mother's lap and wrapped her arms tightly around her neck.

"Mom, will you sleep with me tonight? At least until I fall asleep?"

"Of course, Honey. Come on…"

Shawn's phone alarm rang. He sat up and glanced around the room to get his bearings, then saw his phone on the end table next to the Ryans' living room couch. The low light glowing behind the windows indicated it was either side of sunrise by a few minutes. 5:45. He called Amy's father.

"So far, so good," Ed assured him.

Sally rushed in, tying the belt of her robe. Sam followed behind, wearing a t-shirt and sweatpants.

"Ed, Sam and Sally are here—the kids' parents. I'm at their house. Can I put you on speaker?"

Shawn set his phone on the ottoman and the three of them leaned in.

"Good morning, folks. Amy's stable, her vitals are acceptable, and she's still unconscious. But the doctor said that with severe head injuries that's not unusual, and not to take that as a bad sign."

"Thank God…" Sam put an arm around Sally's waist. Shawn took in a deep breath.

"She's in getting a CT scan right now, from her head to her knees. They need to determine the extent of internal injuries, if any. They haven't gone into her broken leg yet. The bleeding seems to have subsided. X-rays show they need to put in a couple of plates, but that can wait for the moment. Too soon to tell if there's permanent brain damage. They're hoping they got the drain in soon enough. The first scan didn't show any blood or damage inside her brain, just buildup on the outside. Any news on who did this to her?"

Shawn said, "Not yet, sir. A sergeant did a preliminary assessment of the scene last night and collected some car parts. Dave, the other deputy who was at the scene, is meeting me at my house this morning. We're going back there to see what else we can find. Then we'll come to Fargo. I'm assuming Amy is in ICU?"

"Yes. I'll call you if there's any change. I'll see you later today."

"We should be there before 10."

Angel and Danny walked in, both rubbing their eyes.

"Hey, kids," Shawn said softly. "Amy's doing as well as can be expected. Still not conscious, but stable. Thanks, Angel…for last night."

"You're welcome. There's a lot more where that came from."

The kids turned and shuffled back toward their bedrooms.

Shawn checked the time on his phone again. "I better get going." He felt the whisker stubble on his face. "Need to clean up a little before I start my day, I guess."

Sally asked, "Got time for me to make some coffee to go? It'll only take a couple of minutes. Might as well scramble a couple of eggs. Do you like venison brats?" She waved him toward the kitchen without waiting for an answer.

"Thanks," Shawn said. "That would be great."

She noticed him staring at their special coffee mugs.

"Just a little thing Sam and I do. He and his second wife—she passed away—that's how they started their day. And we've been starting ours that way for over 13 years now."

"That's nice," Shawn said. "Sweeten my coffee with a morning kiss. Heard the song, but never imagined anyone doing anything like that." Shawn paused. "You know, I think I told you Amy and I went out last night. We met at The Smoky for supper and a couple of drinks."

"Yes, you mentioned it. How'd that go, if I may ask?" She cracked two eggs into a pan.

That question was like putting a quarter in Shawn.

"Turns out we arrived at the same time and almost ran over each other hurrying up the steps to the deck. Frank and Marla were sitting at the deck bar—you know, Frank Davis, the sheriff, and his wife? He asked us to join them.

"We got seated and our waitress came out—Missy. She said, 'Hi, Shawn and Amy!' Like we'd been there a hundred times together. I glanced over at Amy and caught her smiling. I know I saw her bite her lip. It seemed so natural, so easy—at least on the surface—but I could barely eat my burger, my gut was twisted into such a darn knot. Frank and Marla left first. We did the math and split our tab. I walked her to her truck and asked if she was gonna try to get her job back. And she said, absolutely, and I said that was great. I couldn't think of any more small talk—my mouth was all cotton. You're gonna laugh, but I didn't know what to do or say next! So I chose to make a complete fool out of myself. I stuck my hand out to shake hers! Can you fuckin' BELIEVE it? Sorry, I don't usually say fuckin'…"

Shawn's back was to Sally and he couldn't see she was grinning. She didn't want him to feel embarrassed.

He continued, "Last evening, I didn't say anything to Amy about maybe another date, and was kicking myself the second I walked away from that stupid handshake. I couldn't sleep for being such a dumbass, and then she called to let me know that she was gonna check out someone who was parked up beyond her gate. I said I'd be right there. And now this…"

His voice cracked a little. "Sally, you know, Amy reminds me a lot of you. You might not realize this, but folks are jealous of you two…more so of you, Sam."

Sally chuckled. Sam furrowed his brow.

"Oh, phooey," Shawn said. "That didn't come out right. Sorry, Jammer…"

Sam admitted, "Yes, I would have to agree I'm the more fortunate of us two."

Sally turned from the kitchen stove and gave him a thumbs-up.

Sam said, "Before I met Sally, I'd pretty much given up on sharing anything like what we have now. Lucky for me, she hadn't..."

"And lucky for both of us," Sally said as she pushed the toaster lever down, "there was a little Angel watching out for us who wouldn't take no for an answer."

Sam said, "One thing I wanted to ask you about last night, Shawn. When you had that vision—the blue halo. Have you been able to see things like that your whole life?"

"I was afraid you were gonna ask me that," Shawn said. "But that's okay. The answer is yes, but I pretty much shut it off a long time ago. Once in a while, I'd see a ghost somewhere, but would just ignore it. It never occurred to me that I might be able to conjure up help, like Angel does. By the way, I wonder if Amy knows she has a ghost in her house. An old guy, and he stinks...but not as bad as the kids did last night."

"Why did you shut it off?" Sam asked. "It's a gift."

"When I was real little, my mom just blew me off when I'd tell her about things I saw when I was sleeping. That really ticked me off, and I became a rebellious little pain in the butt, which pretty much stuck with me for a long time, as you know. We had a neighbor woman who was a genuine psychic. She knew about me, of course, and went to my mother and asked her to believe me. The next time I brought up something, it was a dream about my dad, who I never knew, and who I had never even seen a picture of. I described my dad to her to a T. I know that because when I was older, I did find a picture of him. She beat the living shit out of me. So I kept my mouth shut, and became mad at the world."

"So, Jammer, now what?" Shawn asked.

"I'd say just live your life, all of it, including your gift. Your moments will come to you without asking. Who's to argue with—or judge—what God or the Universe or whatever you want to call it gave you? No one."

Sally set a mountain of breakfast in front of them. She gave Shawn a little kiss on the top of his head. He smiled up at her, with his fork poised to dig in.

They hadn't heard Angel come from her bedroom. Danny was with her. He looked confused.

"You guys…" Angel sucked in a deep breath, looked to the ceiling, and squeezed her brother's hand with both of hers. "I need to tell you something."

"What is it, Honey," Sally asked softly.

"What happened to Amy—it's all my fault. It should never have come to this."

Angel squeezed her eyes shut and dropped Danny's hand. She covered her face and began to sob.

"Come on, Sis. It's not your fault," Danny said as he embraced her.

She pushed him away. Sam sat with his mouth half open, his eyes pleading.

Sally asked, "What? What are you talking about?"

"I didn't tell the truth…I was afraid to."

"The truth?" Sam asked. "You didn't lie about anything, did you…?"

"Danny doesn't even know. That day in front of the old post office—what was said. I swore Danny to secrecy—convinced him, Mom, that if you heard what

Dylan said—he said that you like it when the guys in the bar grab you by the...that you'd have more terrible nightmares."

"Oh, Angel..." Sally cried softly.

"That's not all. Dylan also said that I like it when I get grabbed like that."

"But you said to just ignore them," Danny said. "I never gave it a second thought."

"Had I cooperated with the trial," Angel said, "I couldn't have lied. I would've had to explain why Dylan would say that..."

Danny put his arms around his sister and she sobbed onto his shoulder. "What...?"

She turned back to the table. "A couple of days before that—the day we got mixed up about me getting home after softball practice and I began walking home—the boys, they got me...held me down...and..."

"Oh no!" Sally sobbed. "Come here, my baby..."

"Those fucking sonsabitches!" Sam yelled as he pounded the table with a fist.

Angel curled up onto her mother's lap, her arms around her neck and head against her mother's chest.

Sally asked through her tears, "Why didn't you tell us?"

Angel sniffled and drew her knees up tight. "I was afraid nobody would believe me. The boys said they'd tell everyone I let them do it—my word against theirs, four to one. That my 'trick' to get them in trouble would backfire. It was my and Cindy's secret. And then this happened to Amy...it's all my fault. I should have remembered to charge my phone. I shouldn't have been walking home alone..."

"Oh, Sweetie…" Sally patted her daughter's back and kissed the top of her head. "None of that is your fault—getting attacked, or what happened to Amy."

Shawn said just above a whisper, "Danny, Sam, please let me take care of this. For now, don't say anything to anyone about it. I'll wait until next week to get the paperwork going. Just want to concentrate on Amy's case for now."

Danny nodded and placed his hand on his sister's head. "I promise…" She put her hand on top of her brother's.

Sam had his hand over his mouth and breathed heavily. His eyes were squeezed shut. Sally knew it was déjà vu all over again for him.

———

Shawn ducked under the yellow police tape and walked up the trail to the point of impact. He glanced at the spot where Amy had lain. Flies were buzzing. Rich had left the number placards the night before in the left tire track.

"Dave, let's get some more pictures."

Dave pointed toward the gate post. "Want me to call fire to wash that down?"

"Please."

Dave called dispatch with his cell. "No hurry. If they can get here before we clear in around 15 minutes, that would work. Thanks."

After calling dispatch, Dave turned his attention back to the numbers. "I bet the hood's pushed in, too."

Where they had found Amy, Rich had spray-painted an approximation of her outline in orange. The pool of blood where her head had been was still shiny.

Dave held the tip of the tape measure at the farthest number and Shawn backpedaled to the gate post. He shook his head. "Seventeen feet, two inches. I think it's safe to assume she didn't stumble this far." He closed his eyes for a second.

"Waddya think?" Dave asked. "She was right about here when she was struck, where the left tire track is? Considering the injuries we already know about, she was hit by the vehicle's right front and thrown backward. I don't see any evidence to suggest the vehicle braked or even slowed. Why didn't she jump out of the way?"

"Maybe she didn't have time?" Shawn suggested. "Let's look up the trail for signs of rapid acceleration."

In another hundred feet, the clover had been buzzed away to the soil by spinning tires in two places—the left front and the right rear. "Something that's all-wheel drive," he concluded.

They measured the distance between where the front wheel had spun and the point of impact. "That's 109 feet—a pretty good head start," Shawn said. He surveyed the scene between them and the road. "If it was an accident, who would just leave Amy here like that? To be honest, I don't see any evidence the driver took evasive action—no skid marks, no brush crushed off to the side. This looks to me like assault and battery with a deadly weapon, maybe even attempted murder."

Shawn snapped his head up, forcing himself back into the present. "Amy's cell phone. We were talking just a few minutes before…this all happened. You remember if she had it in her pocket, or if the emergency crew grabbed it?"

"Nope, didn't see it," Dave said.

"I wonder if it's here someplace?" Shawn pulled his phone out. "I'll call it. But the battery's probably dead."

It rang six times until her voicemail message came on, but they heard no ringtone. "Remind me to check for it when we get to Prairie to Pine."

"Want to clean up here?" Shawn waved his hand at the markers. Dave nodded. "I need to make a phone call."

Shawn paused near the painted outline and whispered, "Don't you worry. We'll find out who did this."

"Judge Belden, hello, it's Shawn Elliot. Sorry to bother you so early."

"No problem, Shawn. What can I do for you?"

"You'll be seeing it on the news anyway. Somebody ran down Amy Wilson. Remember, she's the Ryan kids' teacher? She was almost killed. In the meantime, we got the Ryan kids home safe. I'll have Greg bring you a temporary order to consider, allowing Daniel to stay at home, and have him set up a hearing on Monday. I'll notify Holly. She's going to be very relieved."

"Whew..."

"One more thing, Judge. Angel Ryan is ready to testify. I'm sure you don't want me to expand beyond that, out of court."

"Thank God."

Shawn ducked back under the police tape, and headed up the trail for one last look around. Dave met him by the gate post with a handful of numbered markers, a stack of cones, and a camera on a strap around his neck. He pointed up the road. An open-top grass fire jeep was heading their way. Close behind was a small green hatchback that Shawn recognized.

"Wait a minute before taking the tape down," Shawn said. "I got a feeling someone's gonna take some pictures, and I might just help her…"

Dave looked over his shoulder. "Aw, man. Just what we need, Stewart making up shit again."

Judy Stewart, a reporter from the *Detroit Lakes Press*, was known among law enforcement and local government for her "creative" writing. She never missed a chance to sensationalize a story, take a comment out of context, or—and this seemed to be her specialty—make the cops and public officials look like the Three Stooges. She had a scanner in her car and often beat emergency responders to a scene, usually parking as close to the action as she could to get photos, even pictures of the cops arriving— without lifting a finger for the victims, of course. She was perpetually in the way, and for a diminutive, dark-haired 50-something-year-old who looked like a lunch lady, she had skin as thick as a rhino's.

Shawn called his boss, Frank. "You know about last night?"

"Yup, I was listening. Amy Wilson, right?"

"Uh huh. It could have been worse, but not much," Shawn said. "We're hopeful though… Anyway, guess who just ducked under the police tape and is stalking this way with a camera around her neck and a notepad in her cloven hoof? You want to handle it?"

The county sheriff sighed heavily. "No, just give her the nuts and bolts and let her make up the rest on her own."

"She might be able to help without knowing it," Shawn said. "Newspaper comes out tomorrow, and she'll have this online within an hour or two. You know, we have some car parts that were busted off where Amy was struck. Can I show them to Stewart, maybe even let her take a picture? Let the driver know we're on the trail?"

"I see what you're getting at," Frank said. "Go for it. Don't cut her any slack though."

"You got it, chief. I'll update you later. Bye."

"Good morning, Mr. Elliot," Stewart chirped as she strode up the trail. "Waddya got?"

"Hit-and-run?" Shawn pretended to be confused, hoping that would compel her to become more rabid than usual. "Wait a minute, Dave," he said, to keep his partner from walking away with the handfuls of crime scene investigative markers.

Stewart's hand was poised to begin writing on her notepad. "Victim got a name?"

Shawn filled her in as to Amy's name and age, who responded, and where they had taken her. Per protocol, he declined her request for Amy's condition. Stewart scribbled as fast as she could.

"You know, we've got a bag with broken car parts in my trunk from up there. We suspect they're from the vehicle that hit Ms. Wilson. I suppose you could photograph them..."

Not used to such cooperation, Stewart jerked her head back in surprise and suspicion. "Are you playing me?"

"Dave, bring those numbers and cones and put them back where they were best you can. I'll get the car parts." He turned to Stewart. "I assume you want some other pictures too?"

"I get it," Stewart hollered. "You want the paper to do your work for you."

"Call it a public service. Just think, you might win an award for helping bring a criminal to justice. Or at least get a raise."

She turned in her tracks a couple of times, looking around, then walked toward Dave, who was replacing the numbers where the shards were. Shawn, on his way back, was just ducking under the police tape. Stewart had reached the outline of Amy's body and was raising her camera.

"NOPE!" he shouted as he began to run toward her. "Not that…" He positioned himself between Stewart and the outline.

"Editor doesn't print my photos of victims anyway, not even outlines." She stepped to the side and raised her camera again. "Just for my own personal archive. What's the problem? This is so unethical," Stewart growled. "The cops choosing my shots…"

Shawn asked, "By the way, how come you didn't chase the ambulance here last night?"

"At the casino. When I got back to my car and heard the chatter, your dispatcher wouldn't give me an address."

"Oh, that's okay," Shawn said, faking sympathy. "The *Stone Creek Record* was here. Might want to check their website to see what you missed. But you'll be the first to get a shot of the headlight lens parts. I glued them back together this morning just for you."

"Hmmph!"

Shawn added, "One more thing, if you need a head-shot of Ms. Wilson, I suggest you check where she used to work—Stone Creek School."

"Used to work?" Stewart checked her notes.

"Yeah, I heard she got fired after just one year and a couple of days of teaching summer session."

Stewart's brow furrowed. "Is that so? Why'd she get fired?"

"You'd have to ask the school—maybe the principal, Esther Kellogg. Or Ms. Wilson's attorney, Joan Adair. Word on the street is that Ms. Wilson is going to fight it, though."

Stewart was again scribbling as fast as she could.

"Okay," Shawn said to Dave with a wink, "let the fire department in so Ms. Stewart can get her shots."

CHAPTER 16

FIGHTING LIKE A MOMMA BEAR

The two officers headed to the hospital to check on Amy.

On the way, Shawn dialed Ed Wilson. "How's Amy doing?"

"She's still not conscious. They say she's serious but stable. CT scan showed three broken ribs. Viv's got the sketch the doctor made for us—just a sec. Okay, three broken ribs, heavy bruising on her right chest, a bruised liver and lung, but nothing else internal wrong. That's good news, right?"

Shawn couldn't find any words.

"You still there?"

"Yup. Yup. Go ahead."

"Brain injury is still draining a little—no compression into the brain tissue. She's stable enough, so they just took her into surgery for her leg. It will be at least a couple hours. The doc assured me that once that's done, assuming there's no complications, Amy should just be on the mend. She'll be in a wheelchair for a month or so. We're all hopeful there isn't any permanent brain damage, but they won't know for sure until she regains consciousness. Just be patient, the doc said."

Shawn replied, "Considering what she's been through, this sounds about good as can be expected. Is there anything we can bring you later this morning?"

"No, that's okay. Amy's brother, Tony, is on his way up from the cities. He's got a list of things to bring that Viv gave him—enough for us to stay at least a couple of days."

His next call was to Sally. "Spread the word about Amy, please. What I need right now is Joan's number. I'm pretty sure she'll be getting a call or visit from a reporter at the *Detroit Lakes Press*. And I let it slip on purpose that I heard Amy got fired. So I'm pretty sure she headed right over to talk to Kellogg at the school.

"If Kellogg's dumb enough to tell this reporter why she fired Amy, or even admit that she did, this could work in our favor. You know, begin building a groundswell for Amy that she deserves, maybe even get people talking about who might have done this, keeping their eyes open for cars with front-end damage. Although reporters shouldn't be covering juvenile legal issues, trust me, this reporter will figure out an angle to bring this all out into the open—the kind of pain in the butt who might do us some good without even realizing it. Might even want to hint about Danny and Angel running away…and why."

Sally replied, "That's pretty solid thinking on just three hours of sleep."

"Thanks. This reporter's name is Judy Stewart. Please keep checking the *Detroit Lakes Press* website to see what she's posted. Also, the *Stone Creek Record* site. They made it out to the scene last night. The two papers feed off each other like bloodsuckers. They make it a competition to see who can scoop the other."

"Shall I tell them about Angel's healing circle at two o'clock? She and her friends are calling around. Will you be back for it?"

"Sorry, I don't think so. Probably won't get to see Amy until later this afternoon. Dave and I are gonna hit the car lots and body shops over there, see if we can get lucky and match up the headlight parts we found last night. It's a long shot at best."

Sally said, "Well, make sure you call us later, okay? And FYI, Angel's planning another circle for noon on Saturday."

"Oh! Almost forgot. Joan's cell number…"

"Thanks, Sally, I got it. Actually, would you mind calling her instead? Don't want to make it totally obvious that I'm pulling strings here."

"Of course. She'll understand."

"Before I go, how are the kids doing?"

"I can't thank you enough," Sally said as her voice began to crack. "Just peeked in their rooms—both sleeping like babies…my babies."

"How about Sam? How's he doing? I could tell that what happened to Angel hit him pretty hard."

"Well, right after you left this morning, without saying a word, he went out and began loading the canoe into the old truck. I poured him a thermos of coffee and made him a peanut butter and jelly sandwich. When I ran it out to him, he was at the truck door, facing away from me, wiping at his eyes. He turned to me and said, "Those were the longest two goddamn days of my life…' "

————————

Dave pulled up to the loading area in front of the hospital to drop Shawn off. Parking was at a premium around the large medical complex. "I'll go park over by that church," he said. The church was a block away, on the other side of a parking lot that held at least 300 vehicles. "When I walk back, I'll bring the headlight parts with. I think I'll poke around."

"Sounds good," Shawn said. "When you're done, come on up to ICU. It's on the second floor—you'll see the signs."

Shawn's heart started racing as he walked through the automatic doors. A knot in the pit of his gut bordered on claustrophobia. He stood off to the side in the busy foyer and took a deep breath, hoping that would quiet his racing heart. He hadn't felt this helpless before, even when his mother was dying the year before last. He touched his stomach with his fingertips. He thought, *Mother Mary?*

He stood in the doorway of the ICU waiting room. It smelled of coffee. There were about a dozen people— some conversing, some reading, a couple of them staring at the television on the wall. There were two middle-aged couples.

A man called, "Shawn, over here." How had they known it was him?

Ed and Vivian Wilson stood and hurried toward him. Ed was about Shawn's height—six feet plus. He had a full thatch of salt and pepper hair that was cut modestly short, parted and combed to the side. Shawn could tell that Ed worked hard and watched what he ate. His forehead was starkly pale starting halfway up to his hairline, though the rest of his face was bronze and lined deeply, evidence of outdoor work.

Ed stuck out a calloused hand. "Nice to meet you."

Vivian took Shawn's other hand with both of hers. He was struck by how blue and bright her eyes were, just like Amy's. Her posture, slim build, and energy defied her age. She had allowed her hair to turn gray naturally, with slight streaks of black mixed in. But it was handsome, Shawn thought—hair tucked behind her ears, long to her shoulder blades, straight and thick.

Ed pointed to a long bench against the wall near the elevator. "Can I get you anything—coffee, juice, water, a doughnut?"

Shawn realized his mouth was dry. "Water would be great. Thanks."

Viv was still holding Shawn's hand in hers and she led him to the bench.

"So how are you guys holding up?" he asked.

Her eyes were moist. "I'll be so glad when this surgery is over and she's conscious, and I can talk to her and know she's still our Amy."

A nurse in scrubs with a face mask on her forehead came through the double doors indicating Authorized Personnel Only. She looked around quickly and saw Vivian. Ed returned with a bottled water.

Viv stood and rushed toward her. "Janet…?"

"She's doing okay," Janet assured them with a smile. "It went more quickly than we anticipated. The tear in the femoral artery was minimal."

She turned and added, "And you must be Shawn Elliot. Ed and Vivian have given their permission for you to have family privileges in the ICU. That way you can be there anytime, if Amy has anything to offer for the investigation."

Ed said, forcing a smile, "That's wonderful news about her leg."

"They set the femur. Yes, a couple of plates and screws to hold everything in place. They were doing the closing when I left. When she gets back to her room, if you want, I'll pull the x-rays up on the computer to show you. Shawn, I'm sure you'll want a copy for the investigation."

Shawn hadn't thought of that detail. "Yes, thanks."

Janet continued, "The orthopedic surgeon says that once the bone is healed and she's had a couple of months of physical therapy, except for the scar, you'll never know it happened."

Viv grabbed one of the nurse's hands. "When can we see her?"

"She'll be in recovery a couple of hours. Then another CT scan of her head and an EEG, just as a precaution. Please don't worry—all standard procedure. We're going to keep her in ICU overnight. Why don't you all go have some breakfast or take a walk. There's a nice patio on the south side of the building. It's a beautiful day."

Ed looked around for a window and noticed one behind the receptionist's desk. "Why, yes. I hadn't noticed. I guess it is a beautiful day."

Janet said, "She's a strong young woman and fighting like a bear. We're all shaking our heads about how well she went through this surgery. Now you just try and ease your minds, okay?"

———————

Ed's phone rang. It was Tony. "Just walk toward the main building. You'll see us on the patio."

Tony was tall, maybe six feet five inches. He reminded Shawn of an uncle who had won the state high school long jump championship back in the 50s—slim, leggy, and boney. He looked to be about Shawn's age.

"Oh yeah, you and Amy had dinner last night," Tony said with a nod and an approving wink.

Dave had joined the group as well.

"What's that?" Tony asked, pointing to the plastic bag.

Shawn explained, "Headlight fixture parts from the vehicle that hit Amy. It's a long shot, but Dave's been out here looking for a match on the make and model."

Dave said, "We've got our work cut out for us."

Shawn said, "Since it'll be a while before we can see Amy, we're gonna check some dealerships and body shops in the area."

Tony said, "I hear there's a new Dakota Territory Sports store out by West Acres. You want to check out some vehicles over there while I shop for a new pheasant gun?"

"You bet!" said Dave, an avid sportsman himself.

Shawn smiled. "I'll do some checking around here on foot. Got the pictures on my phone. Dave, you go ahead."

Dave followed Tony, who was already several long strides ahead of him.

Shawn turned his attention back to Viv and Ed. "I'm sorry, but I shared the updates on Amy I received last night from the ambulance crew with Amy's friends. Very unprofessional of me. Also what you've told me so far today. I won't do that again without your permission."

"Don't worry about it," Viv said as she patted Shawn's hand. "Amy's told us how Stone Creek is like having another family. Anything you hear from us or anybody caring for Amy, yes, let the folks back home know how she's doing—as much or as little as you feel is appropriate. We're appointing you our official spokesperson. You okay with that?" She looked into his eyes for an answer. Shawn didn't dare try to speak. He only smiled, bit his lip, and nodded.

He pulled his phone from his shirt pocket. "Speaking of family, I've got some really good folks I'd like you to meet—Sam and Sally Ryan, parents of the two kids Amy told you about."

Shawn halfheartedly checked some headlights from vehicles parked in the lot and on the street, but he couldn't get Amy out of his mind. He wandered well out of the perimeter of the hospital's sprawling reach, through a comfortable-looking neighborhood of nicely kept older houses, all the way to a park along the Red River. He stood and watched the water flowing past. It reminded him of Sam canoeing that morning. He wished the river in front of him had some solace, some answers for him.

He checked the time on his phone. In his mind, he said to the river, *Exactly 26 and a half hours ago, I was content, living what I believed in and worked so hard for: the rest of my life, a comfortable and satisfying existence doing what I love. I never imagined another life, and I was not only satisfied with my simple path, but actually looking forward to it.*

"I know what you're thinking, Sonny," said an older woman, startling Shawn.

He turned in surprise to find the source. He hadn't noticed her sitting there when he'd walked past the bench.

She was thin and wrinkled, and wore a wide-brimmed straw hat. Wearing slacks and a baggy sweatshirt, she was dressed for comfort. She sat up straight and patted the bench seat next to her. There was something very wise and worldly about her that made him comfortable.

He asked, "How do you know what I'm thinking?"

"Experience. When you been around as long as I have, you can tell just by watching, feeling with your heart."

"How long have you been sitting here?" Shawn asked, leaning forward.

"You wouldn't believe me if I told you!" She laughed, tossing her head back. She lowered her voice. "I've found that the perfect people show up in our lives at the perfect times. Trust in the process, take your time. Or run to it like goddamn hell if you must! That's what I always did!" She threw her hands up and clapped them together.

Shawn's phone rang. It was Ed. "Excuse me, I need to take this." He stood and walked toward the river for some privacy. "Yes, Ed? She's asking for ME? I'll be there as soon as I can." He listened for a couple of seconds. "Not exactly sure where I am. By the river, in a park. I can see the top of the hospital though, five or six blocks away. See you soon."

He turned back to the bench. "Nice meeting you, umm…"

"Cassandra. I never did like that name. Did my level best to be anything but a goddamn Cassandra." She smiled and patted her chest over her joke. "Heh, heh, heh! Nice meeting you, too, Shawn."

He took off at a jog. Suddenly, it occurred to him that he had never told her his name. He skidded to a stop and looked back. There was no one on the bench. He scanned left and right among the huge cottonwoods and maples, then sprinted back to the bench and frantically looked up and down the asphalt path.

"CASSANDRA!" he yelled, then dashed to the river's edge.

Had she made it to the river and fallen in, in those few seconds after he'd left her?

Two women dressed in scrubs were power-walking up the lawn along the river. Shawn called to them, "Hey, did you see an old woman get up from that bench and leave?"

"Nope," one woman said. They kept moving and she continued over her shoulder, "Just you sitting there, and then running back and forth. Too much coffee?" They both laughed and kept moving.

Shaking his head, wondering if he was losing his sanity, he walked closer to the bench. Cassandra's old crinkled straw hat sat upon it, with a fresh red rose in the crease. He looked around again, picked up the flower and smelled deeply of it, then picked up the hat. A flutter traveled up and down his spine, tickling him from inside. Something wonderful, magical seemed to fill his being.

Sam was leaning against the school courtyard wall next to Sally when his phone buzzed. "Shawn!" he whispered. "Give me a sec. Hang on…" He and Sally scurried out of the courtyard and around the corner from the foyer.

Sam answered, "Hey, Shawn! Any news?"

"Oh, right. You're at the healing circle. How's it going?"

"Man, there's gotta be a hundred kids here, and about half that many parents watching quietly. Angel gave everyone instructions, sort of like she did last night. She told us she was gonna use the term *God* so as not to offend anyone. She's leaving out the Mother Mary part, but she's pretty sure she'll be here. So that's what's going on here. You sound out of breath. How's Amy?"

"Let's just say I was out for a walk, and Ed called about five minutes ago. She just regained consciousness and was asking to see me. Heading over there now."

"That's wonderful," said Sam.

"One more thing," said Shawn. "Do you know a Cassandra, an older woman?"

"Hmm, now why does that sound familiar? Oh! Cindy and Carrie's great-grandmother. She died a couple of days ago. A real pistol, I've heard. Why?"

"Well, I found her hat…"

Sam said, "Heh, heh. I can hardly wait to hear the story. For now, I better slip into the courtyard and give Angel the good news."

Angel watched as her dad approached, then dropped Cindy's and Danny's hands, and stood up. He motioned her over so he could whisper in her ear. It was as quiet as the dark side of the moon, and all eyes were on the father and daughter.

Angel's face lit up like the Fourth of July. She punched her fists to the sky and hollered to the heavens, "Amy's conscious and talking! Thank you, God!"

The crowd cheered and the children all rushed to surround Angel, like she had pitched a no-hitter to win the World Series. The parents closed in behind the children and joined hands with each other. Joy was everywhere, like the stars in the night sky.

Angel shouted, "Great work, everybody! She's not out of the woods yet, so I'll see you here tomorrow at noon, rain or shine!"

While everyone filed out through the foyer, the school custodian approached Sam, leaning forward on his broom. "Good thing Kellogg ain't here…"

"Oh? Why? Where is she today?"

"Don't know. Secretary said she called in sick. And then that reporter from the *DL Press* came by to get a photo of Ms. Wilson. I was in the office, cleaning. Secretary couldn't get a hold of Kellogg for permission, so she emailed the picture to the reporter's phone. Kellogg's gonna hit the roof about that…and this." He nodded toward the exiting crowd.

"Go ahead and show her the rose," the nurse said. "But then we'll need to keep it out here until she moves to her room tomorrow."

Shawn paused in the doorway. Amy's eyes were closed. Her parents sat on either side of her—Ed leaning back in a chair with his eyes closed, and Viv leaning forward, holding her daughter's hand. The lights were low. Amy's right leg had a heavy cast on it and was supported an inch off the bed by a sling. A bandage circled her face, holding a gauze over the gash on her head. Small tubes delivered oxygen into her nostrils. Her face was otherwise just as beautiful as Shawn remembered.

Viv noticed Shawn standing there and smiled. She leaned close to Amy and whispered, "Shawn's here." Ed snorted awake from his brief nap. Amy's eyes fluttered but didn't open.

Viv motioned for Shawn to come closer. "They took the drain out." She pointed to the top of Amy's head. "Seventeen stitches. Whew..." She looked over at Ed and nodded her head toward the door.

Shawn missed that signal between the Wilsons, he was so fixed on Amy's face. Viv carefully stepped around him. She met Ed at the door and smiled at him through a tear in each eye.

Shawn was frozen in his tracks, his mind blank but his heart racing. "Please, Mother Mary..." He reached over and gently picked up Amy's hand. Her eyes fluttered again, then opened to slits. Her mouth and eyes formed a tiny smile. Still holding her hand, he shuffled closer. Without thinking, he leaned down and kissed her gently on the forehead.

Amy mumbled, "I'm so sorry. Should have waited..."

He straightened up. "No, it's okay. It's okay. Everything will be fine." Smiling, he showed her the vase with the rose in it. She squeezed his hand. The nurse came into the room and he handed her the vase. He sat in Viv's chair, sliding it closer to the bed. He held Amy's hand with both of his. She looked so helpless. He hung his head and bit back his tears. He looked at her face again. She looked like a sleeping baby, so at peace and content.

When he had composed himself, he slid the chair back carefully and stood next to her. He leaned down and kissed her on the forehead again. He could feel her gentle breath against his cheek. "Just rest now," he whispered. "I'll be back in a little while."

He found Ed and Viv in the waiting room. "I need to ask you something. Did they give you Amy's personal belongings?"

Viv replied, "Yes, there's a bag of her clothes in a closet behind the receptionist station. I just glanced into it. Which reminds me, I need to take those things back to my cousin's where we're staying and get them cleaned up."

"Was her cell phone in there?" Shawn asked.

"Not sure," Viv said. "Why?"

"Just a hunch," Shawn said. "It's possible that Amy might have taken a picture of the vehicle that hit her. We didn't find her phone at the scene."

Ed suggested, "Well, let's go take a look."

The receptionist led them into a small conference room. Slowly, one article at a time, Shawn began carefully emptying the bag: all the earrings in a plastic baggie; Amy's blouse, with bloodstains on the back; her bra, which the ambulance crew had to cut off of her; blue jeans with an empty phone caddy clipped to her belt; panties; socks; and finally, on the bottom, her tennis shoes. Shawn shook his head. "Darn it! We must have missed it at the scene somehow."

"How about the hospital in Detroit Lakes?" Ed asked.

"I'll check," said Shawn, "but they're usually very good about keeping a victim's things intact. She could have lost it in the woods, I suppose. I'll stop by and visit again on my way out of town, if that's okay."

Viv engulfed Shawn's hand with both of hers. "Yes, please do."

Shawn and Dave met at a Ford dealership near West Acres and got permission to peruse the used car lot. After an hour of getting nowhere, Dave suggested they check with the dealership's body shop. The manager informed them he had no clue what kind of vehicle the shards were from. "I've helped out law enforcement before, but I'm afraid there's just not enough to go by here. I couldn't even tell you if this is from a Ford. Sorry, fellas."

"Shit," said Dave as they walked back to Shawn's car. "Now what?"

"The cell phone," Shawn said. "We have to find it."

———————

Amy was more lucid when Shawn came to see her the second time. Ed and Viv excused themselves again to give the two of them some privacy.

He leaned down and whispered, "Hey, it's Shawn." She reached for his hand, which he willingly gave her. "Amy, your cell phone is missing."

Her eyes suddenly inched open a touch more, and she squeezed Shawn's hand harder. "Find it," she whispered as she squeezed even harder. "Yes, find it…"

Shawn asked anxiously, "Is there a picture on it of the vehicle that…?"

Amy nodded and then closed her eyes. "I…I… think so."

He could see she was smiling again. "Come here…" she whispered. Shawn put his face close to hers. "You gotta nice firm handshake…"

He kissed her on the forehead. "Hmm…good kisser, too," she teased, sounding a bit intoxicated from the pain meds.

"We'll find the phone, Amy. Get some rest. And hang onto your hat tomorrow at noon. Angel's having another healing circle for you at the school then. She had one today at two. Sam said at least 150 people showed up—and not just kids."

She bit her lower lip. "One more kiss? A few inches farther south? I don't bite…very hard."

Shawn could tell that the pain meds were really taking over. Still, doubting she would remember a thing about the last minute, he cradled her face with his fingertips, and began slowly closing the inches between them, unsure how much of a kiss to share. He held her gently, like she could shatter into a million pieces. When their lips finally met, Shawn closed his eyes and said to himself, "Dear God, don't ever let me forget this moment."

He felt a light touch on his shoulder and whispered to Amy, "Better get back to work. I'll come see you tomorrow, okay?" He straightened up and turned to see who had come up behind him, but they were the only two in the room.

———

Shawn called Frank to update him on their progress, or lack thereof. "Glad you're still over there! Just got off the phone. Fargo TV wants to do a story about Amy. They saw it on the *DL Press* website. They're hoping to get it on the six o'clock news. Can you head over there now?"

"I'm on it," Shawn replied. "And then Dave and I will be hurrying back. Amy's cell phone is missing. It's gotta be at the scene. She said she thinks she may have gotten a picture of the vehicle just before…"

"Let me know if you need extra help," Frank offered. "This would be a perfect exercise for your Explorers."

"Great idea!"

"Frank, one more thing. The school principal, Esther Kellogg, didn't show up for work today."

"I know where you're going with this, Shawn, but be very careful," advised Frank. "You can't go fishing unless you have some bait first. Find that cell phone, and in the meantime, let's hope for a break."

"I got a call from Greg Pearson, too," Shawn said, "wondering how Amy is doing, and if we're getting anywhere with the investigation. I asked him how it went with Chandler after Judge Belden's new order, which removed the CP from the case for now. Greg was there when she went into the judge's chambers to get the order. She claimed she's actually relieved to be off the case, considering the 'total lack of cooperation' from law enforcement. And then said she was gonna go back upstairs to hand in her resignation and clean out her desk."

"Hmm," Frank said. "For starters, go do that interview, and then find that cell phone."

Tony Todd, a veteran reporter and anchor, met Shawn outside the studio. Cameras and lights were being set up next to the brick building facing several large cedar shrubs, sculpted into globes three feet across and shoulder-high. Todd, in his fifties, had dyed-brown wavy hair, sculpted as perfectly as the shrubs. His artificially tanned face made some people wonder if maybe orange really was the new brown.

"This is my first interview," Shawn confessed, shifting uncomfortably, unsure what to do with his hands.

"Piece of cake," Todd said, his exceptionally white teeth gleaming in the sun. "I ask the questions, you answer them. If I ask something you're not at liberty to discuss, just say so. Sometimes saying that has as much impact as answering the question." He winked at Shawn. We'll want a close-up of the auto parts. You brought those, right?"

"I did. I'm nervous," Shawn admitted. "What if I can't hold them still enough?"

"Then we'll do a still shot. But you'll be okay. Act like it's just you and me in a bar having a drink and talking about fishing. Ignore all this the best you can." Todd waved at the equipment.

"I'm also going to ask you about the allegations on the *Detroit Lakes Press* website, of course."

"What allegations? I haven't seen their story yet."

"You haven't? I don't want to surprise you with anything. It's not that kind of interview. Let's go inside and I'll show you."

Shawn motioned to Dave and they followed Todd inside.

Sure enough, Stewart had taken the bait. She'd said that "reliable sources wishing to remain anonymous" had informed her of Amy being fired from her teaching position just two days before, for allegedly aiding and abetting a juvenile runaway and his accomplice sister. Stewart further wrote "many parents suspect the juvenile boy was set up to commit the two assaults, precipitated by other students harassing the boy's sister for conducting her religious gatherings before school." She had also written that the Stone Creek principal, Esther Kellogg, was unavailable for comment.

"Frank," Shawn said into his phone, "have you seen the *DL Press* website story?"

"Finally!" Frank exclaimed. "We got her telling the truth! Quite frankly, I'm surprised her editor let her run with it that way."

"Here, let me put you on speaker. The anchor, Tony Todd, will be doing the interview. We might as well decide ahead of time what I can say."

"Hey, Frank," Todd said.

"Been a while. Anyway, if you want to ask Shawn questions about the *DL Press* article, he'll be answering by simply saying, 'The Becker County Sheriff's Department has no comment at this time.' Will that work for you?"

"Sure will, but you owe me one," Todd teased. "We're not usually into making someone else's news coverage our story. You still have my number, right, in case something else comes up we can post and air first?"

"Do my best. Thanks, Tony."

"Dammit," Shawn swore under his breath after an hour of inch-by-inch searching for Amy's cell phone with Dave. He went back again to the point of impact and closed his eyes, trying to imagine in which direction the phone could have been propelled.

Dave joined Shawn. "It's gotta be someplace from this point on toward the road."

"We'll get the Explorers out here anyway," said Shawn. "With an impact this violent, it could have caromed. It might even be wedged up in a tree"

Dave looked at his phone for the time. "You'll be on in 15 minutes. Let's go to The Smoky and watch. Don't know about you, but a tall Beam and water sounds awfully good right now...chased down with another one."

The officers took a tall table in the back of The Smoky near one of the large flat-screen TVs. About half of the 80 people or so in the dining area were out-of-towners—summer folks or people from surrounding towns like Park Rapids, Detroit Lakes, or Perham. Like the locals, most of them knew that the best burgers and BBQ were this side of Fargo.

"I'm so sorry, Shawn," said their waitress Missy. "News travels pretty fast in a small town."

"Thanks. Guess I'm gonna be on TV."

"Which channel?"

"Fargo."

She nodded at Dave. "I know what your poison is. How about you, Shawn?"

"Just a bottle of Premium. Thanks."

Missy returned with their drinks. She pointed the remote and switched to the Fargo news.

A couple of patrons protested when Missy changed the other TVs from baseball games and fishing shows. She whispered, "A local schoolteacher everybody loves was run down by a car and almost killed. They're looking for whoever did it. Maybe you can help?"

Tony Todd began the broadcast.

"Tragedy struck today when a schoolteacher, Amy Wilson, age 23, was the victim of a hit-and-run and nearly killed early this morning near Stone Creek, which is in eastern Becker County. She is in serious but stable condition at Prairie to Pines Medical Center, where she was airlifted from Detroit Lakes."

A photograph of a smiling Amy in a canoe appeared in the upper left of the screen.

"I spoke with Sheriff's Investigator Shawn Elliot earlier today for an update on the situation."

Video of the taped interview played.

Shawn explained, "We've got parts from the right front of the vehicle that hit Ms. Wilson, from a clear, plastic headlight cover. It's not much to go on, but if anyone knows of a vehicle with recent damage to the right front, we're asking them to call the Becker County sheriff's dispatch center." There was a close-up still photo of Shawn's hands holding the parts in the right half of the screen while he made that statement.

Todd continued from the outside shot. "Sources have stated that Amy Wilson was fired from her teaching position at Stone Creek High School just two days ago, for alleged collusion in helping hide a runaway boy who had been sentenced to juvenile detention. Are you investigating a possible connection between the accident and Ms. Wilson's situation at the school?"

"There are a lot of rumors, but the sheriff's department has no comment on them at this time. However, we will certainly follow up on every lead we're given. I can tell you our focus right now is on finding the vehicle that hit Ms. Wilson. Any help from the public would be greatly appreciated."

The screen switched back to Todd at the anchor desk. The Becker County sheriff's dispatch center phone number was across the bottom of the screen, and picture of the headlight parts was on the right half.

Todd concluded the story. "According to Investigator Elliot, possible charges could be as serious as assault with a deadly weapon and/or attempted murder, plus several lesser charges, including leaving the scene of an accident, failure to render aid, and trespassing."

Shawn felt a tap on his shoulder. He turned slowly. It was Angel, grinning with eyes bright and arms wide. Behind her were her folks and Danny. She stood on her tippy-toes and just about squeezed the life of out Shawn, her head buried in his chest. "She's gonna be fine. I know it…"

"Mind if we join you?" Sam asked.

Most of the locals in The Smoky either knew Shawn or knew of him, and of course they knew the Ryans. A few at a time, they approached the table.

"Nice job, Shawn!"

"Anything we can do, Sally and Sam?"

"I'll keep my eyes open…"

"Noon tomorrow in the school courtyard, right? We'll be there."

One of The Smoky's owners, Big Dan, came over to the table. "Folks, I'm comping all of your dinner and drinks tonight. Pardon my French, ladies, but Shawn… just find that fucker."

CHAPTER 17

PASTORS FROM THREE CHURCHES

The nine Explorers met Shawn and Frank at Stone Creek City Hall at 9 a.m. They were all wearing their blue uniform shirts, jeans, and matching baseball hats. The 6 boys and 3 girls ranged in age from 15 to 18. Four kids piled into Frank's car and three into Shawn's. One of the parents took the other two. They convoyed south out of town to where she was run down, and assembled at the trail near the edge of the county road.

The kids stood in a neat row facing Shawn, all eyes glued on him.

"So here's the plan." Shawn turned and pointed. "That gate post there is where Amy was found. I know this is gonna be hard, because you all know her. It's even hard for me, and I barely know her. But this is why we train so hard—to set our feelings aside and perform our jobs. Sheriff Davis and I are so proud of you Explorers. The whole community is. You ready?"

"YES, SIR," shouted a proud chorus. Everyone straightened up.

"Here's what we have. We think the point of impact was about 17 feet farther up the trail from that gate post with the sign on it. That's where we found the headlight parts. Deputy Dave and I searched every blade of grass, under every shrub, and around every tree, under the assumption that Amy's phone was knocked out of her hand and went flying. Obviously, we didn't find it. So we need to expand our search. As you can see, the woods are very brushy, and there are quite a few trees blown down. At times, you'll have to get down on your hands and knees. Out here near the trail, watch out for poison ivy.

"Seth, you're in charge of setting up a perimeter. How far from the point of impact do you think you should begin the search?"

Seth was their student captain. He was a three-sport athlete at Stone Creek, but had always played a supporting role: a guard in football, the sixth man on the basketball team, the second starting pitcher in baseball. Average height and average weight, brown hair buzzed in a military cut, he didn't stand out physically, nor did he attempt to draw attention to himself. But he gobbled up the duties of being an Explorer like a dog that hadn't eaten in a week. He had led the Stone Creek Explorers to five firsts and seven other top fives at the state convention and competition that spring. And he'd earned a scholarship to attend law enforcement school that fall.

Seth stepped forward, turned, and addressed the group. "At home earlier today, I took my old cell phone and threw it as far as I could."

Neither Shawn nor Frank had suggested such an experiment, but they exchanged raised eyebrows and nodded.

"Assuming Amy's phone is a similar weight to my old one, it could have gone as far as 175 feet. Not that I think the impact could have propelled it that distance, but there's also a possibility that the perpetrator could have thrown it. Make the perimeter 70 long paces, but not overly long steps. That should be pretty close to 200 feet."

Shawn leaned in toward Frank and whispered, "I like how he thinks."

"What do you think, sir?" Seth asked Shawn. "Shall we mark off a square area of 200 feet in each direction of the four points of the compass?"

"I like it!" Shawn unlocked the trunk of his car, and the Explorers hustled into action. His phone rang. He saw it was Ed Wilson.

Ed said, "Hey Shawn, somebody wants to talk to you!"

Shawn heard some rustling as Ed handed the phone to Amy.

"Shawn?"

"Yup. How ya doing?"

"Had a pretty good night. I'm in my own room now. Now that the drugs are wearing off, my ribs are sore as heck, but I'll make it. Hey, did you bring me that rose?"

Shawn wondered how lucid Amy had been during their two visits. "Yes, the rose is from me. Sort of."

Amy covered the phone. "Umm, could I have a minute? I need to talk to Shawn about something."

Amy asked tentatively in a whisper, "So I'm not sure if I was dreaming or... Did you and I...um...kiss?"

"That part you remember, huh? Whew, I was hoping I left some sort of impression."

"A very good impression. I'm glad I didn't just imagine it. I saw you on the news. Between you and that reporter, I'm sure you got a lot of folks talking."

"We've received a few calls about Kellogg and folks wanting to lend their support to you and Angel and Danny. Nothing yet on the headlight parts. We're out at your place right now—Frank and the Explorers and I are gonna search the woods for your phone. Do you really think you might have gotten a photo of the vehicle?"

"I was trying to, but the next thing I remember is being here. I don't recall anything else."

"Can I come see you this afternoon?"

"Oh, you don't have to drive all the way over here again today..."

"I know I don't have to," said Shawn. "But I want to."

"You do?"

Amy noticed her heart monitor was picking up its pace.

"I do. I'll head over right after the healing circle at noon. Like I said yesterday, hang onto your hat around that time."

"You make sure you say hello and thanks so much to Angel and the rest from me."

Suddenly, a woman appeared at the edge of the county road. "Hey," she shouted, "Heard about Amy. That's just awful."

"Hang on, Amy—I'm guessing one of your neighbors is out for a walk."

"That's probably Ginny. Is she wearing a blaze-orange highway department vest? She walks to the bridge and back home every morning. Sometimes all the way to my house for coffee before she heads back, or if she needs to duck in out of the weather. Or if she's seen the sow bear and her four cubs. Then I give her a ride home."

Ginny, recently retired from her registered nurse job in Detroit Lakes, had been substituting her previous several miles a day on the hospital floor for four miles of "roadwork," she joked to her friends.

"Hang on, Amy." Shawn walked over to introduce himself.

"Whatcha looking for?" Ginny asked.

"Amy's cell phone is missing. Ginny reached into her vest and pulled out a beat-up cell phone. The screen was shattered and the back was crushed and scratched deeply by pebbles and asphalt.

"Could this be it?"

"Where'd you find it?" Shawn asked.

"Back there on the curve, other side of the bridge a block or so," Ginny replied with a shrug, pointing over her shoulder with her thumb. "It was off the gravel shoulder, just into the grass."

"Amy, what color's your phone?"

"Minnesota Vikings purple and yellow, the mascot on the back."

"Bingo," Shawn whispered. "I think Ginny found your phone."

Frank walked over and Shawn handed him the phone. "I think it's Amy's," he said. "This lady found it down the road…Ginny, Amy's neighbor."

Frank peered down the road. "Must have landed on the perp's car hood. Let's get it to the FBI in Fargo right away," said Frank. "Sometimes they can retrieve data or pictures. I don't know about this one, though…" Frank tightened his mouth and shook his head. "Go ahead, get going." He handed the phone back to Shawn.

The Explorers had divided into four teams, and had already stepped off 200 feet in each direction. Several of them had their phones out, using their compass and GPS apps. Orange surveyor's tape was being hung to mark off the search area already.

"I better tell them the search is off," Shawn said.

"Nope," said Frank. "I'll have them do an arm's length search of just one quadrant—good practice."

He turned to Ginny. "Think you can remember the exact spot you found the phone?"

"No problem. Right where I climbed a tree the other day when the sow and cubs suddenly came out to the road and stared me down."

"But bears can climb trees," Shawn remarked.

"Now ya tell me!" Ginny replied. "Tell Amy to get well soon and put the coffee on."

Frank whistled the kids in. "Amy's neighbor, Ginny, found her phone down the road. In the meantime, let's leave the ribbons up in case this isn't it. Instead, let's go process the scene where the phone was found."

"Amy, I'm on my way to Fargo," Shawn said.

"Oh. I guess you won't have time to come up here then..."

"Oh, it could be a day or two or three before they find anything in your phone...or determine they can't. I'll just be dropping it off. Yup, I'll be up."

"Should I brush my teeth before you get here this time?" Amy said, slurring her words a little.

"Are you on painkillers?" Shawn asked.

"Took a hit of Demerol just before you called. But... well...I refuse to answer that question. Call my attorney!"

"No, forget my attorney. I jus' want you present..."

He could hear the phone being fumbled. "Amy... Amy?"

"Hi, Shawn. Viv here. Looks like our little girl has gone to La La Land."

———————

An hour before the healing circle was to begin, the Palmers and Skogquists convened with the Ryans and Joan in the winery tasting room.

"Strange, huh," said Nathan. "The morning after Amy's run down, Kellogg misses work and Chandler resigns."

Ally asked, "Angel, did you say Kellogg's address is down in Perham?"

Angel nodded. "Ya. I wrote it down someplace."

Ally said, "We've got Gram's visitation at the funeral home down there Sunday evening. We can drive past Kellogg's house when we're down there, see if anything looks fishy."

Carrie offered, "Dale and I will be driving over together. We can do that. Probably better us than you grown-ups, right?"

Angel slid off her barstool. "I'll go get the address." She ran out the door to fetch it from her room.

"Any more news on the four boys?" Joan asked.

Cindy said, "Carrie dropped me off in town again yesterday afternoon. Nobody had seen them."

"So much is adding up," Joan said. "Not that this is a surprise to us—they have to be the ones who were watching Amy's place that night. Or somebody connected to them. Boy, would a smoking gun be nice so Shawn can start digging," Joan lamented. "I hope it's on Amy's cell phone and they can retrieve it."

Sam added, "Shawn said it may take a couple of days."

"Still, it wouldn't hurt to drive past Kellogg's today, too," Joan said. "Too many strange things going on. It wouldn't surprise me one bit if they clear out for a while, make themselves hard to find."

"This really blew up in their faces," Sam said. "Chandler seeking revenge on us by setting Danny up—then staking somebody out to call it in if they spotted him. Kellogg is obviously helping her. Little did they know that Judge Belden isn't gonna make Danny go to juvie. They dug their own graves with that." He shook his head.

Angel returned and handed a scrap of paper to Carrie, the corner off a sheet from a yellow notepad. "I wrote it down here again, just to be safe."

"Thanks. Dale and I will head down there right after the healing circle," Carrie said as she stuffed the paper in her shirt pocket.

———

Word about the Saturday healing circle had reached far and wide. The pastors from three of the churches in Stone Creek—ELCA Lutheran, Catholic, and Church of Christ—stood together by the foyer entrance, two older men and a young woman, who looked to be around 30 years old. Sam recognized them from an article in the *Record* that detailed their joint efforts to serve the community as one, providing funeral service meals, collaborating on fundraisers, and coordinating youth outreach programs. At first sight, Sam was concerned, but they were all smiling.

"Angel, I'm Pastor Mary Jo. Can we join in?"

Angel was practically speechless. She bowed her head and mumbled, "Amy would be honored."

Sam was grateful that Angel had again agreed to his advice about leaving the Universe out of it for now and giving God full billing. After all, he had reasoned with her, certainly He had more important things to do than worry about what people called Him.

When the Ryans entered the courtyard, Sam said under his breath, in surprise, "Whew! Would ya look at this?" He squeezed Sally's hand.

The crowd had at least doubled from the day before. More than a dozen colorful helium balloons were tied around the big red pine's massive trunk. The air was still and they barely moved. Some read *Get Well Soon,* others were heart-shaped. Others were in clusters—plain balloons with streamers hanging from them.

Sally whispered into Sam's ear, "Is Stone Creek the best little town on Earth or what?"

Sam recognized Marion, the owner of a local wholesale nursery. She and a helper each had two five-gallon pails full of cut flowers of various varieties. They were passing them out and telling the folks that afterwards there were several large plastic vases by the big pine to place them in. Marion smiled and gave Sam a thumbs-up.

Angel looked around. "You guys are amazing!" she shouted. The throng became quiet, awaiting her cue. She glanced over at Pastor Mary Jo, who was dabbing at her eyes with a tissue.

"What we're gonna do here today is really simple." She gave the same instructions as the day before, while turning and working the entire crowd.

"Usually, we hold hands, but today, let's just hold the flowers. And then every time you think of Amy the rest of the day, don't be surprised if the palms of your hands feel warm.

"Let's get started." Angel closed her eyes and began swaying gently with her friends, who were circled around the tree. There was no breeze in the courtyard or outside of the school, but the balloons began dancing. Several people noticed, and there were soft murmurs coming from parts of the crowd. Many were feeling of the palms of their hands with their other hands or against their cheek.

Sam opened his eyes to see what the murmuring was about. He saw the balloons moving and then looked past them. Up on the school roof across from him was a small-ish, middle-aged woman, snapping pictures—Judy Stewart. Shawn had warned him about her. He wondered to himself, *How the hell did she get up THERE? Broom maybe?*

There was shuffling in the foyer, and soon the aroma of fresh-baked goodies wafted out into the crowd. Angel turned around. At the foyer entrance stood a dozen people, all holding baking dishes, trays, and cake pans of fresh cookies, doughnuts, and bars. Angel looked to Mary Jo, who nodded and smiled. They were from the kitchen crews of the three churches.

"WHOA!" Angel exclaimed, catching everyone's attention.

Mary Jo found her way through the crowd to Angel. "Nice work! Want me to take over from here?"

Angel's eyes welled up and overflowed. She hugged Mary Jo with all her might. "Yes, please. I can't believe this…" she cried as she squeezed tighter.

Mary Jo prayed, her eyes closed and her hands folded, "We thank God for this bounty…and for each other."

Many in the crowd said softly, "Amen."

Sam stepped toward the big pine tree. "I got a call just before we got here about Amy. Call it luck, great care, good genes, being young and strong, your love, or the grace of God, she's doing better than the doctors expected she could. In 36 hours, she's gone from critical to serious to stable."

Some of the crowd erupted into cheers and high fives. Others bowed their heads and said private thanks. Many hugged the person nearest them, whether they knew them or not.

———————

"Hmm…" The FBI tech was surrounded by a variety of electronic machines on a horseshoe-shaped workbench. He looked like a gangly, disheveled high school senior. A framed certificate hung askew on the wall: B.S. in Computer Science from Cal Tech, Steven L. Halston.

"I've retrieved data from worse, but this is pretty bad."

Shawn asked, "What are the chances you can get anything?"

"Too early to tell. Have to look inside and see how the chip processor has fared. And then remove it, because the usual connection we would use to read it on a remote computer is damaged. Getting at the chip won't be too big of a deal. The trick is to find a way to see what's on it. What exactly are you looking for?"

"The victim may have gotten a picture of the vehicle that struck her."

"If you've got 10 minutes, I can tell you whether this is a five-minute job or possibly a five-dayer."

"Go for it."

Steven had the phone open in half a minute. He shook his head. "Damn…"

"What?"

"It's a mess in there. All I can do is put the chip in a phone just like this one and try it."

Steven walked over to a cabinet and found a phone similar to Amy's. He took it apart next to her open phone and exchanged the chip, then put the substitute phone back together. "Here goes nothing," he mumbled as he turned it on.

"Dammit. Let me try hooking it to this laptop."

He typed in a command and shook his head. He typed another. Finally, the monitor flickered. An image of Amy's home screen appeared, the background a photo of her and Ed smiling, sweating, and wearing tool belts covered with sawdust from working on her house.

Shawn smiled instinctively. Steven clicked on the camera app icon. Nothing changed on the screen.

"Well, it's possible that picture file may be accessible, but I will probably have to use every trick in the book," Steven said. "The bad news is that I won't be able to work on it until Monday. Expecting budget cuts from Washington. The special agent in charge has cut all overtime and even comp time for us techs. The only reason I'm here now is because the boss owed your sheriff a favor."

Shawn let out a heavy sigh and ran his fingers through his hair.

"Here's my number." Shawn handed him a business card. "Please let me know as soon as you find anything…

IF you find anything. I'm heading over to Prairie to Pine to check on the victim now."

Carrie and Dale pulled up to the curb across from Kellogg's house. A large dark-colored dog dozed on the front stoop. It looked like a cross between a black Lab and a pit bull. Its coat was brindled with light brown.

Dale turned to Carrie. "Could this be the dog we saw that night?"

Just then, the garage door began to open slowly. They could see someone walking around behind the vehicle in there—a woman wearing a long dress. When the door was fully open, she grabbed the SUV's door handle. Suddenly, she noticed the car across the street and did a double-take. It was Kellogg. Her eyes and Dale's met for a split second, then she turned and disappeared back into the house.

The kids could see somebody moving quickly past a picture window to the right of the front door. The dog jerked its head up as the door opened a foot. A bald man with fuzzy gray hair around the edges grabbed the dog by the collar and dragged it inside, slamming the door.

The kids looked at each other in disbelief. Carrie pointed at the garage. The door was closing. Someone was drawing the drapes shut. "Heh, heh. How does payback feel, assholes?"

"Let's get outta here," Dale said.

Carrie took another look at the house. The left edge of the drapes was being held back a couple of inches by someone peeking out. She couldn't tell if it was Kellogg or her husband. Carrie reached out the passenger window as high as she could and waved with an exaggerated sweep of her arm. Dale, however, gave them the finger.

———————

"Shawn, where are you?" Sam asked over the phone.

"Out getting some fresh air with the patient and her folks."

"They got her up already?"

"In a wheelchair," Shawn said. "Here, say Hi."

"Whew, Sam," Amy said. "How's it going back there?"

"You sound great!" Sam exclaimed. "The reason I called is I have some news for Shawn."

"Here he is. Tell everyone hello for me…and tell them thanks."

"What's up, Sam?" Shawn asked. "Should I put us on speaker? Nobody around us here on the patio."

Sam told them about Dale and Carrie's trip to Perham. "Is that enough for you to go question them? If Kellogg's husband was driving that car, apparently he's not the person who hit Amy, but it's pretty obvious he alerted the driver of the vehicle that did."

"I'll talk to Frank and the county attorney. I'm not sure if our eyewitnesses saw enough to go there. But maybe."

"What do we do in the meantime? I sure wish I knew where Chandler lives."

"So do I," said Shawn. "Frank called her ex-supervisor for an address. Just a PO box on file, in Pelican Rapids."

"Oh! One more thing. Do you have your laptop with you?"

"It's in my car, other side of the parking lot. Why?"

"Just go get it and call me back. Something I want you guys to see—Amy and her folks, too."

———————

"Can Amy see the screen?" Sam asked.

"Ya, I'm sitting next to her. Where do you want me to go?" Shawn asked anxiously. Amy had one arm hooked around the crook of his elbow with her hands clasped together. She leaned toward the computer screen and squinted her eyes.

"Your ol' buddy, Judy Stewart," Sam said.

"Oh, no," Shawn whispered. "What'd she write now?"

"Just go to the *DL Press* website."

"I'm way ahead of ya. Where to now?"

"News. The link to the original story about Amy."

"Ya, Stewart called me this morning and I gave her a rather short update on Amy's condition. And I told her the investigation is ongoing. Short and sweet. What did she turn those two sentences into?"

"Just click on it," Sam said impatiently.

"Here we go. What the…?"

Above a photo that Stewart had taken from the school roof that noon showing the packed courtyard, a caption read: *Hundreds turn out in support of hit-and-run victim, Stone Creek School teacher, Amy Wilson.*

Below it was a second photo—a close-up of Angel holding a pink rose, her eyes closed—for all the world looking like a real angel.

"You guys there?" Sam asked. "HELLOOO?"

Amy broke the silence. "I don't know what to say. Angel…she did all of this?"

"Well," Sam began, "she and Cindy started it, but it seems to have taken on a life of its own."

Amy laid her head on Shawn's shoulder and smiled. "Sam, how do I thank Angel, the other kids, you guys, everyone?"

"Two things I can think of, right off. Get well soon. And don't give up on your job. The kids need you."

"And I need them."

Ed said, "Thanks, Sam. Hope to meet you in person someday soon."

"Me, too," said Viv, touching under an eye with the back of her finger.

"Me, too, you guys," said Sam. "Bye."

"I need a nap, Shawn," Amy whispered into his sleeve. "And something for these ribs."

Ed and Viv watched together, arm in arm, as Shawn wheeled Amy slowly toward the corner of the building, carefully steering around holes in the sidewalk to avoid jostling her ribs. Their little girl seemed so frail, her leg sticking out front like a chunk of cord wood covered with a blanket, an IV bag hooked to a pole above her. Ed didn't know if he should give hell to God for allowing this to happen to his Amy, or thank Him.

Before they rounded the corner to head for the automatic front doors, Amy reached back to hold Shawn's hand. He stopped and placed his other hand on top of hers and kissed the top of her head.

Mother and daughter sat together on the porch swing.

"So what's the deal with Amy and Shawn?" Angel asked innocently.

Sally teased, "Why do I feel like you're asking me a question you already know the answer to?"

"Just making sure. He got more emotional after Amy had been…you know…than I would have expected by a cop. It made sense the next day when Cindy said a friend of Carrie's saw Amy and Shawn out with another couple the evening before having dinner at The Smoky. She said Amy barely took her eyes off Shawn the whole night— even when he wasn't looking at her—even when she reached down for her food!"

"Your dad and I introduced them that morning. Not really as a setup, but…sort of. Amy had volunteered to help us figure out what's going on. We invited her to a meeting with Shawn."

They were quiet with their own thoughts for a minute, both smiling to themselves. Finally Sally put an arm around Angel, who snuggled against her shoulder. Sally pushed her heel against the deck to make the swing move and asked, "How ya doin' otherwise?"

"Sorry I can be such a crab sometimes."

"Would you like to talk to somebody, I mean, besides your dad and me?"

"I don't think so. I hardly ever think about it. I'll be fine. But I do think about Amy a lot."

"You know, your whole life, you've always thought of others first. And I'm so grateful to have a daughter who would first of all think to protect Danny and me after you'd been hurt like that." Sally kissed Angel on the top of her head. "And now you've taken on this guilt about Amy. I wish I could magically wave that away. But I know better than to try to reason this out with you." She chuckled. "That's something else I've noticed these 13 years."

Angel gave her mother a playful elbow to the ribs, looked up at her with a smile, then snuggled tighter.

Brushing a wisp of hair off Angel's face, Sally whispered, "We won't push, but just know, we're here in any way we can be."

"Thanks, Mom. I love you."

"You too, Honey."

Sally began humming softly.

Angel listened for a short while, and then said quietly, "You and Daddy's wedding song… Can you sing the words too, please?"

How could anyone ever tell you
You were anything less than beautiful
How could anyone ever tell you
You were less than whole
How could anyone fail to notice
That your loving is a miracle
How deeply you're connected to my soul.

Sam, Sally, and Shawn came in from the winery, each carrying a glass of a 2016 red. They sat at the kitchen table.

Angel announced, "Danny and I are making supper tonight."

"No, I'll get it," Sally said absently. "What would you like?" She turned to the kids for an answer. They were both leaning with their bottoms backed against the kitchen counter, arms crossed and eyes narrowed.

"We got it, Mom," Danny insisted. She noticed a plastic coffee can of dried morels on the counter. The kitchen sink held four grouse thawing in water. She walked over and dipped her hand into it.

"First of all—remember, you thaw poultry in cold water, not tepid."

Angel responded, "Don't have time for that, if you want to eat before midnight. I've seen you do this exact thing a hundred times!"

"Well, maybe a couple times, but certainly not more than 10," Sally answered in her own defense.

When Angel was in charge, especially if self-appointed, it was best just to stand back and take your orders. Danny knew that. So did Sam. That day, Sally was a little behind on that particular learning curve when it came to matters of her kitchen.

"Whatever," Sally acquiesced as she sat back down. Angel turned to the other sink and began spritzing the dried morels in a colander to reconstitute them. "Make sure you don't overdo it with the spray. What are we having with the grouse and morels?"

Angel recited, "Grouse slow simmered in mushroom sauce, with morels, bacon, onion, and bay leaf. Wild rice with bacon bits, onion, and a little chicken broth."

Danny was at the stove sautéing half a dozen strips of bacon that had been cut into half-inch wide bits.

Angel ordered, "You guys take your wine, head up to the fire ring, and start a good one. And put the swing-away grate on the rod, please. Danny and I will bring up the Dutch oven in the other golf cart. And a pan with the rice, ready to cook. Hey, Shawn, hope you like bacon in your grouse sauce and wild rice. Everything's better with bacon in it, right?"

"Love it," Shawn answered obediently. Like Sam, and unlike Sally, he had picked up on who was really the boss.

Danny poured a couple of tablespoons of bacon drippings into a hot wok. They sizzled and sent up a small cloud of smoke, captured by the oven hood.

"Can I at least get the plates and stuff?" Sally asked as she rolled her eyes at Shawn and Sam. "Don't get that pan too hot," she warned, as Angel dumped in the reconstituted morels, which sent an even bigger cloud into the oven hood.

"Mom!" Angel mumbled sternly as she stirred the sizzling morels.

"How about a vegetable?"

Danny said, "Morels, onion bits, and bacon are as close to a vegetable as we're gonna get tonight." He waved his spatula. "This is a celebration, not cafeteria food."

"Bread?" Sally asked. "We could think about eating better around here. Don't ya think?"

Both kids turned to glare at their mother. She raised her hands in front of her with the palms out. "Okay, just trying to help!"

"You wanna help?" Angel said. "Grab the plates and stuff and go build a fire! And don't forget to check the wind this time before you choose a spool table to set. PLEASE."

About five years ago, they had recycled four big wooden spools from the road ditch that were spray-painted "free." They had been emptied of the communication cable when the cable company had run it underground. After several coats of varnish, they made an appropriate woodsy addition to the fire ring area for sitting on or standing around, or as serving platforms for weddings and other parties. But Sally had a history of setting the table exactly downwind of the smoke coming from the fire.

"Come on, Shawn," Sam said, as he got up to leave the kitchen. "Let's go get the golf cart before somebody ends up with a meat cleaver stuck in their forehead."

Miffed, Sally silently filled the big picnic basket as instructed and left the kitchen without another word. She had her hand on the front door screen latch and stopped. "Umm…make sure you use bleach and spray down everything the raw grouse touched. And throw that dish rag in the laundry."

"MOM!"

Before she could shut the door behind her, a wooden spoon came flying from the kitchen and rattled at her feet. She fired one last shot. "Wash this spoon, too, please." She opened the door and tossed it underhand back toward the kitchen.

Sam and Shawn pulled up in the electric golf cart to collect Sally. Her mouth was open, her free hand on a hip. "They threw a wooden spoon at me! Can you believe those kids?"

Sam really could believe Angel would take over in front of Shawn. He was certain she was performing the Impress-Him-by-Proxy thing on Amy's behalf, standing in for her favorite teacher, trying to win her all the brownie points that she could with Shawn. But that little game had gone right over her mother's head. In fact, Sam contemplated, maybe Sally herself was trying to play it.

It was almost dark. The kids were wearing down. Danny tossed two pieces of split jack pine on the fire and poked at the chunks with a limb to make sure they were arranged to eventually flame all around and burn completely to ashes. Sally sensed it was time to leave the two men to themselves. She, Angel, and Danny packed up the picnic things. Neither Ryan child lobbied to stay back and tell stories around the fire like they usually talked their folks into. They still hadn't caught up on their sleep from their runaway adventure.

Sam held up an open bottle of wine and looked through it against the background of flames. It was two-thirds full. "Shawn and I won't be too far behind you."

Sally blew him a kiss. "Bye, Honey." The golf cart whirred away down the hill.

"You wanna call Amy?" Sam asked. "I can go walk down the trail for a while if you want some privacy. Just whistle when you're done. I'll go down to the clearing and say hello to the full moon." He topped off his miniature Mason jar with wine and quickly disappeared from the fire's glowing reach.

Shawn held his finger above the phone screen. There was something going on inside his chest that he remembered feeling before. It was a tightness, like the same old fear. She answered on the first ring.

"Hey, Amy. How ya doing?"

"Hi, you! Thanks for calling. I'm doing okay. Just fine."

"Your ribs?"

"Gotta be careful how I move, but it's a little better."

"Your leg hurt?"

"Not too bad. Still taking a hit of painkiller now and then for that and my ribs, but cutting back."

Shawn opened his mouth but nothing came out.

"Shawn? You okay?"

"Had a picnic tonight with Sam and Sally and the kids, up here in the woods. Angel and Danny cooked the whole thing—a feast to die for, washed down with plenty of wine. Their fire ring is such a pretty spot. Did you know the Ryans got married up here? I was thinking…when you get better, I want to bring you here."

"It's a date." Amy said softly. "Now how about a nice, friendly, firm goodnight handshake?"

"You already got the only one of those you're ever gonna get from me."

"Okay, then. Close your eyes," Amy said softly. "Imagine me an inch from your face, me holding your face with my hands. That's how I would kiss you goodnight if you were here."

"That was wonderful. But I gotta ask, are you on drugs?" Shawn joked.

"Just a few," Amy teased back.

He gulped hard. "G'night, Amy…sleep tight. I'll call in the morning and be over in the afternoon."

"G'night to you, too."

Shawn stepped toward the fire and gazed into the flames. That tight feeling in his chest had disappeared. It had been like the feeling he recalled from tech school, the reason he rarely called for a second date. The same feeling as when he'd call his mother at the bar and tell her he was hungry and there was nothing to eat, not even dry cereal, and she'd laugh at him in her drunken cackle. He had soon quit calling her. Better to go to bed with a stomach churning from emptiness than with an aching heart.

He felt a comforting hand on his shoulder. "Sam?" But Sam was still off in the dark woods somewhere down the hill. Shawn smiled. "Thanks, Mother Mary."

He whistled and heard Sam whistle right back, perhaps a hundred yards away. Shawn refilled his glass and inhaled the scents of the forest deeply. He felt light, almost weightless, a certain kind of peace within him.

From the edge of the fire's glow, Sam could see Shawn's wide smile. "How's Amy?"

"I asked her on another date," Shawn said as he held his glass toward the heavens. "I told her about the fire ring. In fact, would it be okay if we come up here some evening? All of us, I mean. There's something about this place—you guys, the kids. I want her to experience this."

"Of course, We'd love to have you. Hey, you gonna be okay to drive home? I can't tell if that goofy look on your face is from the wine or…whatever. I asked the kids to turn on the porch light in the first guest house, assuming you've seen enough of our couch. In the morning, Angel can fill you in about the search for Chandler's residence. It's not going that good—a needle in a haystack type of deal. Maybe you can help her fine-tune her search."

"That would be great! I still have the overnight kit in my car." They packed up the golf cart and started heading down the trail. "One more thing, Jammer. I've…never really felt like this before. What do you think is happening to me?"

Sam laughed. "The flu. It's gotta be the flu…"

CHAPTER 18

LOOKING FOR CHANDLER

Angel sat in front of her computer while Danny and Shawn looked over her shoulder.

"The problem is, although Pelican Rapids is in Otter Tail County, which is huge, it's within six miles, as the crow flies, of three other counties, a couple of which are also huge. I haven't had any luck doing a name search. The property could be in her husband's name, but we don't even know if she has one. Or she could be renting."

"I know it's going to be a lot of work," Shawn said. "What do you think about just checking the townships and cities within 15 miles of Pelican Rapids for now?"

"Yup, Cindy's riding over. I can put her on Danny's computer and we can search separate areas."

Angel chuckled. "Ya know, I was lying in bed this morning and thinking about possible shortcuts. It occurred to me that Chandler probably lives in a cave. Know of any geological formations around there where the bedrock comes to the surface that she could crawl into?"

Shawn chuckled. "I'll let you know if I think of any."

Entering Amy's room, Shawn asked, "Where are your folks?"

"Come here," she said. "I owe you one, remember?"

She held her arms out wide. "Be careful of my ribs." He embraced her carefully.

"You smell so good. Oh, my folks—I sent them home last night. Told them to take today off. Start the smoker and put in ribs for supper. Go to church and out to lunch. And bring me some ribs tomorrow. Gawd, I love Dad's smoked pork ribs!"

He sat on the edge of her bed and reached for her hand. "When do you think you'll get out of here?"

"Saw the leg doc this morning already, and the internal medicine guy with him. I start occupational therapy tomorrow, learning how to get in and out of bed by myself, on and off the pot, in and out of the wheelchair, and eventually how to stand again. They said I need to take it slow. And then if I'm still on pain meds when I've got all those things mastered, I can't be alone when I go home. I could be here another week."

"And then where will you go?"

"Haven't really figured that out yet. Can't go to my folks' place—that old farmhouse is certainly not handicap friendly. My house, same thing."

He squeezed her hand. "I know where you can go..."

"No, not your place, if that's what you're gonna say. Absolutely not. That's not the way I want us to start out, me being such a load."

"Start out?"

"Remember last night I said I had something to tell you?"

Reaching to brush hair away from her face, he asked in a whisper, "What is it?"

"I had a default speech ready. I was gonna thank you for being such a good friend on such short notice. But that would have sounded like, 'Hey, thanks for changing my flat tire, see ya!' I don't know if it's the drugs, getting knocked on the head, or what's going on. And I don't want to scare you off..." She bit her lip. "When I'm not higher than a kite, and can think, it's mostly about you. How long has it been?"

He smiled and said without having to pause to do the math, "Three days and two hours, give or take. As a matter of fact, I told Sam last night that something was going on with me. He said I probably have the flu."

Amy put one hand to her mouth and the other over her broken ribs and giggled. "Well then, I hope you caught it from me."

He picked up her hand and gently kissed the back of it. "Back to where you'll go when you get out of this place. Last night, I stayed in the Ryans' guest house. Cute log cabin, all on one level, open floor plan, stone fireplace. Even a washer and dryer and dishwasher. But here's the unbelievable part. There are handicap bars in the bathroom, and bolts in the ceiling above the bed and tub for chains and handholds. Sam told me he was just getting the place ready for retirement in a couple of years.

"Then he admitted he'd put all that in for his cousin, Alvin, a paraplegic Vietnam vet who comes up a couple weeks every June and cruises the trails with his wife in a golf cart, checking out birds and wildflowers. Sam takes him canoeing on the river, up to the fire ring. In fact, the last five or six years, the Ryans have hosted disabled vet deer hunts and spring turkey hunts. Danny and Angel guided a turkey hunter this spring to a monster tom, at least for these parts. Almost a state record. Angel even filmed the hunt. There's a picture in the guest house.

"Anyhow, sorry…got off track. Sam said the cabin is yours, as long as you need it. All you have to do is keep their kids out of juvenile detention the rest of this summer and they'll call it even. Plus, he said, when you're able, it never hurts to have a bartender prettier than him for weddings."

"I…I…can't accept that. Besides, what about their guests? Their relatives? I can't impose like that."

"Listen, Sam pretty much insisted, said they're not expecting company until later in August. There's nothing they'll need help with from his two older kids in the vineyard until harvest in September. If someone does come up, there's plenty of room otherwise."

"Gosh, please tell them thanks for such a generous offer, but I really can't…"

"But why not? Your folks think this is a great idea."

"My WHAT?"

"It's pretty much a done deal. Everyone thinks it's the perfect solution."

Shawn dialed his phone and handed it to Amy. "Here, you tell them you're turning them down."

"Hello," said Angel. "Is this Amy? Shawn said you'd be calling."

Amy rolled her eyes at Shawn and shook her head. "Angel, my little dear," she began apologetically, "I can't possibly take you guys up on the offer to stay with you. I'm so sorry."

"Aww, man. Why not?" Angel asked.

"Well, to be honest, I don't really know at this moment. This just happened so fast. And I don't want to put anybody out on my account."

"Maybe this will help you decide to come here," Angel said seriously. "If you don't, I'm gonna kill myself! No, not really…"

Amy tossed her head back onto the pillows, burst out laughing, and dropped the phone onto her belly. She put a hand on her broken ribs and tears began pouring from her eyes. Shawn could hear Angel shouting, "WAIT! AMY? I won't really!"

He picked up the phone while also laughing. "I don't know what you just said to her, but she'll be moving in, in about a week."

"Great! I gotta get back out there! Dad fired up the skid loader after you left, and he's skimming off the topsoil. We're doing the prep work to pour a concrete sidewalk from the cabin's front door to our back door, so Amy can get back and forth. Oh! When can we come see her? I'm sensing a shopping trip with mom to Fargo is in the near future. Won't be today. We've got Gram's visitation this evening down in Perham. And the funeral at ten on Monday. Maybe right after that."

"I'm sure that will be fine. I'll warn Amy," Shawn teased.

As Shawn walked to his parked car, he reported, "Nobody home at the Kellogg house, Frank. Just a dog in there barking and growling. No car in the garage. Drapes open. I'm off to the funeral home for Gram Palmer's visitation."

Frank asked, "Can you go back later and watch the street for a bit?"

"Sure. I'll call Perham PD to give them a heads-up to be on the lookout for an SUV with a broken taillight. If one of us sees one, we'll back the other up. Extra set of eyes and ears won't hurt."

"I'm sure I don't need to remind you, but I will—make sure you have your body camera on. The bigger question we need to answer is who exactly was driving the car that hit Amy. Sure hope that FBI tech comes through…"

CHAPTER 19

ONLY ONE TAILLIGHT

Nightfall was complete, or as complete as it can get in a small town with a streetlight on nearly every corner, and porch lights and interior lights still on for half the houses. It was 10:30. An SUV with the left taillight out drove past Shawn.

"Bingo." He stuck the magnetic police light to the roof and sped to catch up. That flashing and one chirp from his siren was all it took for Kellogg to pull to the curb, half a block short of her house.

"Well, well. Deputy Elliot," Kellogg said as she rolled down the driver's window. "Aren't you just a little out of your purview?"

"I noticed you've got a taillight out. License and registration, please. Perham PD will be here in a couple minutes. I was actually gonna stop by and have a chat with you anyway, Ms. Kellogg. Who is this with you?"

"He's my husband, David. Why?"

"Why don't you go ahead and give me your keys, leave the dome light on, and keep your hands where I can see them," Shawn advised in a steady, stern voice.

"Well, for the love of… Are you ARRESTING us?" Kellogg demanded. "Should I be calling our attorney? This is ridiculous!"

"Please do as you're told." Shawn kept an eye on them as he talked into a hand-held radio. "Yup, it's them," he told Otter Tail County dispatch.

The response crackled back. "Officer's ETA is two minutes. Need anything else?"

"Not for now, thanks."

Shawn instructed, "David, I'm gonna need your ID."

"I…I…don't have it on me. Why would you need that? I wasn't driving."

"Sir, when the officer gets here, you understand that we will check you for one?"

Kellogg demanded, "What is this all about?" She unlatched her door and pushed it open hard, smashing it into Shawn's thigh and kneecap. "I'm warning you, Ms. Kellogg. Just stay put."

"Dispatch, send additional backup, please. Subjects are uncooperative. The driver, Esther Kellogg, just attempted to exit her vehicle after being instructed to stay inside it. And now her husband, David, last name unknown, just exited the vehicle. He appears to be running toward their home, three houses east on Chokecherry. Backup should use extreme caution. I don't know what he's up to."

"Copy that."

"I'm gonna subdue and cuff Ms. Kellogg. Whether we do it standing up against her vehicle or on the asphalt, that's up to her. I'll let you know when she's been neutralized."

Kellogg shrieked, "This is because those kids were here snooping yesterday! You and your badge will fry in Hell, Elliot! This is harassment, clear and simple! I happen to know you and Amy Wilson are more than just casual acquaintances."

"Step out of the car," Shawn ordered tersely. "Keep your hands above your head where I can see them."

"Are you really going to cuff me? Wait until my attorney hears about this!"

"No problem. He can watch it all on video." He touched the camera pinned to his shirt.

Shawn heard the Perham police car approaching from a block away, its siren blaring. There were also sirens on Highway 10, to the northwest and southeast. The Perham car screeched to a stop, its headlights washing over the front of Kellogg's SUV. She was cuffed, her hands behind her back, standing awkwardly with her back against the car, her chin stuck out in defiance.

The driver of the Perham squad was one of Shawn's former Explorers, Dean Aaron.

"She's all yours for now," Shawn said. "I'm going to their house after her husband. Three doors down, on the left."

"No, wait!" said the young officer. "Backup will be here in less than two minutes!"

"I'll be careful."

Shawn quickly slid into his car, peeled out around the SUV, gunned it, then screeched to a stop, his car at an angle, the headlights illuminating the house.

Dean blurted into the microphone on his epaulet, "Becker County's by himself, walking toward the house. Get backup here immediately! He has his weapon out and has now entered the premises."

A muffled shot rang out.

"SHOT FIRED! I repeat, shot fired!" Dean yelled.

Kellogg slumped to her knees and began sobbing. "DAVID! My David! Elliot shot him…"

Dean shouted into his microphone, "I'm leaving this perp here by her car. She ain't going anywhere. I'm going in…" He began sprinting toward the house.

Dispatch responded, "Perham, please wait for backup!"

Inside the otherwise dark house, Shawn's headlights cast a shaft of light through the opening in the drapes, across the living room into a hallway. Peeking around the door, Shawn saw David in the hallway, a pistol pointing at his mouth. A large dog lay dead in the middle of the living room, a pool of blood spreading on the carpet.

Shawn leveled his weapon on the man's chest. "David, please, put the gun down. It doesn't have to be like this."

David was sobbing. "You guys aren't gonna put me through the same thing as you did to my brother. I'm not going there…"

As Dean ran up the front steps, the second shot rang out. "SHAWN!" He yelled into the microphone, "Another shot fired!" His weapon gripped tightly, arms held straight out, he carefully approached the front door.

Shawn said, "I'm okay, Dean. Put your weapon down. He's dead. So is the dog. I don't know if you wanna come in here."

"Sir, I'm not an Explorer anymore. I need to do my job like you taught me, according to the oath I took. What is it? Did you shoot him?" Dean stepped inside and stopped cold when he saw the body sprawled in the hallway. He put a hand on Shawn's shoulder.

Shawn was eerily calm, his arms hanging loosely by his side, his weapon in his right hand. "He shot himself. It's a mess. You better get back to the woman."

Just then, the Highway Patrol screeched to a stop in front, further lighting up the front of the house. Dean met the trooper halfway cross the yard. "Perp's dead in there. Shot his dog and then himself. Deputy is fine. His name is Shawn Elliot. I've got a second perp back by my car—an older woman. She's cuffed. I better get back there."

Dean pressed the button of his microphone as he headed back to his car. "Situation is under control. Shawn Elliot is okay. One perp is dead in the house. Self-inflicted gunshot."

"Elliot?" The trooper, a woman, stood outside the door. "State Patrol. I'm coming in. Can I turn the lights on?"

Shawn holstered his pistol in the carrier below his left armpit. "Yup, go ahead."

"Have you checked the premises for other people?" she asked.

"No, ma'am. Haven't had a chance."

"I got it." The trooper, gun drawn, stepped around the dead dog and entered the hallway. She stood spread-legged over David's body as she looked into the first room on the left, careful not to step in the pool of blood. She checked a room to the right and another at the end of the hall.

"Clear down here," said the trooper. "I'll check the basement."

―――――――――

Shawn said into the phone, "Frank?"

"Ya, I've been listening. You okay?"

"Yes, sir."

"What's the victim's name?"

"David something. Haven't gotten that far yet, but I know his last name is different from his wife's. What should we do with Kellogg?"

"Find out if she and her husband have next of kin. And have dispatch get a hold of them. We won't make her go through this—losing her husband—without some support. Give her the Miranda, but don't name any specific charges at this point. You can tell her we're holding her for questioning and possible complicity in Amy's hit-and-run. I'll talk to Perham and Ottertail County, have her taken directly to our jail.

"We need to question her and get her statement, if she'll cooperate. Of course, she gets counsel before any of that, if she requests it. I'll send a car down to pick her up. Work with Otter Tail in the meantime—help process the scene. And then follow our car back to DL. Give her one shot at cooperating. If she won't, see you first thing in the morning."

There was a pause, and then Frank said, "Good work, Shawn."

"Thank you, sir. We still don't know who hit Amy, but...that's not important right now. We'll connect the dots. But I don't want Amy to learn about this over the phone or on the news."

"Do you think your friends the Ryans would go over and tell her for you, like first thing in the morning?"

Shawn looked at the time on his phone. "It's 11:00 now. They've got a funeral here in Perham at 10:00 tomorrow morning. I guess there will be time. Yes, I'll ask them. Oops, now my phone is ringing. It's Amy. Talk to you in the morning."

He went outside and headed for the far side of the garage, where he could have some privacy. "Yes, Amy?"

"Are you out late, working?"

"Yup, following up on leads about who hit you. I'm down in Perham. This might take a while."

"Find out anything?"

"Working on it…been a long day. And when I'm done here, I have to drive back up to DL before I go home."

"Would you mind if I did a ride-along…you know, in my mind? I can't sleep anyway. This wrinkly old woman with blue eyes, she keeps popping into my dreams, shaking her bony finger at me. She was saying things like 'Call him, goddamnit! What are ya waiting for, an act of Congress? You're only 23, and ya ain't getting any younger.' It was pretty vivid. Crazy, huh?"

"Sounds like Gram paid you a visit!"

"Who?"

"I'll tell you about her next time I'm over," Shawn kidded. "Yes, I'd love for you to be my ride-along home tonight. I'll call you when I'm on the road."

"Are you okay?" Amy asked. "You sound tired. Are you sure you should put in this many hours?"

"Just building up paid time off that I'm going to spend with you at Sam and Sally's. How's that sound?"

CHAPTER 20

THE UNRAVELING

Amy said, "Whoa! To what do I owe this visit so early in the morning?" Then she noticed that the Ryans' smiles seemed forced. "What's wrong?"

"Shawn's fine. Everyone's fine," Sam said.

"Hugs first," Sally said. "I know…your ribs."

Sam stepped in and gave Amy a gentle kiss on the forehead while she patted him on the back.

He began in an even, serious voice. "Shawn made some progress in your case last night. They're almost certain it was Kellogg's husband who was parked up on the other trail. Shawn was staking out their place. He stopped them for a taillight out near their home. Kellogg's husband got out and ran to their house. Shawn went in after him. The guy…umm…took his own life."

Amy covered her eyes then squeezed her temples. Sally grabbed a couple of tissues for her.

"Oh God! That guy had a gun…Shawn could've been shot!" She dabbed at her eyes. "Oh Jesus. What about Kellogg?"

Sam stepped aside to let a nurse access the IV. The conversation stopped as they all watched the nurse push a small syringe's contents into the piggyback. "You should be good for a couple hours. And you'll be fine for therapy after lunch. Get some rest, hon."

Sam continued, "Kellogg's in custody in DL. When Shawn tried to question her early this morning, she demanded to see her lawyer. He offered to call her next of kin, but she said she has none. They've been trying to contact her husband's next of kin, a brother and sister, but no luck finding them so far."

Amy pointed to the IV. "Hardly slept last night. Goofy dreams. We've only got a few minutes. What about Chandler?"

"Still haven't found out where she parks her large carcass. Angel and Cindy have been scouring the property records of four counties."

Amy squeezed her eyes shut. "How are the kids taking it?"

Sally said, "Angel's taking it pretty hard. When you're better, and things have settled down, would you mind talking to her? She feels like the accident is her fault."

"Of course, I'll talk to her..." Amy smiled through her tears. "Oh, that poor dear."

Sally leaned forward and kissed Amy on the forehead. "We better head back for the funeral. Angel wants to come see you afterwards. Is that okay? Danny does, too, but he and Sam ordered cement and they're gonna do the pour on the new sidewalk this afternoon."

"I can't thank you both enough for all this."

Sally said, "We're happy to do it. What goes around, comes around."

Before the door to the stairway had shut behind the Ryans, Amy was calling Shawn.

"Sam and Sally just left here for the funeral. Thanks for not letting me get the news all by myself. You're the most thoughtful person I've ever known. I could get used to this."

"I could get used to you, too," Shawn joked.

"I know you're busy. Don't feel like you have to come over today. I'm doing okay. Not sure what to expect from therapy. I'll probably be crabby after."

"I have some good news," Shawn said. "The FBI tech just called. He said he's gotten into your phone further than he had hoped for at this point, but it will take some sorting through it."

"I still don't know if I got a picture."

"Keep your fingers crossed."

"Will you have to come over for it if he finds it?" Amy asked anxiously.

"No, he can email a copy to me. I'm sorry."

"I'll be having plenty of company today anyway. Sally and Angel after the funeral. My folks—they're bringing me Dad's barbecued ribs for supper. He said he made an extra rack just for you."

"An entire RACK?" Shawn said. "Oh, I hate to turn down an offer like that! But I have no idea how Kellogg's interrogation might go, and if we do get that picture off your phone, and with a plate number, I'll be tracking that down right away. I'll keep you posted. I'm going on three hours of sleep again. I'll see ya tomorrow for sure. And I'll call later if there's any more news about your phone."

CHAPTER 21

CLICK

Shawn shoved a piece of paper across the table to Kellogg and her court-appointed public defender, Megan Richards. Kellogg's makeup was streaked and her eyes were puffy. She hadn't slept a wink overnight.

It was almost noon. Richards had been in court all morning. She was only two years out of law school, but was known for being perfectly well-prepared even though sometimes she'd be representing over 20 clients in one day. When the clerk called a case, she'd set the file in front of herself, but rarely had to open it to state her client's plea or explain their position in a settlement offer. But she was also a realist.

Before looking at the paper, Richards stated, "For the record, did you or anyone connected with the sheriff's department monitor my client's telephone call or trace it?"

"No," Shawn said flatly.

She pulled the paper closer so she and her client could read it. Shawn watched Kellogg for any kind of reaction. She did raise her eyebrows a fraction.

"What is this?" Richards asked.

"This is the owner of the hit-and-run vehicle that ran down Amy Wilson. Ms. Kellogg, do you know this person?"

The ladies whispered for about half a minute.

Richards said, "What has this got to do with my client?"

"Her husband was parked up the road a quarter mile away on another trail. The two vehicles, one on each side of Amy Wilson's driveway a few blocks away, are suspected of being on the lookout for people coming and going at her home, which is approximately 18 miles from the Kellogg home."

"I'm still not getting the relevance."

"Eyewitnesses saw a driver, a dog, and a vehicle whose descriptions match Ms. Kellogg's husband, their dog, and their SUV. They also observed the driver of that vehicle make a phone call before he sped away without his lights on. We suspect he alerted the driver of the second vehicle that he had been discovered, and to get out of there. Seconds later, the eyewitnesses heard tires squealing near where we found Amy Wilson, who was lying unconscious, critically injured."

Richards sat up straighter in her seat and adjusted her glasses. "Okay then. One observation and one question. That could have been anybody in the first vehicle. And secondly, how do you know that is the vehicle that hit Amy Wilson?"

Shawn slid over a photo of the vehicle taken from the front, its license numbers clear.

"This vehicle was parked on Amy Wilson's property, up a side trail 50 yards. She approached it from the front and took a picture with her phone just before she was hit.

Also, we recovered part of a headlight assembly that broke off in the collision. We are securing a warrant to search the property of this vehicle's owner. Also, we've noticed that the owner of this vehicle has the same last name as Ms. Kellogg's husband."

Richards and Kellogg again whispered, but only for a few seconds.

"I need to speak to my client in private," Richards said, as she and Kellogg slid their chairs back.

Shawn picked up the phone. A jailer entered and escorted the women to a small conference room across the corridor.

Sheriff Davis had been observing the interview with county attorney Greg Pearson from behind the one-way mirror. They met Shawn at the doorway. "Nice work, Shawn. I hope Richards can talk some sense into her client."

Shawn responded, "It sure looks like Kellogg was privy to the stalking and the hit-and-run. I hope she'll fill us in on the Chandler connection. Greg, any idea what we can charge Kellogg with?"

Frank said, "Let's go to my office." He called out to the jailer standing by the conference room door. "Joey." He waved him over. "When they come out, offer them coffee or whatever. But don't come get us for another 10 minutes, okay?"

In Frank's office, seated around a table, Greg picked up the conversation. "Conspiracy laws are complicated. I'm not sure that applies in this case, even with what they did to Amy. I doubt it was their intent to hit her. For sure, the driver will be charged with several counts. I'll make some calls and check out Minnesota's law regarding failure to report a crime. Also, child endanger-ment laws—you know, mandated reporting. Kellogg is a mandated reporter. If she knew the other boys were bait-ing Daniel Ryan, that law could apply, also concerning the other boys' safety. An argument could be made that she was setting them up to get hurt. As far as conspiring to set Daniel up—again, I need to do some research."

"What if she wants to cut some sort of deal?" Frank asked.

"We're not sure what to charge her with yet, other than interfering with Shawn at the stop last night. No deal for now. Let's just see what she's willing to provide. I know Megan Richards very well. In fact, I wish she worked for us. If her clients want to talk and hang themselves, she won't stop them. However, I'm quite certain she's advised Kellogg not to talk."

The jailer knocked on Frank's door, and the men headed back to the interrogation room.

Richards opened the conversation. "My client wants to tell you what she knows."

Shawn looked at Kellogg, who had a soaked tissue covering her eyes. Richards saw him raise his eyebrows in surprise. She shrugged and sat back.

"Let's start with the relationship between your hus-band and the owner of the vehicle that hit Amy Wilson. Do you know who was driving that vehicle?"

"Yes, it was David's brother, Elroy."

Shawn pointed to the copy of the vehicle's registra-tion. "This address, is this where Elroy lives?"

"Yes, it is. David and I had gone to see them the evening before. We were on our way home when you stopped us."

"Them?" Shawn asked.

Kellogg fidgeted with a tissue on the table and took a deep breath. "Dorothy Chandler. She's David and Elroy's sister—my sister-in-law."

"What relationship do you or they have with any of the boys who were involved in the assaults concerning Daniel Ryan?"

"Billy Anderson is Elroy's grandson."

"Do you know who bought the dirt bike for Billy and the gifts for the other three boys?"

Kellogg shook her head. "I told her right from the beginning to just let it go—that Billy and his friends could get hurt. Dorothy bought the gifts."

"Let what go? Does this have anything to do with Sally Ryan's custody evaluation back in 2004, when the judge charged Ms. Chandler with favoring Ms. Ryan's husband?"

"Not really. Dorothy's grudge—the whole family's— goes back to before that."

"A grudge against Sally Ryan? For what?"

Kellogg began to sob. Richards handed her more tissues and whispered, "Take your time."

Kellogg clenched her fists. "This is about Sam Ryan. He ruined our family. Took our brother away from us the year before."

"Which brother?"

She whispered, "He died in prison, a year ago. Duane Whiting. They figured since Sam Ryan took away someone they loved, and all their livelihoods, they'd take away someone he loved."

"How did Sam take away their brother and livelihoods?"

She took a deep, shuddering breath. "Their grandparents had set up Duane, the oldest, with their car dealership. The other kids weren't official partners—it was all in Duane's name—but the grandparents made him promise to take care of the other three. Half the yearly profits were split between the three other kids. Duane was a heckuva businessman. Nobody in that family worried about money…until Sam Ryan came up with that cock-and-bull story that Duane had molested him when he was little. And then the cops started digging, and these liars kept coming out of the woodwork. Before we knew it, Duane was in prison, the state seized all his assets to pay the fines and civil suits, and suddenly everyone was living hand-to-mouth."

Kellogg now looked less repentant and more angry. She sat up straight and looked Shawn in the eyes. "At first, the only thing Dorothy could think of was to take Sally Hunter's baby away from her. When that didn't work out, she just bided her time. Then, after Duane died in prison a year ago April, the pain returned full force.

"That's why I came out of retirement—to have a connection with the Ryan kids. The Whitings were willing to settle for just one of the Ryan kids taken away, so Sam would truly understand what it felt like to have someone he loved ripped away, even temporarily. But when Amy Wilson got hit, the plan was over. David and Elroy vowed they'd never go to prison like their brother did."

"But why stake out Amy Wilson in the first place?"

"They didn't know at the time that the judge was going to go spineless and drop the charges against Daniel. Considering how pathetic you were at hunting down the kids, they wanted to do it themselves, then call to have them picked up. It was pretty obvious that Amy was help-ing them. The question is why couldn't YOU figure that out? So the last two Whiting brothers are gone now..."

"Elroy's gone, too?"

"Last night, I called Elroy and Dorothy. When Dor-othy told him about David, he jumped into his car and drove away. She stayed on the line. A minute later, she heard a gunshot. She said there was no need for her to go look."

Shawn turned to the one-way mirror. "Frank, get somebody out there."

Frank pushed the speaker button. "Already on it."

Kellogg was almost bragging. "Even before David died, Dorothy didn't care where she ended up. She just wants to make sure Sam Ryan pays for what he has done, and hurts as badly as he made them all suffer. Then she can die happy."

"What does that mean, exactly?"

Kellogg began to weep into her hands.

Shawn stood and demanded, "Where's Dorothy Chandler?"

"She only said she has big plans in Perham today. She has a gun..."

"Oh shit—the Palmer funeral! The Ryans were there. Frank! Get a jailer in here. I need to make some calls."

Shawn punched at his phone as he hurried from the interrogation room.

"SAM! Where are you?"

"What's going on? I'm home working on the sidewalk."

"Where are Sally and Angel?"

"With Danny and Cindy. They all went up to see Amy, took the flowers from the healing circle."

"I thought Danny was going home with you, to work on the sidewalk?"

"Changed his mind. Said he had a feeling he should go to Fargo with them. Why, what's going on?"

"Did you see Chandler in Perham this morning?"

"Yeah, she was lurking as usual. Why?"

"I'm just gonna give it to you straight. Chandler is Duane Whiting's sister. Kellogg was married to a brother, the one who shot himself in Perham last night, and there's another brother we're pretty sure also committed suicide last night."

"Oh, fuck. You don't think she might have followed them to Fargo, do you?"

"That's exactly what I'm worried about. I better get Amy right away. Chandler's gone crazy and is likely dangerous."

———————

Shawn yelled into the phone, "AMY! Who's there with you?"

"Hey, you! Sally and the kids and Cindy. You should see what they brought me! Vases and vases of flowers! Wait a minute. What's going on?"

"Amy, it's Chandler. She blames Sam for ruining their family because he blew the whistle on her pedophile brother. Kellogg says Chandler has nothing left to lose. Buzz a nurse and get Security up there right now. She's got a gun! Get everyone out!"

Shawn waited for her to respond, but heard nothing.

"Amy? AMY!"

Finally, she responded, her voice trembling, "Too late…"

Chandler stood with her back to the door, her arm stuck through her purse handles, holding a small automatic pistol. "Who's that on the phone?" she demanded.

"Shawn…Shawn Elliot."

"Gimme the phone," Chandler ordered while waving the pistol around. "Everybody, behind the bed. NOW!"

Cindy and Angel were already there by Amy's side. Sally sidestepped next to Cindy. Danny followed, keeping his eyes locked on Chandler. Everyone's eyes were wide with fear, except Danny's were narrow and angry.

"Mr. Elliot!" Chandler said into the phone, feigning cheerfulness. "I found these runaways for you again!" She chortled. "And their mother, and another little whippet up here with their former schoolteacher. Help me pick out which Ryan pays Sam Ryan's debt for the lives of my three brothers."

"Ms. Chandler—Dorothy—please, just walk away. It doesn't have to come to this. I'm begging you!"

"I'm putting you on speaker so we can all hear this." She set the phone down in Amy's lap then stepped back, her butt blocking the door.

"Heh, heh. Sally, have you figured it out yet? Do you know who I am?"

Sally shook her head.

"I'm Duane Whiting's sister. And I've been waiting 14 years for this."

"Who's that?" Angel demanded.

Sally replied, "A serial pedophile your dad helped get put away back in 2004. He died in prison last year."

Chandler asked, "Why the hell couldn't Sam Ryan have just kept his mouth shut, like the rest of us did? His big mouth cost us not only Duane, but also our livelihoods that he worked so hard to provide for us. And now my other two brothers are gone. All because of Sam Ryan."

A wave of déjà vu washed over Angel. She became faint and fell sideways into Cindy before flopping forward onto Amy's bed. Sally pushed past Cindy and slid both arms around her daughter. Angel began sobbing. "That boy in my dream before they were gonna take Danny away. It wasn't him. That was Daddy, wasn't it?"

Chandler said, "Okay, pay attention. Do you remember your kids wouldn't repeat what Dylan said, words that sent Danny into that rage by the old post office? What Dylan said was my idea. Hell, if the President of the United States can say it, might as well use it ourselves, huh?"

"That's not the real secret we were keeping," Danny warned through clenched teeth. "Those boys also said that Angel liked it when she got grabbed like that. A couple of days before that, they got Angel alone…and did that…and worse. Angel didn't even tell me at first. She was afraid I'd do something terrible. And I would have."

Chandler swiveled the pistol and pointed it at his chest. "That's news to me. My advice to you, Angel, is to just get over it, like the rest of us did—except for your dad."

Danny took a small step toward the end of the bed, his eyes still steady and narrowed.

Angel cried, "You are so goddamn evil! I hope you rot in Hell!"

"Danny, NO!" Sally screamed.

"Okay, little fella," Chandler warned, "you just made up my mind, you chip off the old block. This world doesn't need two Sam Ryans anyway…"

Chandler wore a confident grin. Danny took another step toward her. Her pistol was still leveled at his chest, only the end of the bed separating him and the gun.

"Ms. Chandler," Shawn pleaded through the phone, "please don't harm these people. I know you are suffering some great losses. You have been through so much. But not because of these kids or Sally or Amy."

Danny slowly stepped around the bed and closed the gap to only three feet from the end of Chandler's gun barrel.

"DANNY!" Angel shrieked. "You are my brother and I love you more than anything. Don't let her—PLEASE! I'm begging you."

Sally yelled through her tears. "Get that gun off him! You're gonna have to take me first!" She rushed around the end of the bed and pushed Danny aside, knocking him to the floor.

She walked right up to Chandler's gun barrel. "Do it! You fucking goddamn coward piece of shit. Do it, and go rot in PRISON!"

Cindy had covered her eyes and convulsed with sobs. Angel was whispering something to herself. Amy had hung her head and closed her eyes, arms wrapped tightly around herself. Danny stared at his mother from the floor, his face etched with fear.

Danny begged, "Mom, don't pay for her sins…please."

Chandler tightened her finger to the trigger.

Amy screamed, "DON'T!"

Chandler closed her eyes. "Here's to you, Sam Ryan."

Click.

The door suddenly flew open. A hospital security guard tackled Chandler, knocking the pistol from her hand. She fell face first onto the floor between Danny and his mother, bloodying her nose. The guard had Chandler's hands behind her back in an instant. A second guard had her cuffed before she could even protest.

"Get off me, you thugs," she growled.

Amy picked up the phone with trembling hands. "Oh my god. It's over, Shawn. They got her."

The guards yanked Chandler to her feet. Two Fargo town cops rushed into the room. One picked up the pistol, pulling the clip out and ejecting the round in the chamber.

Chandler stood defiantly, her head held high.

"Just a second, please, officers," said Danny. He faced Chandler, a head shorter and less than a third her body size. Blood from her nose dripped onto her manly blazer. "Here's something for you to think about in prison. And if you do get out alive, a reason to come looking for me. And I hope you do."

Danny spit in her face. Chandler winced as the wad hit her in the left eye. The sputum hung there for a second, and then a glob of it dribbled onto her cheek. "We'll see, little man Ryan. We'll meet again…I promise."

"You'll wish we hadn't," Danny growled to her back as a security guard and a cop shoved Chandler through the doorway.

Amy held her hands out and motioned for them all to lean in. "Give us a minute here, Shawn," she whispered.

"Hands," Amy said. "I need to touch all of your hands." She squeezed her eyes shut, and the tears ran. "My friends…my blessed friends. Thank God for you, and thank God we're all still here."

The Fargo cop examined the pistol and the cartridge from the chamber, focusing on the primer. The firing pin had made its proper dent in the cartridge's primer. "Did she pull the trigger?" he asked. "Hmm, never seen this kind of ammo misfire..." He scratched his head.

Angel whispered in Cindy's ear, "Gram..." Cindy nodded and smiled.

"These amazing flowers," the officer said as he looked around Amy's room in awe at all the overflowing vases.

He looked at Amy first, and then Angel. "Oh! Saw you on the internet at the school over in Minnesota, the other side of Detroit Lakes. Nice work!"

He pointed to the green vase on the windowsill. "Red roses. My favorite."

"Roses?" Amy asked.

"Ya. Those two are so perfect...and fresh."

Angel turned and looked at the roses. Her face lit up as she picked up the vase. She turned and handed it to Amy, whose lips were parted.

Angel got that fluttery feeling up and down her spine. "Well, it looks like your rose has a friend."

"Did you hear that, Shawn?" Amy said into the phone. "How did you do that? Special delivery?"

"Oh," he joked, "it helps to have friends in high places. Amy, save me a seat for the rib supper. I'm gonna finish up with Kellogg, and then I'm on my way. Call you when I'm on the road."

"Kids," Amy instructed as she held her hand over the phone, "cover your ears, please."

They did...sort of.

"Shawn Elliot, I love you," she said with a sigh. She looked around at the smiling faces and rolling eyes.

"I love you, too, Amy Wilson," Shawn said. "More than you could ever imagine."

"Didn't hear a thing!" said Danny.

"Me either."

"Me either!"

"Sally?" Shawn asked. "Want me to fill Sam in? Tell him everything's okay?"

At the mention of her husband's name, Sally suddenly broke down sobbing, slumping to the floor beside the bed. Danny caught her as best he could, and then sat next to her, squeezing her like she'd fly off the Earth if he loosened his grip even a tiny bit. "Mom...Mom. We're all fine. This is all behind us. It's over."

"Goddamnit," Sally whispered through her tears, "don't you ever, EVER, stand in front of a gun, for me or anyone. I couldn't bear to go on without either of you, or your dad."

Angel whispered, "And don't you be a hero either, Mom. Deal?"

"How did I ever end up with a couple of kids like you?"

Danny answered, acting annoyed, "Oh geez. Do you really want me to tell Dad's stupid story about how you guys made Angel?"

Sally buried her head in Danny's shoulder. He could feel her laughing. "Please, no..."

CHAPTER 22

OVERNIGHT

Shawn returned to the interrogation room.

"What happened?" Richards asked.

"Yup, Dorothy Chandler followed them to the hospital. Had them at gunpoint. By the grace of God, it misfired. Dorothy's in custody."

He slammed the table with the force of pent-up anger and fear, shaking a finger at Kellogg. "Do you realize how close she was to killing somebody? You knew she was this unhinged!"

Kellogg hung her head and began sobbing. "Mr. Elliot, I'm so sorry…but so thankful nobody was hurt."

"Now help me fill in the blanks about this family. I need to make some sense of these Whitings."

Esther Kellogg wove a tale of a horribly dysfunctional family: an uncle molesting Duane at around age 10, then Duane, when he became a few years older, began molesting his siblings. If their parents knew, they had turned a blind eye. That is, until Duane was 16 and they caught him having sex with Dorothy, who was only 12 at the time. That summer, they sent him to live with their father's parents in the country, which, Kellogg admitted, coincided with Sam's story about Duane molesting him.

Even as adults, Duane had a sick stranglehold on his siblings: the money. If anyone told the family secrets, they knew they'd be cut off. When Duane was convicted and the money was gone, David and Elroy seemed almost relieved, but they were still too ashamed to reveal the family secrets. And Dorothy took over as head of the clan, vowing revenge against Sam Ryan. The brothers fell right back in step, and Kellogg joined the effort to punish Sam. But nobody was supposed to get hurt—or die.

"Amy Wilson…" Kellogg said through her ears. "She didn't deserve this. Nobody did."

"Ms. Richards," Shawn said, "I've talked with the county attorney. For now, we're just charging Ms. Kellogg with interfering with the traffic stop last night. There will be a bail hearing later this afternoon, and I'll recommend to the county attorney that Ms. Kellogg be released without bond."

Richards asked, "Do you think for now you can release Ms. Kellogg into my custody? I'll take her to my office, and we'll call her sister from there. She's offered to take her in."

Kellogg sniffed and swiped a tissue across her nose. "I promise I won't do anything stupid. I'm not going to meet my maker with unfinished business, like my brothers did. I have to make arrangements for David and Elroy. And someone needs to be there for Dorothy. She'll need somebody to lean on, and to take care of loose ends."

"Yes, that will be fine," Shawn said. "If you'd like, I can call a crew to take care of the…inside of your house. That will take a day or two."

"Thanks, but I'll pay for the cleanup. I'm never going back into that house, though." Kellogg reached out and touched Shawn's sleeve. "Oh, Mr. Elliot. Are you going to see Amy Wilson anytime soon?"

"Yes, I'm heading to Fargo in a bit. Gonna meet Sam there."

"Please tell her—and Angel and Danny and the others—I am so sorry we put them through all this. Ask them if, in time, they might consider forgiving me."

"Yes, I will."

"Esther," said Richards, "I need a minute with Mr. Elliot."

He left the room, followed by the attorney.

Richards said, "That was quite a break you just gave her. And no bail? Of course, I appreciate that on behalf of my client, but may I ask why?"

"Everyone deserves at least one break. I truly hope she'll make the best of hers."

———

Amy attacked her occupational therapy like General Patton chasing the Germans across France. The bulky cast didn't slow her down one bit. There wasn't much pain in her leg, but the cracked ribs demanded their due. She remarked to her nurse, who saw the intense pain on Amy's face whenever she had to use her upper body, "A little rib pain isn't gonna kill me…or even slow me down."

She was discharged the Monday following Chandler's arrest, after the stitches were removed and another bulky cast was put on. X-rays confirmed that significant mending was already taking place, ahead of schedule. Her doctor firmly ordered that her only mode of transportation at the Ryans' place should be the wheelchair with the leg prop for two weeks, at which time they'd remove the cast and do another round of x-rays. By then, she could possibly get a lighter cast and use crutches.

"Count on it," Amy promised her doctor.

———————

Ed and Viv were waiting at the winery with Angel and Danny when the party bus from The Smoky pulled in late that afternoon, with Sam at the wheel and Shawn riding in back with Amy. It was the only vehicle they knew of large enough to haul Amy in a wheelchair. Besides, it had a handicap lift. Sally pulled in behind them.

Amy's parents had stopped by her house ahead of time to pack up a list of things she wanted. It was a noticeably tough day for her, with all the jostling and excitement, and even some anxiety. Sally had pre-cooked a simple supper—a couple of pans of venison sausage lasagna and a salad fresh from the Ryan garden—which they ate in Amy's cabin.

After dinner, Amy gave a huge yawn. "I think I need to call it a night." She did look tired, and her eyes had become heavy.

Angel volunteered, "I'll stay with you tonight, okay?"

"Oh, thanks, Angel," Amy said, her eyes darting sideways to Shawn. "But you've all done enough already. I'll see you first thing in the morning, Sweetie, okay?"

"You guys go on," Shawn said, with a wave of his hand toward the front door. "I'll clear the table."

Sally put an arm around Sam's waist and they began following the others. She kissed him on the cheek. When they reached the door, Sam went out first, and she paused and turned. Shawn was standing behind Amy, his hands gently massaging her shoulders.

Sally said, "Amy, please call if you need anything, okay?"

———————

Sally was at the kitchen sink, scraping a lasagna pan that had soaked overnight. She gazed up at the cabin, smiling.

Angel came flying around the corner from the hallway, pulling a sweatshirt down over her head. "Crap! I overslept! I better go check on Amy! She's probably lonely…"

Sally turned to her daughter and pointed out the window. Angel snuggled up beside her mom, placed a hand on her shoulder for balance, and stood on her tip-toes.

"Huh, what's Shawn's car doing there? Did he come back over already this morning?"

"Oh, his car's been there all night…" She patted her little girl on the head. "Maybe you'd better call first."

OTHER BOOKS IN THE
CANOES IN WINTER **SERIES**

 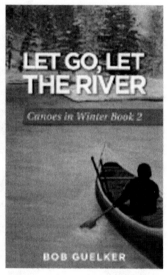

ACKNOWLEDGEMENTS

For book 3 of the *Canoes in Winter* series, I once again truly appreciate the efforts of "the team," without whom Stone Creek would forever be stuck in the bowels of my computer. My cover artist, fellow Nevis-ite Amelia Woltjer. The back cover art was a painting that sent chills up and down my spine when she first showed it to me (not to diminish the beautiful front cover art); my editor, Julia Willson, for her patience and gentle guidance, not to forget her exceptional skill with language and story; and my book producer Julie Anne Eason, for taking all these parts and putting them together into a real book in record time, while calmly advising me over and over, "Don't worry Bob, we'll make the deadline…"

ABOUT THE AUTHOR

A handful of years ago, my son mentioned to my first ex-wife that I had retired.

Curiously she asked, "From what?"

My path through life has been akin to floating down a winding river—around every bend there's a new view, an unknown place to explore, and people I've never met. Along the way I've been blessed with a multitude of jobs, and I've witnessed such an expansive spectrum of humanity–from the sublime to the not so. My last job before retiring was writing, editing, and producing our small-town weekly newspaper.

I grew up just north of the Minneapolis city limits, when the north end of Anoka County was still *country* (and you could actually make it to Minneapolis in half an hour). There I hunted, swam, canoed, played ball and fished to my boyhood heart's content.

I stayed put for a while into adulthood, but upon approaching middle age, I realized the suburban sprawl had crept up and surrounded me. Home had become someplace claustrophobic. I joke that one Friday in 1984, I went "up north to the lake" and decided never to go back home. (Actually though, it was a planned move for our whole family.) I spent the next eleven years in west-central Minnesota–away from the big city traffic jams and with my beloved outdoors just steps away.

But the river of life beckoned. Twenty-one years and two divorces later, I looked around the next bend in the river, and found the quiet, friendly little burg of Nevis. It was smack-dab in the middle of northern Minnesota's beautiful rivers, lakes, forests, and hill country–the kind of place I'd always dreamed about living. I didn't realize it then, but I was finally home. For good.

There's no better place on earth to live. And write.